A THUNDER OF CRUDE

Brian Callison was born in Manchester and
educated at Dundee High School before entering
the merchant navy in 1950 as midshipman with
Blue Funnel Line, sailing mainly on cargo liners
to the Far East and Australia.

On leaving the sea he studied at Dundee
College of Art. He has held several administrative
posts, including managerial directorship of a
construction company and general manager of
a large entertainment centre.

He served several years in the territorial army
with the 51st Highland Division Provost
Company, Royal Military Police, and now
maintains an active connection with the sea as
Head of Unit, Royal Naval Auxiliary Service.

His phenomenally successful first novel, *A
Flock of Ships*, was published in 1970 and has
been translated into nine foreign languages.
Since then he has published a series of bestselling
novels, most recently *The Sextant*, *Spearfish* and
The Bone Collectors.

BRIAN CALLISON

A Thunder
of Crude

FONTANA/Collins

First published by William Collins Sons & Co. Ltd 1986
First issued in Fontana Paperbacks 1987

Made and printed in Great Britain by
William Collins Sons & Co. Ltd, Glasgow

Many Liberia flag vessels sustain
standards of maintenance and manning
equal to any other nation's sea carriers.

Most oil companies do invest
responsibly in safety and anti-pollution
measures.

Some don't. Or details are overlooked.
Or quite ordinary people make
mistakes.

Whereupon a terrible Thunder of Crude
is heard.

The Ship

When she first appeared off the bay, materializing soundlessly, or so it seemed, from out of a winter's sea mist that was trying every bit as hard as it had done for centuries past to deny all hint of horizon west of the offshore pinnacle of Sgeir Garth, she might well have looked like some spectral Leviathan to any landsman watching from that very edge of Scotland. A trick of the imagination; an insubstantial monster slowly rising out of wreathing gossamer strands, all greyed and fuzzed and shimmering.

But she wasn't – a mirage, that was. And certainly not without substance either for, while even her awesome bulk might have been unremarkable in comparison with some of her younger, still more technologically ambitious sisters, nevertheless that gradually crystallizing shadow remorselessly closing with the mainland represented one of the largest mobile structures yet created by man. Long enough to accommodate two football pitches laid end to end and still leave room enough for the more euphoric supporters to riot in; wider than a ten-lane autoroute; higher from bottom to top than a seven-storey office block; she carried in the vast caverns of her welded steel belly seventy-six thousand metric tonnes of Arabian Heavy and a further forty-one thousand tonnes of Arabian Light. Crude oil, that was, sweat–milked from desert sand and transported all the way from Mina al-Ahmadi in the Persian Gulf – enough, once refined, to keep a typical family motorcar fuelled and running for fifty-five thousand years, give or take a decade or so.

Or, of course, to run fifty-five thousand average family motorcars for one year.

Her name was *Calauria*. As she came closer, and the spectre took on unmistakably solid form, even the most lubberly of landsmen must have concluded that such a seaborne colossus could only be something called a supertanker, which she was indeed; though mariners, who tend to use more specific if somewhat less romantic abbreviations for everything, would simply have referred to her laconically as a VLCC – a Very Large Crude Carrier.

Of course no observer, landsman or seaman, could possibly have guessed, during those careful hours as she inched her way into the sea loch and crawled towards her discharging berth on the offshore jetty – slipping ponderously through the two-mile-wide entrance formed by the sheer rock face of Roinn Tain, surmounted by its ruined fortress cap of melancholy Dùin Feadda to the north, and the more gentle seawashed ledges of Riddock Skerries to the south – at the potential for horror which was also being imported beneath those acres of rusted steel plate. Nor could he have dreamed that the alchemy of catastrophe had already begun to foment within that mammoth before them.

Certainly he would never have accepted that he might even then be witnessing the supertanker *Calauria* in the process of making her very last landfall.

Or that *Calauria* and her complement, as well as the sea loch of Quarsdale, and its deep-water oil terminal and tank farm situated on the point known as Sròine Rora, could all be destined to fashion tomorrow's headlines.

To say nothing of two thousand-odd ordinary residents of the quiet Scottish burgh of Vaila: people who lived and laughed and loved and argued and were sometimes jealous of each other just as people in any other community were, and who – again like

8

most of us – never anticipated that some truly awful experience would impinge upon their largely unremarkable lives.

But then people, by definition, tend to avoid thinking The Unthinkable. Until, without warning, it becomes: The Reality.

CHAPTER ONE

Late afternoon: FRIDAY

'Slow astern, please, Captain. Starboard twenty!'

The docking pilot carefully enunciated the command – or was it a request? There's a fine diplomatic line between orders and guidance when you've got a master pacing his own bridge in nerve-tuned anxiety while a complete stranger takes over his ship. But then, in close and foreign waters the master only knows his ship while the pilot nurses hard-won acquaintance with the local dangers; knows intimately which submarine hazards the vessel briefly entrusted to him might foul, to say nothing of what currents and tide-rips and assorted maritime plagues might cause her to do.

'Engine slow astern. Right twenty the wheel,' Bisaglia translated harshly across the width of the huge bridge deck. Then he leaned far out over the port wing and frowned anxiously seventy feet down into the cold, black and, by now, barely moving water between them and the offshore jetty; just checking that Pilot McDonald really was taking the same action with *Calauria* as he himself would.

The responses were less strained: liquid Italian.

'Engine slow astern . . .'

'Right twenty the wheel, sir.'

'. . . engine running slow astern, sir.' Chief Officer Spedini's confirmation came almost in time with the clang of the telegraph.

'Wheel's twenty to right, sir,' General Purpose Rating First Class Forlani supplemented deadpan in his odd Cosenza brogue. He looked and sounded professionally bored as he invariably did, yet, particularly when manoeuvring, Forlani's presence at the helm always reassured the Captain. His was a competent boredom.

'Midships the wheel.'

'MIDships.'

'Midships the whee . . . Wheel's amidships, sir.'

The scarred bridge rail began to vibrate fractionally and even from that awesome height Captain Bisaglia could detect the thresh of white water creaming and whirlpooling forward from the counter.

'Stop engine.'

'STOP her, Spedini.'

'Stop eng . . .' CLANG, clang. 'Engine stopped, sir.'

All way, all fore and aft movement, was now off the ship. She loomed inert, little more than an old-fashioned heaving line's length from the offshore jetty.

'Wind's still gusting fae the sou' west. Keep a wee bawhair o' strain on forr'ad, Jimmie,' Pilot McDonald chatted into his hand-held VHF radio. Then he leaned comfortably on the window ledge and peered one-seventh of a mile ahead, out past the bluff bow and the matchstick figures of Second Officer De Mita's fo'c'sle-head crew to where the terminal's lead tug, the *William Wallace*, sat squat and steaming gently on the end of its tow. A second company tug, *Robert the Bruce*, had charge of the VLCC's stern; two more tugs – pusher tugs with funny padded-coir noses – were already nuzzling into *Calauria*'s starboard plates ready to ease her great bulk laterally into its berth.

It didn't matter that this final delicate manoeuvre would be monitored not by human judgement alone but also by an electronic-eyed Doppler Docking system located on the jetty, with the fractionally closing distances remaining between ship and berth constantly relayed to Pilot McDonald via his VHF link: Bisaglia was still anxious and would remain so until full autonomy was restored to him, and *Finished with Engine* rung down from his bridge.

'Go *on* then, Pilot: get your bloody headrope across to the jetty, dammit,' the Captain urged silently, despite the awareness that such an achievement would provide only psychological comfort at this stage of the docking process: a

11

single line ashore could snap like rotten thread if *Calauria*'s bulk took charge under the press of the keen Scots wind topping the short seas building in Loch Quarsdale: just as alien now to his warm Mediterranean blood as ever it had felt.

But they'd been on stand-by for three hours now; nearly two since sliding between the Heads, teasing and coaxing and persuading the unwieldy VLCC through the gathering darkness into position off the jetty. The Captain's outward phlegm was more a product of tight self-control than of complacency. Like most big ship masters Bisaglia felt more nervous within sight of land than ever he did when the great rollers spawned off Cape Agulhas hissed in serried ranks to challenge his suddenly puny Goliath with their most awful power.

He was also acutely aware that, even though *Calauria*'s own enormity might appear breathtaking to the unversed, her greatest bulk was still hidden – only twenty per cent of her was visible; loaded as she was, eighty per cent lay concealed beneath the surface. And allow eighty per cent of a hundred and whatever thousand tons to begin drifting, even at the rate of a few centimetres an hour, and you have one hell of a job to bring it to rest again. Bear in mind also that your single screw may only, because of the limitations of its design, be able to produce less than one fifth of its ahead braking power – one carelessly-given engine command could generate a momentum which might still wreak havoc even ten minutes later.

'Ah,' McDonald said cheerfully, as the navigation lights of the line boat finally appeared under the bow and they began lowering the eye of the headrope down into it. 'I was wondering for a minute if they hadn't been able to start yon bloody engine again.'

'I was wondering for that minute if I was not going to have to let go my starboard anchor and sit my ship here until they did,' Bisaglia retorted grimly, involuntarily. Then he hurriedly forced a smile to take the sting out of the remark, because he was by nature a pleasant man and immediately realized that here was an example of that mercifully unique British humour; the Pilot had only been joking.

12

The elderly Steward Gioia clambered up the tread-worn internal stairway to the bridge, carefully positioning a tray holding a silver-plated coffee pot, cream, sugar and two china cups beside the Captain's port high chair. He bowed before retiring, stiffly formal in his white jacket.

Gioia had been deputy head waiter of Rome's Ambasciatori Palace Hotel until responsibility for twelve children, a wife's incessant haranguing and the marginally more attractive money the sea provided had proved too strong a lure. He still insisted on maintaining standards though; as did the Captain himself whenever possible. Indeed, in moments of wistful reflection Bisaglia looked upon Gioia and himself as fading anachronisms in an equally faded ship: all three of them now reduced by circumstance into serving employers whom, in years gone by and at the peak of his professional career, a more selective Captain Bisaglia could have afforded to deny.

Once the ship could have scorned such second-rate owners' dreams of acquisition too: would have been beyond their purse. When new she'd been the pride of a great British tanker fleet. Only now, commercial viability strained by the ever-escalating costs required to maintain her to British Flag standards – as well as having been drained of all tax-efficient benefits by soulless accountants without a drop of salt in their veins – she had found herself replaced by an even greater ship; had been summarily discarded for little more than scrap value into foreign hands.

And pressed back into service immediately: without a Swiss Franc having been spent on her needs. A maritime mammoth . . . a superseded supertanker.

But then, didn't most of his present crew find themselves in that situation? Wouldn't most of them have been happier to be sailing under their own Italian Flag rather than an ensign of convenience such as the one *Calauria* currently flew? Perhaps they could even consider themselves fortunate – at least, having all been contract-hired by the same crewing agency in Genoa, they messed with their own countrymen instead of alongside Greeks, lascars, Chinese, Eurasians and whatever other hard-case flotsam drifted into the pool of seagoing unemployed. It was very much a hirer's market.

13

In today's maritime recesssion the most qualified of ship's officers, the most arrogant of seamen, the most highly skilled of marine engineers, were well-advised to consider deeply before refusing a berth of any kind.

At sixty-seven years of age, with or without a shipping slump, even a Captain lost his pride . . .

'*Grazie*, Nino.' The elderly master gestured towards the coffee tray. '*Per favore*, Pilot. Please help to yourself when convenient.'

The sternrope began to go ashore next; snaking through peat-dappled water astern of a Panoco Terminals personnel launch currently doubling as berthing backup. The glare of floodlights was beginning to take yellow precedence over waning daylight now; picking out the jettymen gathered in anticipation by the quick-release hook of the most northerly mooring dolphin. It was still raining steadily; a dreich, misting Highland evening.

Archie McDonald spoke into his VHF again, this time too rapidly for Bisaglia to follow, then nodded towards the coffee.

'Much appreciated, Cap'n: and thanks for demolishing the language barrier, by the way.'

'It helps avoid confusion. Though they would have understood you anyway, *signore*: most seamen are familiar with English manoeuvring commands – midships; port thirty degrees and such . . . My Chief Officer, *Signore* Spedini, speaks it quite well in general, as does Chief Engineer Borga.'

'You haven't had to pilot some of the Jap Flag tankers,' McDonald said feelingly. 'Or the Koreans. They're no' all as fluent, believe me.'

Calauria's master smiled again. It was a wry smile this time. To the Pilot it seemed as if there might have been a trace of irony there as well.

'But perhaps I have the advantage. I once spent . . . some time in your country. Many years ago.'

Only a girl got off the Fort William bus. Well, she was more a woman, really: in fact she was definitely a woman when the bus finally drew away and Duggan got a good look at her through the Range Rover window.

She stood there for a moment outside McKay's, the Spar grocers where the Vaila Cross bus stop was situated: tall; long dark hair tumbling over a black leather coat; good legs – hell, fan*tas*tic legs! She put the case down, staring uncertainly towards him in the gathering darkness. He gave her a vague smile then started the engine, preparing to go back to the depot and return in time to meet the next bus.

She walked hesitantly over to catch him. 'Panoco Oil? Mister Duggan?'

He said involuntarily, 'Christ, *you* aren't Herschell, are you?'

She looked nettled. It made her even more attractive.

'I presume your chauvinistic image of the press has been gleaned from nineteen-forty Bogart movies?'

Duggan fell out of the Rover door in embarrassment and shook her hand. 'Gee, I'm sorry. Look, I'm just the monkey usually, my boss is the real organ grinder: the Terminal Superintendent. But Charlie's been recalled for conference to the States so I guess that being his Deputy lets me screw things up my own way.'

She smiled a little mockingly. 'One of the privileges of rank – choosing your own mistakes.'

The young man still looked worried. 'Fact is he just left me a memo – Meet initial-F Herschell: *Northern Citizen*. It didn't say whether you were a Mister or a Miss.'

'Neither – I'm a Mrs. I happen to be married.'

His already pink cheeks went scarlet. 'Look, Mrs Herschell: say I just crawl back in my machine and drive round the corner. Then drive back an' start fresh again?'

She picked up her case and handed it to him. 'Call me Fran. And I really am initial-F Herschell, your intrepid ace reporter from the *Citizen*.'

Duggan began to say, 'I thought they were sending their shipping correspo . . .' when he saw the look in her eye. 'You're just about to tell me you *are* the *Northern Citizen*'s shipping correspondent, aren't you?'

'Yes, Mister Duggan,' she answered. Then began to giggle.

'I wish I was dead,' he muttered with feeling.

The reporter called Fran said consolingly, 'Don't. I also happen to be their cookery expert, agony aunt, crime reporter and tea lady. We aren't a very big newspaper . . .' She waved at his Range Rover bearing the *Panoco Oil Terminals (U.K.) P.L.C.* transfer, in yellow letters on slate grey. 'Can we go? It's raining and it's cold.'

'Hell, yes . . . Er, where to first? We've booked you into the Meall Ness Hotel: Mrs McAllister's. Not exactly the Holiday Inn but you'll be very comfortable and you get a knockout view of the loch.'

'I would like to get cleaned up. Then maybe I could go and see the demonstration?'

'You make it sound like a nuclear disarmament rally,' Duggan said. 'It's only a very small demonstration.'

She looked at him sideways as they climbed into the Rover. 'Then why is Panoco Oil so anxious to put its point of view, Mister Duggan?'

He pulled away from the kerb and headed north along the narrow main street, rubbing at the condensation forming inside the windscreen. 'We hope your article will reflect that we do have genuine concern for minority opinions. Just as we have for this self-same environment they claim our terminal puts at risk.'

'You sure it's only minority opinion? They collected enough signatures in Vaila alone to force the Scottish Secretary of State to institute a public enquiry before granting permission to locate your terminal here.'

'We still got it though. And don't forget, the Region recommended acceptance. And the District Council Planning Committee.'

'They had to consider the broader implications: the good of all. They need the income your rates and the port dues bring. And the employment you offer. This is the Highlands; a whole area slowly dying through economic starvation.'

He shrugged. 'Then there's your answer.'

'Perhaps not,' Fran said softly. 'Not if I actually happened to live in Vaila . . .'

16

They drove in silence for a while until she asked, 'You're American aren't you, Mister Duggan?'

'Canadian. And just call me Duggan. Everybody else does.'

'Don't you have a first name?'

He went pink again. Sometimes he seemed more a schoolboy than Deputy Superintendent of a major deep-water tanker terminal. 'Aloysius.'

'I'll call you Duggan too,' she said gravely as they passed a gap in the houses and the windswept length of Loch Quarsdale opened before them. 'Can we stop a minute?'

He pulled to the verge and kept glancing surreptitiously at her ankles as she half turned on the high seat to gaze over towards the terminal. A massive supertanker lay floodlit and almost alongside the jetty, her navigation lights burning steadily. It seemed to fill the darkening horizon.

'Just arriving,' Fran mused. Duggan grinned.

'How d'you know it's not just leaving?'

'Because she'd either be light or in ballast – that one's right down to her marks. And ships don't leave: they either sail or depart.'

'You *are* a shipping correspondent.'

'And married to a sailor. John's homeward-bound. Somewhere near Singapore just now: master of a Scotia Container liner out of Glasgow. The *Highlander*.'

'He's a very lucky man,' Duggan blurted impulsively.

'I know. There are so few commands available in the British merchant fleet nowadays.'

Duggan wasn't sure whether she'd misinterpreted his fumbled compliment or whether she was being deliberately obtuse.

'Liberian,' she mused, gazing at the tattered red and white horizontally-striped ensign still visible over the berthing VLCC's counter, the dirty white star almost lost within the dark blue canton.

'Named *Calauria*. Chinese owners, Swiss managers . . . Italian crew, far as I know.'

She didn't reply, but he could guess what was running through her mind. Liberian and Panamanian ensigns all too

17

often marked vessels being operated by high-profit low-outlay owners these days. Flags of convenience they were called: convenient in that they demanded minimal survey and safety standards, issued inadequately checked licences for watchkeeping officers, ran with skeleton multinational crews and paid starvation wages . . .

'I know what you're thinking, but most of the big FOC hulls we get in here are one hundred per cent safe, Liberian or Panama-registered purely for tax reasons,' Duggan put in, perhaps a little too hurriedly. 'Major shipowners; European certificates of competency; run and maintained to Lloyds or Bureau Veritas A-One Plus standards.'

'No VLCC is a hundred per cent safe, it's the nature of the beast,' Fran retorted. 'No tanker is, come to that.'

'No ship of any type is, considering the proposition objectively.' Duggan shrugged, slightly nettled. 'But then again, neither is a train, an automobile or, f'r that matter, a kid's bicycle. Mobility implies, by definition, some degree of risk.'

She let the point go, still watching the Liberian tanker.

'Where's she from, anyway?'

'Persian Gulf: Mina al-Ahmadi and Kharg. With Arabian Crude.'

'Heavy or Light?'

He eyed her with grudging respect. 'Both.'

'How much?'

Again Duggan suspected the motive behind her casual question – how deep, for instance, would even a small spillage lie over the shingle beaches and the beautiful rocky coves which formed Loch Quarsdale, and over the commercial shellfish and mussel beds below it?

He leaned forward and started the Range Rover, it seemed a good idea. 'A hundred, seventeen thousand tonnes,' he answered shortly.

It was strange how – even to Duggan – *Calauria* all of a sudden looked different as he drove along the coast road towards the Meall Ness Hotel.

Different. A bit older, a bit run-down under the cold, analytical wash of the floodlights; even slightly jaded as she towered – curiously sinister now, as well as breathtaking by virtue of her immensity – above the island jetty off the point called Sròine Rora.

Aboard that same slightly jaded leviathan her Chief Officer, Mario Spedini, was also reflecting upon *Calauria*'s true measure when compared against the scale of natural things. But then, during the past two hours Spedini had found himself gazing for the first time upon the rugged majesty of Scotland's Highlands from his post at the engine telegraph.

Comparatively young at thirty-two to hold a senior deck officer's berth aboard even an FOC hull, the VLCC's Mate had never visited the north-west coast of Britain before, most of his previous tanker experience having been gained between the Gulf and the great Continental oil centres: Europoort, Algeciras, Le Verdon on the Gironde estuary. He'd sailed into Falmouth and Milford Haven a few times; only once before had he voyaged to Scottish latitudes – to the Lowland Firth of Forth's Hound Point Terminal as a young Second Officer.

So he'd never looked upon mountains affording quite such a dramatic aspect, rising as these did from the very edge of the Atlantic to encompass the windswept span of the Quarsdale Loch within their massive geography; wild black silhouettes towering to a scudding cloudbase which parted only sparsely to reveal snow-capped peaks weirdly luminescent in the gathering dusk. To her Chief Officer the familiar dimensions of *Calauria* seemed humbled by such fierce magnitude, but then Spedini was a son of Lombardy, more at one with the sun-kissed plains of Italy.

The clustered yellow rectangles which marked the windows of Vaila were duplicated in hamlets and even more isolated dwellings along the darkening shoreline. They appeared tantalizingly close, yet Spedini knew with the fatalistic acceptance of a big tanker man that they would also prove quite remote from the men on the ship. Because of her draft, and her inherent need for deep water, the offshore jetty against which *Calauria* would lie was a mere sliver of manmade island constructed a quarter of a mile into the loch.

The Mate had only needed to glance at the chart to see that, as was common with most oiling berths in a cost-efficient, to say nothing of a terrorist-apprehensive world, no bridge, no causeway, not even a pedestrian catwalk had been provided to offer convenient access to the nearest mainland point: the terminal where Panoco's storage tanks were situated. It meant that, while the Crude was simply pumped ashore through underwater pipelines, the men who brought the cargo and who worked on the jetty itself had to await passage by boat to escape their isolation.

Harassed as he would be for the next forty-eight hours of discharging, the Chief Officer hoped he would be able to spare the time for a ferry trip in order to visit the town shops. His mother had instructed him to buy some real Scottish tartan to take home; his youngest, most spoiled and thoroughly awful sister had threatened screaming family crisis on his return if he didn't procure at least a Celtic doll.

While the ship was lying off the berth and under the control of the tugs, Spedini took advantage of the lull in engine movements to scan the foreshore and town through his binoculars. Grey stone houses, a church with a stubby spire, few pedestrians, little apparent colour even allowing for the winter gloom. Scotland in January did not appear a jolly place. Occasional vehicles crawled along the wet main street: beetles with glowing yellow eyes affording, at least to him, an impression of comfortable domesticity, of having somewhere warm and welcoming to go. It was an emotion Mario Spedini often experienced when looking from the ship into someone else's country. It was a lonely feeling, a sense of intrusion, of not being a part . . .

He halted momentarily as a movement caught his eye. A white square – a sign or a placard? – wavered at what appeared to be the gates to the terminal. And weren't those people huddled in a tight group as if to block the road?

The British Pilot passed Spedini's station en route through the wheelhouse and misread his interest.

'Aye, you're right, Chief Officer. It's not exactly the Costa del Excitement – our wee borough of Vaila.'

Spedini frowned, his already limited command of English totally confused by the unfamiliar Scottish dialect. 'I am

20

sorry, *signore*? But do you not have a riot in your town, yes?'

'Only four times a year: when the electric bills come through the letter boxes.' McDonald followed the Mate's gaze and grinned. 'Och, you mean the protest?'

'*Si!* The gathering of people at the gate – you call it a protest then?'

'Personally I call it a complete waste of time. Mind you, I'm biased: I work for Panoco,' Pilot McDonald retorted enigmatically before continuing out to the starboard wing with VHF in hand.

He left Chief Officer Spedini frowning doubtfully. Not so much over the reasons for the curious British goings-on at the gate as . . . well, wherever in the world *was* a Scotchman's Costa del Excitement?

One hundred feet away the Captain still leaned on the port wing rail, hunched against the steady rain. Like Spedini he was pondering over an earlier remark made by the Pilot: the comment on his fluency in English. Or more, perhaps, on his own reply.

'I once spent . . . some time in your country. Many years ago.'

Bisaglia hadn't elaborated. It had been so many years since 1940; that demoralizing fleet engagement off Cape Matapan, his subsequent capture by the British.

Over two-thirds of his lifetime now, yet occasionally, in nightmares, he still felt a residual ache in his right leg, fractured when the first incoming shells exploded under his action station in *Fiume*'s gun director; experienced again the stunned disbelief about him, soon compounded by the horror of the heavy cruiser's inexorable capsize; heard the screams of comrade sailors still trapped below decks as the warship finally went down, leaving a fluff-cheeked and tearful *Guardia Marina* Tommaso Bisaglia, then only two months graduated with honours from the Italian Naval Institute in Livorno, to be plucked ignominiously from an oil-subdued sea by one of Admiral Cunningham's triumphant destroyers.

The Italian Battle Fleet had lost two more heavy cruisers and two destroyers in sea-child Bisaglia's first, last and singularly traumatic naval action – as well as suffering considerable damage to the ultimate pride of their Navy, the battleship *Vittorio Veneto*. She'd never left harbour to challenge the Royal Navy again during the rest of the Second World War.

The Captain nodded the water from his cap and concentrated once more on the steadily closing gap between ship and berth. Already they were preparing two of the depot's stork-like Chiksan arms for marriage with *Calauria*'s manifold; the link through which his cargo would ultimately be discharged. A man with the look of an ex-seaman in a white boiler suit, Panoco yellow oilskin jacket and hard hat stood close by the coiled bonding cable, presumably to supervise its early connection to the ship's structure as a precaution against any potentially lethal accumulation of static electricity. Bisaglia guessed him to be the terminal's Pollution Control Officer and therefore the man who carried responsibility for the safe conduct of the offshore jetty's part in the unloading operation.

He assessed the man critically. The PCO certainly seemed alert enough; watching even now as, dimly visible on the main deck, Bosun Egidi scraped industriously to remove grease and paint from a section of the VLCC's port rail.

The Captain stirred, suddenly aware of what would have been, until recently, a quite uncharacteristic reaction. He was, he realized, making a conscious effort to assure himself that this particular key supervisor would . . . well – put baldly – would prove proficient at his job.

Bisaglia frowned uncomfortably, angry with himself; even a bit shaken. Before he'd taken command of *Calauria* less than a year ago it would never have occurred to him to search for such reassurance. The realization that he now felt the need to do so was unsettling.

Oh, not that any experienced tankerman would dispute either the demand for vigilance or the fact that a high-risk venture was indeed about to commence – the transferring from ship to shore of one hundred and seventeen thousand metric tonnes of inflammable oil was no casual undertaking. But working tankships is a routine daily operation in today's industrial world and furthermore – simply because the dangers *are* so clearly appreciated – there exist well tried and internationally recognized precautions; statutory safeguards evolved out of bitter lessons learned over decades since the first barrels of transatlantic oil were carried by the sailing ship *Elizabeth Watts* in 1861. They ensured that key men such as that anonymous PCO down there were professionals; trained to be acutely aware of the hazards and to minimize them.

And then again, an international system of control also exists to ensure the competence of the shipmasters and officers who actually drive the great crude carriers across the world; requiring that they be licensed as risk-worthy, because they, perhaps, carry the widest responsibility of all.

Yet reality, in relation to the safety of the Very Large Crude Carrier, has grounded somewhere between idealism and unpalatable fact. All seamen are aware that what should, in theory, offer a watertight system of issuing international certificates to prove seagoing competency doesn't always accomplish its aim. Indeed, was it not the case that, deep down, Captain Tommaso Bisaglia himself had good reason to confirm that such exceptions did exist?

Was it, in truth, precisely that belief which was causing the elderly master's unease as he stood on his high bridge on that day – causing both his unease and, of rather more significance, his steadily growing sense of guilt?

Bisaglia walked to the front of the wing and gazed unhappily ahead over the length of his undeniably degenerating monster. It seemed a long time now since going to sea had been an uncomplicated, confident pleasure, and a very long time indeed since he'd felt such strange anxiety. Not, indeed, since he and many others had awaited the coming of the British during a grim night off Matapan in 1940.

It was ironic that Junior Naval Officer Tommaso Bisaglia had been present at that particular engagement – had taken part in the only major sea battle of history during the course of which no ship of the victorious side had sustained any damage whatsoever.

It meant that the elderly, now Captain Bisaglia had already

participated in the making of one notable maritime disaster. At least, one until that moment, anyway.

Prior to *Calauria*'s arrival in Loch Quarsdale.

The Ship

For a time she would lie there until the links bonding her to her temporary lair were strengthened. Then she would be further pushed and eased and jollied into position, and bound securely before she was cautiously drained of her reason for being.

It happens to such juggernauts every day: all over the world.

And while it was true to say that the ship carried a master who suffered a not entirely unique apprehension, it would be quite wrong to assume that unease was caused by anything other than an ageing man's mistrust of himself. There was no suspicion in his mind that the vessel he commanded might also present a greater than usual degree of threat. The Captain had served in many ships older and more frail than his mighty *Calauria*. All had carried him safely through such appalling stresses as are to be found among the natural hazards of the seas – always remembering that the British Navy was as unnatural a hazard as one could encounter under the colours of any enemy.

Certainly it was undeniable that Bisaglia had spent his life in ships, and was still alive; that Bisaglia had loved each of his ships, and each had amply rewarded his love . . . which explained perhaps why Captain Tommaso Bisaglia, during the twilight years of his career, would no more have questioned the integrity of his ship than he could the honour of himself.

It was an unthinkable prospect.

But nevertheless in that particular ship the unthinkable *had*, even then, become the possible. The

25

Captain had been in older hulls perhaps, and survived until that day: but as with carthorses and railway engines and human beings and windmills, when assessing the condition of a ship the span of years cannot be considered in isolation. Other factors must be taken into account: her base quality, her employment, the degree of care and attention she has commanded during her working life – all are significant factors.

Highly significant in Crude Carriers. Ominously significant in the case of the Very Large Crude Carrier *Calauria*.

For, as a result of certain omissions within her history she, like her Captain, concealed a subtle decay working beneath that deceptively impressive exterior.

A sequence of events, some initiated many months before in far distant parts of the world, was inexorably approaching conclusion. Already those factors had combined to create conditions under which, by the time Bisaglia's command loomed out of the rain masking the Scottish coast on that raw winter's afternoon, the possibility of her being overwhelmed by disaster hung – quite simply – on a hair trigger.

Whatever form it might adopt: an otherwise tolerable human error; some trifling and commonplace mechanical failure, even some sequence of routine acts, all of them safe when performed in isolation . . . Once such a chance catalyst had been invoked, then the possible would instantly become the inevitable. And the terminal phase of such a transition was already prescribed; its consequence dictated by the constant laws of physical chemistry.

By her inherent vulnerability something appalling must then happen to that most awe-inspiring composite. A terrible thundering would begin within her.

In brutally simplistic terms – notwithstanding the

fact that she, when fully loaded to her marks, displaced well over one hundred and forty thousand tons of ocean during every moment in which she lumbered on her cost-effective high-tech trade – by the time she moored close by the burgh of Vaila, the surely indestructible behemoth *Calauria* already ran an odds-on risk of . . .

Well . . . of abruptly ceasing to exist.

CHAPTER TWO

Early Evening:
FRIDAY

While the pensive Captain Bisaglia presided conjointly with Pilot McDonald in supervising the final berthing of his Flag of Convenience supertanker *Calauria* and, coincidentally, of one hundred and seventeen thousand metric tonnes of Arabian Crude; and while reporter Fran Herschell was being greeted most warmly and shown to a neat little bedroom by her hostess of the Meall Ness Hotel; and while her Panoco guide, Deputy Terminal Superintendent Duggan, sipped a welcome glass of McEwans in the downstairs cocktail lounge and brooded over the approaching public relations storm already signalled by his attractive but strangely disturbing charge, many other people were going about their daily business on and around the shores of Loch Quarsdale.

Take the primary reason for Fran Herschell's visit for instance – the 'riot' observed by Chief Officer Spedini.

It was, in fact, the opening round of a perfectly orderly protest by the Quarsdale Fishermen's Association – hardy souls who'd lined and netted the loch since long before the great tankers came to Quarsdale – against a threat to their livelihoods which they contended had been increasing ever since the construction of the offshore jetty some seven years previously.

It was a protest which enjoyed the qualified support of a majority of the burgh's residents. But then, most of those residents – unlike VLCC Pilot Archie McDonald – didn't actually work for Panoco Oil, and a cynic might claim that a man's attitude towards the environment in which he lives does tend to be fashioned by the source of his pay packet.

To be fair, it wasn't only the fishermen who were actively campaigning. In fact, if you had occasion to be chatting about Vaila's interests, and the talk came round to public concern and the voices which demanded most strenuously to be heard in the affairs of the community, then you would hear one name repeated often: that of local Councillor Mrs McLeish, from the big house on Fariskay.

Apart from possessing a somewhat strident voice Councillor Mrs McLeish also held the fearsome reputation of being a Woman Of Example. Which was why she was standing as firmly as she'd done every day for the whole of the previous week, accompanied by seven other good ladies from the Quarsdale Women's Action NOW Committee, in the middle of the service road leading to the Panoco Terminal – or, to be more specific, in the middle of the road and right between a banner demanding *Protect Our Traditional Fishing Grounds* and the main gate, leading not only to the company's tank farm but also to the landing place where all employed on the offshore jetty were required to embark in the company personnel launch.

They would stay there until those men, forced by economic circumstance to fish all day in the small fleet of inshore boats, had eaten and dressed yet again for the winter night, and made their way down to the terminal to campaign resolutely for someone at government level to take note of their rising concern.

Even – or so it seemed to the less optimistic, especially in the small hours – for someone at government level tae bluidy well care!

It was true to say that the Chief Constable of the region already *had* taken note. And having done so, certain prudent measures had to be taken, as was always the case where demonstrators insisted upon demonstrating and thereby afforded even a slight possibility of obstructing other persons in the pursuance of their lawful business. Whether or not the Chief Constable felt sympathy with the principle was immaterial.

Thus it was that twenty-year-old Constable Hamish Lawson of the Highland Police Force stood equally resolutely between the aforementioned Councillor Mrs McLeish and that same terminal gate; it being his solemn duty under Law to protect the uninvolved citizens and lieges of the Borough of Vaila – to say nothing of the American Panoco Oil Corporation's multi-million dollar investment in Scotland – from whatever threat of war, civil riot, commotion, thuggery or general awfulness might be offered at any moment by the said Councillor Mrs McLeish.

Well . . . by Mrs McLeish and the other seven ladies comprising the day-shift spearhead of her environmental protest, of course.

Most particularly, Hamish had to ensure that Councillor Mrs McLeish didn't persist in standing in the middle of the road when a motorcar or lorry wished to enter or leave the terminal. Needless to say Mrs McLeish didn't, because for one thing it wasn't that sort of demonstration and, for another, Hamish was the son of her sister Mary, and she would never have dreamed of embarrassing the laddie, not even for political advantage.

So the only unfair part of the arrangement lay in the fact that Mrs McLeish and partners were sheltering sensibly under umbrellas while Constable Lawson – being a police officer and charged by the Chief Constable himself with such a grave responsibility – just wasn't allowed to use one.

'Och, go and have a coffee, Hamish,' Mrs McLeish suggested, worried by the way the rain was soaking through her nephew's short police coat and dripping off the peak of his cap. 'You'll catch your death of cold. And we promise not to storm the Bastille Of The Vandals before you come back.'

There was a mutter of collective urging from the assembled and equally concerned members of Vaila's ecological task force, who not only had known Hamish since he was a wee laddie stealing their apples but, equally, had no desire to be held as accessories before the fact in the murder of policemen by pneumonia.

Hamish, however, merely stared stonily through the drips and reinforced his dogged stance. He'd been protecting the lieges an' so on since three-o'-bloody clock that bloody

30

afternoon while now it was wearing on for half six. It hadn't stopped raining since he started, and his shift didn't finish until eleven. Apart from thinking of all the things he wished he dared say to the Chief Constable he was relishing what he undoubtedly would point out to Uncle McLeish about Auntie Jesse when next he surprised him parked on a 'No Waiting' line.

He still sympathized in secret with the demonstrators though; despite the fact that his official function forced him, like the Chief Constable, to appear strictly neutral. There had already been two oil spillages at the Panoco Terminal since its commissioning: discreetly hushed up; no wide press coverage. No one had made the right phone calls from the burgh.

Hamish had still been attending school when the first, and the worst, occurred. He, like the rest of Vaila's senior pupils, had spent many mornings gathering oiled seabirds from the beaches, helping the RSPB officials who'd arrived full of concern to clean the sad creatures . . . and then watched hundreds of them die anyway with the skin beneath their feathers red-burned and the webs between their toes melted under the corrosive attack of Arabian Crude.

The lobster and mussel catches hadn't been affected to any extent that time. Nor on the second occasion which had seen a smaller spillage of bunker fuel; less of a threat. The fishermen who trawled an already precarious living from the cold waters of Quarsdale had been lucky, Hamish reflected in a brief moment of detachment.

Lucky that was, up to now.

While Constable Lawson got wet, deck hand Wullie Gibb was clattering the lid of a teapot in the *William Wallace*'s miniature galley before hoisting a tray containing six mugs, a carton of milk and an aluminium bowl of sugar already brown-encrusted from the depredations of previous generations of wet spoons. Carefully he eased his way over the coaming and stepped out on to the tug's dim-lit starboard alleyway.

The Engineer was already hovering in anticipation at the

engine room fiddley. In addition to a filthy boiler suit, Burns wore, as ever, his battered cap, red sweat rag and air of impending doom. The lads manning Panoco's waterborne plant out of Neackie Harbour aye reckoned Tam Burns was a straight clone o' Engineer McPhail from the *Parahandy* stories. Wullie balanced the tray while the Engineer poured himself a mug and ladled five heaped spoons into it.

'Hae some sugar,' Wullie encouraged.

'It's bad for me. Gie's me furred-up arteries,' Burns denied himself morosely.

'It's polly-unsaturated fat does that. Onyway it'll make a change fae your fluttery heart,' Wullie pointed out reasonably. 'An' the varicose veins an' the migraine, an' the cirrhosis o' the liver an' a'thing else you reckon you got already, Tam.'

The towing wire from the VLCC's bow scraped and screeched briefly across the strongback as the tug veered fractionally.

'Wan spark!' Engineer Burns brooded. 'Only needs wan wee spark an' we're a' blown tae buggery!'

'Better gie the Skipper his tea then,' Wullie grinned. 'In case he passes me on the way up wi'out a mug in his hand.'

Mind you, Tam Burns had been predicting holocaust and cataclysm from every VLCC that had berthed for seven years, ever since the terminal was first commissioned.

'Aye, laugh while you can, Gibby; ah'm telling you yon's a specially bad one.' The melancholy mariner encompassed the thousand-foot length of the looming *Calauria*, most of it now lost in the darkness, with a wave of his mug. 'Old and neglected an' eaten away wi' rust where you can't see it. Mark my words, laddie, you're lookin' at disaster in search o' a place tae happen!'

But Wullie Gibb knew Burns had been saying *that* for seven years as well.

Onyroad . . . did Tam no' understand that Company regulations were specifically framed to prevent such a ridiculous event from occurring?

*

32

'Lettuce and tomato tonight?' Ella called. 'Or d'you fancy corned beef and pickle again?'

'Fillet steak!' Reg Blair shouted back sardonically. 'Green beans, perhaps just a few buttered courgettes, an' a bucket of chips.'

'Lettuce and tomato,' Ella said resignedly. She came through from the kitchen, wiping her hands. 'Mind you, you *could* cook a hot meal for yourself, you know. Or even warm something up. I can always make a stew to heat in a pot, Reg, and there's a stove where you work.'

'I've told you; on my own in that control room for most've the night, by four in the morning just keeping awake's hard enough, never mind coping with a full stomach. Especially when the terminal's quiet, like while they're ballasting from sea.'

She said, 'I wish you didn't have to do the night shifts. I miss you.'

'What for? Most've the time you're in bed anyway.'

Ella pulled a face. 'That's what I mean. And you know perfectly well what for.'

Blair took his eyes off the television and grinned at her. She was still pretty: still kept herself looking attractive after twenty-seven years of marriage. It gave him a nice warm feeling inside: showed she still felt something for him, too.

'Given yourself away, haven't you? A husband who's spent half a lifetime in the Navy yet you never once suggested you were going short – so who filled the bed when I was doin' my sea-time with the Fleet, eh?'

She didn't smile back. 'The boys were young then.'

'They still are. Ken's only seventeen, while Billy's not exactly an old age pensioner at twenty.'

'It's different. They don't need the same attention. And the life was different when you were on shore-base drafts. Gib; Pompey; Singapore . . . We were always on the move in those days.'

'And now we're settled. We live in Vaila. Scotland.'

'Yes!'

Her answer was short, ominously short. Blair sensed what was coming, they'd been down this road a few times already.

33

He eyed her warily. 'It's a good responsible job – Terminal Expediter. Well paid. And Panoco's a good company . . . most of the time.'

'And you're an ex-Chief Petty Officer RN. And there aren't many jobs around for ex-gunners . . .'

'Now you sound like me.'

'I'm quoting you! You said the same thing when they offered you your first appointment out in Saudi.'

'Come on, Ella. Vaila's hardly Saudi Arabia.'

She looked at the window. The rain spattered briefly on a gust of wind; silver-glistening tears suspended against the blackness outside. It seemed to sum it all up.

'No, Reg. It doesn't rain for most of the time in Saudi.'

He got a bit irritated. 'An' what does *that* mean?'

Ella shrugged. 'Just that . . . Oh, I don't know: maybe I take badly to being buried alive.'

'Not that again! Jesus Christ, Ella, what *do* you want? They don't build bloody VLCC terminals in the West End of London!'

'I don't ask to live in the middle of Oxford Street,' she retorted impulsively, 'but neither do I want to spend the rest of my life being a country girl. Talking to the same faces, shopping in the same shop – and walking half a mile through a Scottish winter, Reg, just for the privilege of doing even that.'

He got up, threw his arms to the ceiling in heavy appeal, and said, 'Jesus *Christ!*' again. She knew they were in for a row then and tried to sidestep it.

'It doesn't matter. I'll go and make up your sandwiches.'

'Bugger the sandwiches!' Blair snapped. 'You just explain to me where we find that sophisticated good life you're searching for, Ella; what proposals you have for gettin' me a draft chit to the grand metropolis – *and* the money to pay for it, o' course – and I'll hand Duggan my notice tomorrow. Right?'

'You don't need to swear. Lettuce and tomato, wasn't it?' Ella said tightly.

'Jesus CHRIST!' Reg shouted for the third time and thumped back into the settee, glaring at the television.

She hadn't been in the kitchen more than five minutes before he came in, all awkward and diffident, and started poking at the sliced tomatoes and fiddling with the lettuce leaves.

But that was only because he still loved her.

'Look,' he muttered eventually. 'There's something you ought to know . . .'

When Reg had finished talking, it was her turn to sit down.

'Jesus Christ, Reg!' Ella Blair whispered forgetfully.

To say nothing of uneasily.

While Wullie Gibb was giving Skipper McFadyen a working mug of tea in the shadow of *Calauria*, and Police Constable Lawson simmered, and Ella Blair digested news which, at the very least, threatened a crisis in the life of her husband, ex-Chief Petty Officer Reg Blair, now Panoco Terminal's current night shift Expediter and Key Operative, a meeting was about to take place in the lounge bar of the Stag – that hostelry across from the Spar grocer up by the Cross which provided a rendezvous largely favoured by Vaila's younger set.

Peter Caird was met with looks of expectancy as he entered. Four of his contemporaries had been waiting, classmates before they left school, now nineteen-year-olds who passionately believed – like so many of their, and indeed the youth of every previous generation – that they alone appreciated the gravity of the world's problems; cherished simplistic solutions to each and every one; and, in addition, felt violent impatience towards their so irritatingly complacent elders.

'Well?'

The doctor's son rather enjoyed his new-found status. He'd never made much of a mark with the others when just another kid in the playground, but it was different now. His having gained an undergraduate's place at St Andrews University, and thus having achieved at least some prospect of building a professional career, earned him a certain respect in the eyes of his erstwhile schoolfellows. Unless they were academically able or prepared to remain permanently jobless, even the most grudging teenager would concede the difficulties of making a satisfactory livelihood in one of Scotland's remotest areas. For the other four the choice was stark: either they would be fortunate enough to find employment in the local farming or fishery industries, or they would be forced to leave home and go down to the cities in search of work.

'It's a big cargo,' Peter announced conspiratorially. 'She'll be here for at least forty-eight hours.'

John McLean, whose father owned the lobster boat *The Vian* and who, for want of a better paid or more promising job holding some future, had been helping to haul creels off Calf Skerry earlier that day, stated with carefully emphasized casualness, 'Oh aye? Then we do it tonight, man.'

He'd purposely kept his response casual, not only to impress Janey Menzies and Shona Simpson with its crisp decisiveness but also to underline his scorn of the consequences implied. More particularly though, McLean had made it sound like a statement rather than a question because he resented Cairdy's superior air and was determined to reestablish his own leadership of the group. Naturally assertive, he took exception to the manner in which a voluntary expatriate had returned during the university winter recess for what was after all just a wee holiday, yet had immediately proposed an unsettlingly militant escalation of what had, until then, been only a vocal disdain for the ecological pussyfooting of District Councillor Mrs McLeish and no-hope local fishermen such as his dad.

Actually he was apprehensive as hell about the possible repercussions of Peter Caird's plan. Trouble was, having started the ball rolling himself, he could hardly admit to having second thoughts, could he? An' certainly not if he were a true McLean.

'But we can't,' Alec Bell protested, eyes concerned behind thick glasses.

'Can't what?' Mclean demanded dangerously. A challenge from Caird was one thing; he'd brook no mutiny fae Specky Bell.

'Can't do, er . . . *It!* No' tonight, John.'

36

'How no'?'

'Cause it's the disco at the church hall, that's how.'

'Jesus H. *Christ*!' McLean exploded. 'You tellin' me a bluidy disco's mair import . . .'

'Well I'M not missing the Friday gig an' that's a fact,' Shona Simpson snapped. 'And neither's Janey here – are you, Janey?'

'I don't really . . .' Janey whispered unhappily, but having been frantically in love with Johnny McLean ever since fourth year she didn't want to be seen to side against him now. She'd hesitated largely because she was even more scared of offending Shona Simpson, who could be a real spitting virago when roused.

'See?' Shona triumphed with tightly folded arms.

'Look, tomorrow night's fine,' Peter refereed smugly; destroying the effect of John McLean's crisp decisiveness at one fell swoop. 'We can do it tomorrow night just as easy.'

He began to grin a clever grin which worried young McLean a lot. 'Och, but are we not going to make them sit up an' take notice then,' he said. 'All the fat-cat, irresponsible Dallas boys running Panoco?'

Back aboard *Calauria* Pilot McDonald watched the hydraulic buffers of the jetty fenders compress ever so slightly as a hundred and forty thousand tons of momentum finally dissipated. It had been a textbook docking. He turned to Captain Bisaglia with straight-faced professional relief.

'Welcome to Scotland, Cap'n.'

More lines and wires snaked ashore to mooring dolphins pile-driven into the bed of the sea loch. Headropes, stern ropes, back springs, fore springs, breast ropes . . . fifty minutes later the mammoth lay fast to the offshore jetty to the satisfaction of both master and pilot: a now passive Gulliver, bound securely by Lilliputians.

It was then nearly seven o'clock on Friday evening and quite dark. Bisaglia watched under the red wheelhouse lighting as Chief Officer Mario Spedini noted *Secured port side to: West Berth; Rora Jetty* in the bridge log, followed by *F.W.E.*

Finished with Engine.

'*Grazie, signore!*' The Captain gave his young Mate a slight, old-fashioned bow of acknowledgement, then turned to McDonald.

'And my thanks to you, Pilot. Now perhaps you will permit my steward Nino to show you to your cabin until the safety checks are complete and we are ready to begin discharging?'

Bisaglia watched as the precise Gioia led the Pilot from the bridge. Archibald McDonald would remain aboard *Calauria* throughout her off-loading operation; not leaving her, in fact, until he had shepherded her once more through the Heads and into the open Atlantic west of Sgeir Garth.

Unlike some masters, who resented what they considered oil company interference, Captain Bisaglia was only too grateful for such transient supernumeraries. While aboard McDonald would act in many capacities: he'd already performed the dual function of river and berthing pilot; now, through his VHF link, he would be available as the primary means of liaison between ship and shore; in conjunction with Chief Officer Spedini and the duty PCO he would oversee the pre-arranged discharging plan; he would act as an additional safety officer, a consultant, a mine of local information and, if necessary, a mediator between crew and terminal personnel.

Captain McDonald would sleep as he could and when he could for at least the next two nights in the cabin specially prepared for him. Job and finish, the pilots called it; on call twenty-four hours out of twenty-four and, it was to be hoped, vigilant in the interests of safety.

Ohhh, Captain Tommaso Bisaglia was *very* grateful to have a man such as Archie McDonald aboard!

But then, Bisaglia had a better reason than most to welcome support from whatever source. You see, even as *Calauria* had inched on her Doppler-guided final approach to the offshore jetty at Sròine Rora, the Captain had felt rather more than a perfectly understandable concern for the several billion lira interests of his owners and charterers.

Captain Bisaglia had also come to accept the brutal truth that he was no longer qualified even to *be* on that bridge at that moment. That, at his age, he would never have been offered command of an Italian VLCC, nor of any European Flag supership owned by a reputable company.

Because they would have suspected, as the honest Bisaglia himself feared, that whatever control he held over the man-made device stretching almost three hundred metres ahead of him had become at least technically inadequate.

And worse: that the nature of the device was such that, while she was discharging, should he as master make one small but critical error or fail to correct some miscalculation on the part of those around him – then his Very Large Crude Carrier *Calauria* might instantly transform itself into nothing less than . . .

. . . well, say for want of a better description – into a Very Large Floating Volcano.

The Ship

The ship would begin to discharge its cargo as soon as the safety checks stipulated by terminal standing orders had been carried out by Panoco's duty Pollution Control Officer, ex-tanker master Michael Trelawney who had, indeed, been the man in white overalls noticed by Bisaglia earlier.

The unloading sequence had already been planned by Chief Officer Mario Spedini prior to *Calauria*'s arrival. It would be a trying time for young Spedini; while the master carries overall accountability, his First Mate, in common with the Mate of any merchantman, shoulders the practical management of all aspects of cargo handling and stowage.

In that connection a detailed procedure for loading or unloading is a vital preparation. Despite its vast bulk a VLCC is still, in basic terms, an unsophisticated concept; not so much a ship as an elongated steel box with a point at one end and an engine at the other. This box is further vertically divided into massive compartments, or tanks, which transport the crude oil cargo itself. Each tank can be discharged by the ship's own pumps either individually or in tandem with others, the permutations controlled by activating inter-connecting and free-flowing sluice valves.

Notwithstanding that, the VLCC is still a waterborne object and, as such, responds to the primary laws of physics. Because of the great weights involved, unless care is taken while displacing its payload the most fearsome stability and shearing stresses can be created, far in excess of those which the vessel was designed to withstand. Buoyancy, for instance, forces an empty compartment upwards; gravity drags a fully loaded compartment down. Empty both ends, keep the middle section full and you have a thousand feet of hull sagging like a monstrous banana. Conversely, pump from the centre of your VLCC only while leaving both extremes fully laden and you have a dangerously droopy boat: bow and stern desperately want to sink, amidships she's become as buoyant as a light bulb. Mariners call that alarming condition 'hogging'.

Discharge one half of your oil cargo from the port – or starboard – side of your vessel but leave the other half still in the starboard – or port – side, and mariners call it a rather silly thing to do. You won't call it anything because you'll probably still be pinned under a hundred and odd thousand tons of capsized Very Large Crude Carrier.

So instant decisions are out. You consider what you're going to do very carefully in advance. You calculate the effect such constantly changing stresses and strains and trims will have on your ship by using well-established mathematical formulae – and long before the time comes to start pumping.

Chief Officer Mario Spedini had – he sincerely trusted – done just that, and hoped to obtain safety clearance from the PCO to begin operations well before midnight. He proposed initially to off-load the seventy-six thousand tonne consignment – or parcel, as the tankermen call it – of Arabian Heavy Crude; then to take on intermediate ballast, not only to equalize the trim imbalances thus created, but also to prevent the vast hull of the by then considerably lightened tanker from rising too high above the surface of the water; becoming too exposed to the pressure of winds alongside the berth and thereby running the risk of ranging against, even snapping the lines which secured her.

Finally Spedini intended to recommence the delivery ashore of their somewhat smaller parcel of forty-one thousand tonnes of Arabian Light.

He anticipated that the first phase, the discharge of the Heavy Crude by *Calauria*'s two steam-driven centrifugal cargo pumps, would take some nineteen hours to complete.

Unfortunately Chief Officer Mario Spedini still had one slight cause for anxiety.

. . . he wasn't entirely certain – not one hundred per *cent* confident – that his discharging plan was correct!

CHAPTER THREE

Late Evening:
FRIDAY

In the Meall Ness Hotel, some distance from but directly overlooking *Calauria*'s isolated berth, reporter Fran Herschell unpacked following her long and uncomfortable train and bus journey from Glasgow. That Highland safari had been necessitated by the abrupt collapse of her own ancient MG's will to suffer any longer or, in mechanical terms, of a crankshaft strained as far beyond its manufacturer's limits by Fran's intolerable driving as any supertanker hull forced to go bananas through the negligence of its mate.

Well, by that and by her boss's subsequent refusal of an abject plea to borrow his car instead. But the *Citizen*'s editor had already allowed Mrs Herschell to test-drive his beloved new BMW, with himself in it, on one previous occasion – a traumatic high-speed flirtation with the Grim Reaper during which his nerves, too, had been strained far beyond their manufacturer's limits.

It was nearly 8.00 p.m. when Duggan finally dropped Fran at the terminal gate. It was dark, and still raining. Councillor Mrs McLeish's committee ladies had by then withdrawn gratefully to their various homes, having been relieved by husbands and sons wearing sensible yellow fishermen's oilskins and the look of men determined to see the thing through. Well, assuming they could reach mutual agreement on a shift system, anyway; whereby one half of the Association could protest in the flesh while the other protested, in a more spiritual sense, from the public bar of the Stag.

Other men were arriving on foot, by car or on bicycles as Duggan stopped the Range Rover. Some already wore

Panoco anoraks and safety helmets. There was a deal of good-natured banter between the two local groups: it seemed a tolerant disagreement.

'Night shift coming on,' Duggan said. 'We work twelve-hour rotas here – eight till eight. The boys prefer it, they get more time off over rest periods.'

'How many?'

'On the graveyard shift? Eleven, usually. A Pollution Control Officer and five others out on the offshore jetty, the Expediter with a pumpman, one gateman and two PPOs – they're our Plant Protection Officers, fire and security men in essence – to cover the terminal. Admin staff and maintenance crews are normally involved in day work only unless there's a pressing problem.'

'The Expediter? He sounds vaguely sinister.'

Duggan grinned. 'Some oil companies call him the Despatcher, conjures up an even more bizarre picture. Actually he's a very responsible guy who sits in the terminal control room and keeps a steady finger on the pulse. He and the Jetty PCO are the real key men.'

'What about the tug crews, and the boatmen who run the personnel launches?'

'Mostly contracted. They work out of Neackie Harbour a couple of miles to the north. It offers the most sheltered berth for the waterborne plant.' Duggan held his watch to the gate lights shining through the Rover window. 'Look, this background material, how about me outlining Panoco's operation – nothing too technical – over supper back at the Meall Ness?'

'You realize you've just tried to bribe a journalist?' Fran said. 'Very successfully – I'd forgotten about eating! But what about Mrs McAllister: won't it be too late to bother her?'

'All fixed: she's leaving us something cold. And it'll beat sitting in the Rover in the rain eating fish an' chips with our fingers.'

Fran opened the door and slipped out, turning up her collar. 'You'll pick me up here again?'

'Nine o'clockish? I want to thumb a ride out to the tanker

45

and have a word with Archie McDonald and the duty PCO about the overnight routine. Meanwhile I'll leave you to face Mrs McLeish alone – that's her over there, Boadicea with a banner. Still here at this time, telling all the men how to demonstrate.'

Fran stared through the falling rain. There was something about the woman Duggan pointed out that made her feel more of a war than a shipping correspondent. 'Oh, dear.'

'Aye.' Duggan grinned with a well-you-asked-for-it air, and started the Rover just as a stocky, middle-aged man passed on a bicycle, heading for the terminal. 'Lousy night, Mister Duggan.'

'Evenin', Reg,' Duggan called, then leaned across the seat. 'The Expediter,' he whispered furtively from behind a cupped hand.

Smiling, Fran watched the Rover drive off, waved through the gates by a young bored-looking policeman. Duggan was nice. A bit immature maybe, a bit too transparent in his interest in her, but nice. And she could hardly blame him for being determined to present Panoco's case in the most favourable light. He was paid to do that.

Her smile faded, leaving her feeling a little guilty about not taking Duggan entirely into her confidence. Unjustifiably so, it was hardly her fault – though ultimately, perhaps, it could prove to her advantage – that a Terminal Superintendent, more suspicious of the motives of the press, had been recalled to the States leaving his young Deputy to handle an apparently routine public relations exercise with some kid reporter from a small provincial newspaper.

Only it wasn't routine at all. Duggan didn't suspect it yet, but there was more purpose behind her visit than that.

Far more . . .

'Ohhh, *damn* Duggan for being so nice and ingenuous,' she reflected, angry with herself for showing weakness. And anyway, hadn't Duggan positively invited whatever Company censure might eventually befall him? The way he'd betrayed from their first meeting a naïvely chauvinistic attitude towards her as a female reporter, presuming that she was incapable of technical or investigative journalism? Even

46

his supper invitation showed that he still assumed her simply to be gathering superficial Page Two copy; the very stuff of classic feminine-interest articles – small town versus State-protected monolith.

Well he – and Panoco – might open the papers one day soon to discover that Fran Herschell's presence in Vaila had held more significance than a mere feature writer's interest in parochial discontent.

She began to walk towards the small group of demonstrators, people who were concerned enough to brave the winter elements all night in addition to following their hazardous trade through the bleak grey hours of daylight.

She wondered who the really frightened one was. The one who'd written anonymously to the *Citizen*. About what he – or even she? – believed was happening behind the locked gates of the potentially explosive Rora Tanker Terminal.

On *Calauria*'s main deck Pollution Control Officer Trelawney, accompanied by a noticeably preoccupied Chief Officer Spedini and a somewhat truculent Bosun Egidi, had begun the safety checks required to be completed before any oil would be moved.

After having confirmed that the anti-static bonding cable was indeed connected to clean, bare metal, he assisted in the realignment of one of *Calauria*'s seven platform-mounted fire monitors – the ship's own water cannon – on to the area of the manifold through which all cargo would pass. He also checked that an adequate number of foam drums were close by. Trelawney further satisfied himself that fire hoses and foam branches were ready connected to the ship's mains. He noted that the hoses themselves were dirty but decided to pass them without test as no signs of severe wear showed in the canvas casings.

A blank was missing from one of the manifold valves. He pointed it out to Spedini who shrugged, seemingly more concerned with whatever else was exercising his mind, then passed the problem on to Bosun Egidi. Egidi trailed off in search of a replacement, muttering under his breath.

It wasn't an entirely novel experience for the PCO. As a

47

safety officer he'd met the whole spectrum of attitudes shown by first mates of various nationalities, ranging from fist-clenching Greek aggression to Korean total bloody indifference.

Trelawney's experienced eye roamed the VLCC's structure as they moved on. This one was a poor ship altogether – heavily rusted decks; topsides showing great blisters of corrosion under a nominal skin of paint; any brightwork, such as varnished accommodation doors, now long faded to a weather-beaten grey. Flag of Convenience in its most unattractive form, in other words. She looked good from a distance but when you got close, really lifted the stones, you saw she'd been allowed to deteriorate through lack of proper maintenance and basic ship husbandry. It probably wasn't the Mate's fault; the kid seemed bright despite his current preoccupation, and too young to have been Chief Officer long enough to matter anyway. He could hardly be expected to perform miracles when his owners themselves refused to provide the necessary hands and equipment.

Yet rigidly planned maintenance and expensive surgery to replace failing structural members became more and more essential the older these monsters grew. Only the Mickey Mouse owners and managers took the short-term gambler's view: didn't really care, didn't re-invest any of their profits with a thought to the safety of others. Take the first generations of big Crude carriers, those even older than *Calauria*. Built by reputable companies in the oil boom of the early sixties and designed to be written off in profit-earning terms within a decade, the PCO had seen some of the ageing originals sold on and sold on yet again to smaller, even less responsible syndicates; still struggling along busy shipping lanes under third- or fourth-hand ownership twenty years later.

Yet a supertanker lost some two per cent of its metal due to corrosive wastage every year it was retained in service. So how the hell did the world escape with the mercifully few major disasters which had occurred so far?

'This ship,' Trelawney called to Spedini as they mounted the fo'c'sle head ladder. 'How old?'

'Ten years,' the Mate replied, then looked anxious. 'But we are certificated, yes? Surveyed las' year in Korea.'

'Oh, terrific,' Trelawney thought cynically. He knew the value of many Liberian condition-surveys. But he'd only asked out of curiosity. His terms of reference were clearly defined in Panoco standing orders; so long as *Calauria* was properly equipped to deliver oil over the succeeding forty-eight hours, and her safety precautions were appropriate, then he would have to pass her. He was neither qualified nor expected to perform a structural marine survey . . . but he could still form opinions; still think secret thoughts.

Sometimes most unsettling ones.

'You have fire wires rigged fore and aft, Chief Officer?'

'Five wires?'

'*Fire* wires,' the PCO repeated patiently. 'I require heavy wire hawsers to be rigged on the outboard side and made fast not more than one metre above sea level.'

'*Si, si!*' Spedini nodded, suddenly enthusiastic. 'In case of the emergency, yes? For your tugs to tow us off the berth – it is there before you to see, the forr'ad wire.'

Trelawney saw. The heavy wire leading from the bitts down through the fairlead was rusted and ancient, broken strands protruding needle-like from the lay. It was a token gesture to the regulations, it would part as soon as strain was applied.

'I must ask you to replace it, please, Chief Officer. With one in better condition,' the duty Pollution Control Officer requested. Wearily.

Peter Caird wasn't enjoying the church hall disco.

Mind you, after having thrashed the night away at real student's union gigs with the rest of the St Andrews freshmen it wasn't exactly a turn-on to shake, rattle an' bore yourself out of your skull to the Presbyterian minister's wife's aerobic exercise records while the holy man himself, carried away by the beat, jiggled the lights on an' off to create an atmosphere more confusing than disco stroboscopic.

It still had its compensations though; largely in the amply

developed form of Shona Simpson, who'd never paid much attention to Peter while they'd been at school but now made it pretty clear she fancied him since he'd asserted himself in his new found leadership role.

She'd made it pretty clear to John McLean, too. The black looks the fisherman's son had been casting towards them flattered rather than concerned Caird. A year ago they wouldn't have; a year ago no one would have dared throw down the gauntlet to John McLean.

But tomorrow night the terminal would offer the real proving ground; the leadership crunch. Certainly Caird was confident *he* would go through with it, but then, maybe he held a psychological advantage over the rest of them – well, he was a student, wasn't he? And people accepted that students, by definition, held strong views and took enthusiastic even if sometimes misguided action to promote them. Apart from which, if some academic 'acquired' a pub sign and hung it outside the local Salvation Army home, or perched a chamber pot on the highest steeple in town, everybody put it down to high spirits and a zest for living. If a working youth – a fisherman's son like McLean, say – did precisely the same thing, he was condemned out of hand as a bloody yobbo.

But that was McLean's problem. Either way, twenty-four hours from now they'd settle once an' for all whether or not McLean was prepared to put risk where his mouth was.

And another thing: it was Peter Caird's scheme; so Caird intended to make damn sure he would be the one to perform the really exhilarating part of the plan; the one who took the boat out to the seaward side of the tanker. Fisherman or no, McLean would have to settle for being a land-bound animal tomorrow night.

Of course no one could have imagined such a dreadful thing at the time, but as it turned out it was a pity the Simpson girl had been bitchy enough to flaunt her admiration for a rival who was – in the opinion of a fulminating John McLean – naething mair than a pretentious, conceited, toffee-nosed bluidy smart ass. For it meant that what had simply been a childish act on Shona's part would ultimately constitute not only the first, but also the most cruel and unnecessary element in the trigger mechanism of eventual disaster.

When Fran approached the group before the Panoco gates she soon discovered, as Duggan had pointed out, that Mrs McLeish was indeed still there, harrying and organizing.

She only needed to listen for a moment to confirm that fact.

Of course Police Constable Lawson was still there too, but policemen tend to be faceless uniforms and hold little interest for the press unless attacking or being attacked *en masse*, performing some heroic deed or – even better, even more newsworthy – indulging in some darkly criminal ploy.

Fran did note vaguely that there was a policeman in attendance, and that was about all. Hamish carried on stoically nevertheless: still protecting the lieges an' that; still performing his solemn duty under Law; still getting wetter an' bloody wetter. And all without even the prospect of getting his name in the paper.

Or not on that particular evening, anyway.

'Councillor McLeish?' Fran asked tentatively.

The lady swung away from her somewhat uncomfortably shifting audience of yellow trainee-demonstrators. They welcomed the diversion. It was to let the authorities see they weren't too happy about the terminal that they were there; no' tae hear Jesse McLeish goin' on about strategy like General Eisenhower afore bluidy D-Day.

'Aye?'

There was a snap to the reply. Brisk, and demanding.

'My name's Herschell. From the *Northern Citizen*.'

'Oh? And why aren't you from the *Daily Express*?'

Fran blinked. 'I don't really . . .'

'Or even the *Sunday Times*,' Mrs McLeish added petulantly. 'Far more people read *The Times* than the *Citizen*.'

'A lot of the nationals' leads are picked up first from local press items. Perhaps they'll send a reporter to see you too,' Fran said weakly. 'Particularly if you wouldn't mind explaining your – Vaila's – side of the dispute, Mrs McLeish.'

The *Action Now* banner above Mrs McLeish shook with

indignation as the Councillor drew herself to her full height and looked tight-lipped. 'It's hardly a "dispute" as you call it. It's flagrant and irresponsible misuse of English-dominated government power.'

'Oh, God,' Fran through desperately, 'She's a Scottish Nationalist on top of everything. She'll bring the "North Sea oil belongs to Scotland" argument up any minute now.'

'Just like our North Sea oil, Miss Hirsel,' Mrs McLeish offered exactly on cue. 'Och, but any analysis of either the geographic or the historic facto . . .'

'Local objections to the Rora Terminal, Mrs McLeish,' Fran pressed more firmly. 'I'm here to look at both sides of the story. If it isn't convenient to talk now, then perhaps I could call on you tomorrow? And it's Herschell, by the way – Mrs Herschell.'

'You're a bonnie lass,' Mrs McLeish said somewhat disconcertingly. She turned and waggled the banner at the fishermen. 'One of you take hold of this – and mind to make sure it's kept in view. Aye, and you, Jamie Kennerty; you see you dinnae go sneaking off to the Stag soon as my back's turned.'

There was a general grinning at the smallest man in the group, who went pink with embarrassment, while Councillor Mrs McLeish tucked one arm into Fran's, drawing her to one side. Suddenly she didn't seem quite so fearsome.

'It will be the young manager laddie, Duggan, who's your host from the oil company?'

Fran nodded.

'Aye, well you hear his side – the official side – first, Miss Herschell. And then you'll maybe come over to Fariskay for a cup of tea tomorrow afternoon? Where I shall tell you the real truth of what people should know.'

At that moment Fran Herschell sensed there was a story.

'That's very kind of you, Mrs McLeish. I'd love to come.'

'Until then,' the Councillor said, 'you might care to keep a few wee points in the back of your mind . . .'

. . . and such was the way of Councillor Mrs McLeish that,

by the time Duggan came back to collect reporter Herschell, he found himself escorting a very thoughtful young lady indeed to supper at the Meall Ness Hotel.

In the vast if somewhat dilapidated master's suite aboard *Calauria*, Captain Bisaglia had eased from his dripping oil-skins and now stood before the bathroom mirror debating with his reflection.

He saw a small stocky man with a walnut-seamed face and steady blue eyes. He noted wryly that the grey hair, only thinning slightly at windburned brown temples, nevertheless looked dry and lacklustre since he'd towelled it vigorously. It had been so black when he first set eyes on this rugged country of Scotland, so strong and glossy. So Latin.

So damnably long ago.

. . . after being retrieved from the debris-strewn sea off Matapan, the then *Guardia Marina* Bisaglia had spent most of his four years as a prisoner of war in a hutted camp north of Perth.

Not only had he learned his English there but also – demeaning at first for a would-be naval officer yet, in the end, oddly satisfying – how to lead a plough and milk an Aberdeen Angus herd; even how to deliver a sow of piglets. At first he and his fellow prisoners had laboured under armed guard; later they worked on trust, as Mussolini grew more alienated from his people and allowed the youthful Bisaglia's homeland to fall increasingly under open Nazi domination – no longer a partner in the Axis so much as an occupied and resentful subject.

In general his captors had been kind to him; finding him an unassuming and co-operative youngster obviously out of his chosen elements. Certainly he'd never learned to hate the British; not even for what their Cunningham had done to his once proud Italian fleet. But Tommaso Bisaglia never had been a convinced *Fascista* in the first place; only a child who'd wanted so much to go to sea.

While now the face in the mirror was that of an old man, or at least of a man too old to command a ship such as *Calauria* with confidence and absolute safety. Certainly he was beginning to find difficulty in keeping abreast of the advances still being made in the development of specialist sea-transport: the lumpish container ships which carried more cargo on deck alone than his first tramp steamer did in total; the double-hulled liquid gas carriers; the animal fat carriers; the OBO ships; LASH ships; BACAT ships; the bulkers; the VLCCs – so-called supertankers such as the declining giant which now weighed so heavily on his conscience.

Even – may the Holy Madonna forbid he should ever be offered the opportunity to command one during this closing phase of his career – the most recent generation of tank ships; juggernauts displacing half a million tons and more, the ULCCs – the Ultra Large Crude Carriers which daily ploughed their fully-automated way across the world's oceans in the charge of complements arguably inadequate for vessels one-tenth their size, yet bearing enough crude oil in one single voyage to suffocate five hundred miles of coastline under corrosive sludge as deep as a man's ankles.

Oh, make no mistake about it: it wasn't *Calauria*'s sheer bulk which gave the Captain cause for concern. She was still only a ship which relied on water to support it – and Tommaso Bisaglia had been, and always would be, a most able seaman. He'd known the oceans as sister, mother, brother, Father Confessor; experienced the exquisite joy of communion with its most endearing moods; suffered its many rages in the calm acceptance that they were his martyrdom – a penance quite reasonably demanded by a merciful God for having permitted him to survive the sinking of *Fiume* and having bestowed upon him, instead, the privilege of continuing to be a sailor for a further four decades.

No, getting his ship from A to B was not the problem facing Captain Bisaglia. He still believed with modest conviction that he would remain a competent seaman for as long as God and his own ageing frame were disposed to allow. And that during whatever precious time *was* left to him he would shepherd his commands, irrespective of size, with a margin of safety as great as any afforded by younger, less veteran masters, simply by using the senses and the sea-wisdom which only experience gleaned over the years could provide.

So why *had* he grown so increasingly uneasy; almost frightened in fact?

The answer wasn't too hard to understand. It was that Tommaso Bisaglia had confronted the truth about himself. The Captain, being a simple and honest man, had slowly and painfully come to terms with his inadequacies; had virtually accepted the fact that, officially-certificated master or not, he no longer possessed the right to claim proficiency in what had fast become not only a high-risk but also a high-technology profession in which seamanship and ocean lore were not enough to rely on. He was actually creating a major hazard by clinging to the command of any vessel as sophisticated and potentially lethal as the VLCC below him.

Captain Bisaglia had finally recognized that his mind, once so sharp when he had been a junior deck officer in tramp steamers of the reconstituted post-war Italian Mercantile Marine and subsequently as a middle-aged master of conventional tankers, now was unable to cope with the unremitting technical pressures of supership command. More and more he found himself forced to rely on the judgement of younger and better educated crewmen such as his present Chief Officer, Spedini.

'Thank you, God, for at least giving me Spedini,' the Captain thought as he stared at his reflection on that bleak Scottish evening. 'Thank you, God, for affording me such a dependable right-hand man.'

It was pitiful consolation for a man who had once been a king among seamen. And worse. For in that consolation there existed the second ingredient that was to fuse destruction. As well as, perhaps, the most exquisite irony of all.

For, down on *Calauria*'s main deck, the dependable right-hand man in question was still trailing uncomfortably in the wake of the Panoco safety inspector, PCO Trelawney, and thinking gratefully to himself: 'Thank you, God, for at least allowing me to serve under *Capitano* Bisaglia . . . thank you, God, for providing a mentor of such long-standing professionalism to correct me, where necessary, in the light of my inexperience.'

But then, wasn't Spedini just as anxiety-plagued as his Captain? Though – in the Mate's case – for slightly different reasons.

It was hardly surprising. The seeds of the Chief Officer's apprehension had been planted some months before; when the Genoa crewing agency – having found a master prepared to sign on for the miserable wage on offer, and thus heavily under pressure to produce a First Mate to fulfil their all-in contract with *Calauria*'s impatient ownership syndicate – had discovered that, recession or not, they simply didn't have a VLCC-experienced officer of any grade immediately available on their books.

Until Mario Spedini, somewhat naïvely, had entered their lair in hopeful search of a berth.

And thus it was that Spedini, admittedly a bright young chap possessing excellent discharges from his previous ships, had unexpectedly found himself being offered the appointment, despite a frank admission that he'd only logged a limited number of years sailing as Second Officer in more strictly supervised European Flagged VLCCs. Before that he'd mainly served as a junior watchkeeper aboard the smaller, conventional tankships.

Needless to say Spedini had jumped at a golden opportunity to attain instant executive status, being not only bright but also susceptible to flattery. It was understandable overconfidence; any ambitious young man would have found difficulty in resisting the lure of wearing three rings on his epaulettes, even though their golden sheen was somewhat tarnished by the knowledge that the salary which went with the job was much the same as that for a Third Mate's berth with a reputable Italian line.

The administrative details had proved simple. An upgraded Liberian certificate of competency had been acquired for him by the agency in much the same manner – according to many cynics – as most Flag of Convenience certificates of competency are acquired; by the payment of money.

Yet already, as he approached the termination of his

second voyage with *Calauria*, harsh reality was beginning to displace his initial euphoria. Chief Officer Spedini had suddenly found himself wanting in practical experience, when he'd somewhat apprehensively discovered himself confronted by the technical problems inherent in delivering two grades of crude oil which would – because one grade cannot be put at risk of contamination by the other – require separate handling.

And further, the young Chief Officer was also keenly aware that Captain Bisaglia, to say nothing of his new owners, would be hawkishly critical of unnecessary delay; every wasted hour a VLCC spent alongside meant sixty minutes less of cargo-carrying profit and a censure for its Mate. That threat alone had afforded Spedini many sleepless hours of mental effort on the run from Mina al-Ahmadi to work out the most efficient and least time-consuming programme for unloading.

Mind you, Spedini still retained confidence, almost arrogant confidence, in his own ability. Having arrived at an answer he was certain he'd got it right, despite the fact that he'd never been called upon to prepare such a complicated discharging plan since nautical college; and then only in theory. His niggling concern lay rooted in the fact that, on this particular occasion, he'd had no way of checking his conclusion.

The shipboard stress computer – the aid that nearly all Chief Officers of today's supertankers, and certainly those less experienced ones such as Mario Spedini, rely most heavily upon to assist with the complex load distribution calculations demanded of them – had, during the course of *Calauria*'s recent passage from the Gulf, become unavailable to him.

Its pre-programmed electronic wizardry had failed . . . and nobody aboard, including her Electronics Officer, had been able to repair it.

The Ship

Lift off her several thousand tons of after accomodation and main deck, then look down at her with a seagull's eye, and the two football-pitch lengths plus a sizeable kick along a third which approximately represented her size, might strike you as appearing rather like a rectangular egg crate.

Admittedly a very *large* rectangular egg crate.

The cargo compartments of the floating almost-box – 'almost' because that sub-partitioned structure did occupy what would otherwise have been a rather pointless gap between her propeller and her bulbous bow and therefore qualified the egg crate *Calauria* to be termed a ship – those cargo compartments were first formed by nine steel dams constructed clear across her hull. Oil-tight transverse bulkheads a tankerman would call them; just as he would refer to the first so-formed triangular space – the bow compartment – as her fore peak. The next section, divided fore and aft into two halves would, for reasons best understood by sailors and naval architects, be known as her port and starboard deep tanks; while the following six cross-compartments were simply termed 'the tanks': number one tank; number two tank . . . all tallying sequentially from forward.

Each of these six cargo tanks proper were then further divided into three sections by longitudinal bulkheads. The central row of sub-tanks thus created were known as . . . well, as her *centre* tanks'. Number two centre; number three centre and so on, while each side tank was called a 'wing tank' –

59

number five starboard wing tank; number six port wing ta . . .

The ninth cavern – which occupied most of *Calauria*'s after end, extended from one side to the other and happened to be the largest compartment of all – was called the 'engine room' by the crew who sailed in the ship, and a 'bloody waste of space' by the accountants, who didn't. But then, they were those same accountants who could condemn a ship to death at the end of its tax-efficient service as if it didn't have a heart and a unique personality of its own – as all ships do, of course – and who haven't yet managed to work out how you can fill a VLCC's engine room with profitable crude oil cargo in addition to using it for propelling the monster from collection to cash-on-delivery port.

Chances are they're working on the idea though, some of those accountants. Along with designs for special immersion suits to enable the engineers to maintain the engine under oil.

Finally there was a smaller tank space right at her stern called the after peak. It meant that in total, thankfully still excluding her engine room, *Calauria* consisted of twenty-four separate steel boxes which could, theoretically at least, transport crude oil.

But in *Calauria*, as with all VLCCs, compromises had to be made between theory and practice.

Because any large vessel must maintain a minimum draft in order to prevent her from falling over sideways – as a cork on the surface might do without some added weight affixed to its base – she must always carry a certain amount of seawater ballast within her when empty of cargo, even in the most placid of weather conditions. But if, as in a supertanker, the crude cargo spaces are the sole receptacles available to contain this unprofitable but most vital balancing medium, then the pumping systems normally utilized in working oil are instead, for at least a part of her time alongside, employed merely in the task of loading or discharging valueless seawater.

And, as Chief Officer Mario Spedini was so nervously aware, time thus frittered away on a safety measure was time begrudged by some owners, in particular those who, like their accountants, didn't actually have to sail in the ship.

Accordingly, a nuclei of ballast compartments independent of the main cargo systems are reserved as non-payload spaces, with which the Chief Officer can juggle and thus maintain the minimum permissible balancing weight within the ship while, at the same time, continuing to discharge oil.

In the case of the VLCC *Calauria*, numbers four wing tanks port and starboard, which were situated roughly midships and on either side of her tipping centre, were therefore separated cross-wise once again into two halves. The aftermost halves acted as conventional crude cargo spaces in the same way as her other tanks, but the forward halves never carried any cargo at all.

These midships wing tanks were known as the Permanent Ballast Tanks, the tankermen called *them* the 'PBTs'. Combined with the capacities of the fore and after peaks and both deep tanks, the Liberian goliath could hold a total of some eighteen thousand tonnes of seawater ballast without compromising the efficiency of her crude tank working.

The PBTs were to prove particularly significant in the case of *Calauria*.

Empty of ballast when she first arrived at Rora Terminal, already deeply-laden enough under the weight of her Arabian payload, they contained nevertheless the element which – if an error *was* made – would surely kill her.

61

CHAPTER FOUR

Late Evening:
FRIDAY

After Reg Blair had relieved Bill Thomson, the terminal's day-shift Expediter, he'd sat before the transfer operations console as he always did at the commencement of his watch, and read the Control Room daily Log.

He noted that the VLCC then being readied to make delivery was called *Calauria*; that she had berthed at the offshore jetty in the loch ahead of him at precisely 1856 hrs; that the duty PCO was Mike Trelawney, and that he had radioed from the jetty on VHF Channel 90 to report that he was boarding almost immediately thereafter. The berthing tugs had returned to Neackie Harbour after being dismissed by Pilot McDonald at 1906, the duty fire tug *William Wallace*, once having slipped the head rope of the tanker, had then confirmed herself as anchored and standing by to seaward of the berth as required under Panoco safety procedures. Finally, no discharging operations had yet taken place.

Next high water at Quarsdale was due at 0114 tomorrow morning. The weather forecast for the next twelve hours promised low cloud with air temperatures of between 4 and 6 degrees centigrade, precipitation giving less than 15 km visibility, and winds west to nor' westerly force 3 to 4. A deepening trough of low pressure in the Atlantic suggested it wouldn't improve any, and would probably get worse.

Blair initialled Thomson's previous entries as read; logged his own commencement of duty; spoke briefly on VHF to Skipper McFadyen aboard the *Wallace* to make sure he'd received the forecast; then sat back to stare through the plate-glass window before him. It was dappled with rain. Just like the windows at home.

That made him think about Ella and her growing unhappiness over their domestic condition. Oh, she didn't go on about it too much; tended to keep it within herself most of the time; but this evening's brief clash had been enough to remind Blair that his wife was still unsettled in Vaila. London-born, she never would resign herself to being a country girl, and consequently they, as a couple, had a problem which could only become aggravated with time.

If they had a lot of time left, that was. Maybe, once Panoco discovered what he'd done, the problem he and Ella faced wouldn't be over night watches any longer: simply over unemployment . . .

Downie, one of the two duty Plant Protection Officers came in and started hunting through a drawer.

'Seen any new torch batteries around, Reg?'

'Stationery cupboard. Top right, I think.'

'Bloody weather,' Downie grumbled, rummaging around. There was rain dripping from the bottom of his anorak and running down his yellow-oilskinned legs.

'Who else is on with you tonight?' Blair asked. It was only to make conversation; the duty watchbill was already listed in the Log.

'Auld Phimister's on the gate. Duggan's given me the new man to break in – McLeod. Seems a cheerful enough bloke.'

'He'll have to be, walking round Rora on a night like this.'

The security man found the batteries and began slipping them into his torch. It was one of the spark-proof safety torches specified for use on the offshore jetty. 'Pity them poor sods picketing the gate,' he said. 'Mind you, they don't have to do it. An' it's a waste of time anyroad.'

Blair looked at him. 'Why is it?'

'Why is it what?'

'A waste of time?'

Downie frowned. 'I dunno . . . OK, so who's going to listen to 'em now? After what – seven years in operation.'

'The company should, f'r a start.'

The PPO looked sour. '*That*'ll be bloody right.' He came over and frowned at the discharging panel. A drop of rain

63

fell from the tip of his nose and splashed a little glistening star on Reg's Log.

'What's happening out there jus' now?'

'Not a lot. Trelawney's safety check's still in progress.'

Downie peered through the window. Floodlit against the blackness the VLCC seemed to fill the frame even though she lay nearly a quarter of a mile away, out in the loch.

'Looks all right to me.'

Reg Blair began to sharpen a pencil; already bored. 'They probably said much the same about the *Titanic*.'

Downie grinned. 'You ever see that cartoon? A crowd o' weeping relatives standing round a bulletin board outside the White Star Line's office; the board reads, "Disaster: latest news". Only there's this anxious polar bear shovin' his way through the crowd demanding, "Never mind the bloody ship – what about my iceberg?"'

Panoco's night Expediter laughed automatically as Downie went back out to begin his rounds, dabbing absently at the rain spot on the Log with his handkerchief.

Where it had landed, his shift predecessor's neat 1856-timed entry had started to go all fuzzy; its text gradually dissolving and radiating outwards in concentric ink-tinged circles.

Particularly one word. A man more given to flights of fancy, less preoccupied with looming domestic crisis than Reg Blair, might well have imagined the letters of the name *Calauria* were slowly exploding to form little oil-black shock-waves.

It wasn't merely an odd drop of rain that was causing havoc aboard the *William Wallace* as supper time approached on Friday evening. Eck Dawson's oilskins scattered gobs of sea-water clear over Wullie Gibb's panful of happily cremating sausages when he barged across the galley coaming at around nine o'clock.

Between the hot plate of the oil-fired range exploding with sharp dehydrating *cracks* of salt-white deposit, and superheated dripping already slopping around the frying pan

64

with the movement of the tug, which instantly erupted and sparked and smoked and hiss-sizzled in frantic protest, it took all Wullie's courage to dodge through the billowing steam to slam a lid over the contents, thus saving them both from the exquisite torments of a thousand hot fats.

'Ye stupit BASTARD!' Wullie roared, which, while hardly to be classed as a proper mode of address to employ when confronted by the Chief Officer of one's ship, was still OK to use on Eck Dawson because the lads ower at Neackie all agreed that the Big Yin *wis* a stupit bastard onyway – not to mention the fact that the *William Wallace*'s Mate had been courting Wullie Gibb's sister for near on nine months now and relied heavily on Wullie's tacit support on the domestic front.

'She's sitting fine to the anchor,' Eck said indifferently, tugging at the snap fasteners round his neck. 'Got a spare cup o' tea goin', Wullie?'

'Ah'm a qualified deckie, no' a cordon bleu chef at a'body's beck and call!' Wullie snarled petulantly. He reverted to a nasal whine. '"Gie's a cuppa tea, Wullie"; "Got any jam, Wullie?"; "Whit's fur the dinner the day, Wullie?" It's time you lads realized there's nae proper bluidy cook signed on aboard these hair dryers they call tugs . . .'

Cautiously the Mate lifted the lid of the frying pan which immediately raged and spat at him in reanimated vituperation. The sausages lay awash in their fury of fat; black and crisp and inedibly overdone ten minutes ago.

'That's f'r sure,' he confirmed with deep sincerity. 'Got ony hot soup then, Wullie?'

A frustrated Gibby stuffed both clenched fists in his mouth, bit his knuckles hard and screamed and stamped all at the same time.

Engineer Burns squeezed into the galley, looking like he'd just been blown out of an oil well, and said morosely, 'Got ony bread fur . . .'

'Don't, Tam,' the *William Wallace*'s executive officer advised. 'Don't ask him f'r onything just now. No' unless you want a crispy fried heid.'

'That'll be hypertension,' Burns diagnosed, irresistibly

65

cued into his favourite subject. 'Jesus, mah hypertension's givin' mah stummick ulcers gyp.'

The tug rolled heavily, awkwardly, as a wave larger than the rest took her on the port bow and snubbed her viciously against the weight of her anchor cable. Fat dribbled out of the pan, blazed briefly as it ignited on the hot plate, then died in a shiny black smear.

'Supper's ready,' Wullie announced, mercurially cheerful again.

'Sausage flambé Quarsdale avec pommes oh naturel,' the Mate offered sardonically. A second roller hit her, whereupon the aluminium pot of boiled potatoes jumped over the servery fiddle and landed on the deck. Wullie Gibb went down on his knees and tried to persuade the crumbling white globes back into the pot with the flat of his hand.

'Correction . . . wi' mashed potato.'

'I thought there wis some experienced seaman said she's sitting fine tae the anchor a minnit ago?' Wullie jeered snidely.

'Skipper'll no' go back to lie at Neackie unless the weather worsens,' Engineer Burns predicted with relish. 'We'll be oot here destroyin' our bodies all night; subjectin' them tae gravitational strains unheard of before on the human frame.'

'Can you ever imagine? That they would build an oil terminal at the exposed end o' a three mile long wind tunnel,' Eck Dawson remarked, almost as an afterthought.

'Just gie's a hand wi' getting the dinner off've the deck,' rejoined an uninterested Wullie.

But then, there was nothing unusual about the comment; no wonder in the Mate's voice at the planners' lack of foresight. Any local – all the fishermen, any of the lads employed on the waterborne plant out of Neackie Harbour had been saying it for years. Marvelling at the way the experts had spent a billion dollars on setting up a VLCC complex at Vaila, yet had never foreseen that, during the prevailing westerly gales of winter, it might prove impossible for any stand-by vessel to moor or anchor to windward of the offshore jetty no matter what the regulations demanded. That, because of the nature of the bottom and the funnelling effect of

66

the surrounding mountains, once the short seas of Quarsdale
built to a crescendo the only place for any ship as small as a
tug to lie without fear of damage would be in the lee of
Neackie breakwater: over two nautical miles from the primary source of risk.

But the forecast relayed from Expediter Blair in the Control Room only predicted winds nor' westerly three to four
for the next twelve hours.

Enough to make supper a shambles and give Engineer
Burns masochistic satisfaction, but not strong enough to
force the tug to withdraw immediate seaward fire and safety
cover from the supership *Calauria*.

Not by ten-fifteen on that particular Friday night, anyway.

Peter Caird had become disenchanted with the church hall
disco long before then.

He'd had some justification. The whole evening had deteriorated in a succession of snide remarks like 'bluidy state-
subsidized students' and 'imported superbrains' from big
John McLean, who'd sat sour-faced and glowering otherwise:
not even dancing once; refusing to be pacified by Shona at
any price. Not that she'd tried that hard, mind. In fact
Cairdy, egocentric to say the least, had formed the naïve
impression that Shona Simpson was really setting her cap at
him, and whatever else displeased him about the social
inadequacies of Vaila, he liked that part.

It never occurred to him that he might be being used, that
Shona's mongrel-cunning female intuition had suggested to
her that the best way of securing McLean's devotion was to
destroy his previous complacency; to create uncertainty and
thus to conquer; to set admirer against admirer and harness
jealousy as a more than ready ally.

So when Peter eventually stood up and declared dismis-
sively, 'Och, this is for schoolkids, not for thinking adults,'
she was quick enough to rise with him.

'You going straight home then?'

'I'll maybe walk awhile first.'

She tucked her arm into his, pointedly ignoring John

McLean. 'Buy me some chips and ah'll walk with you. I . . . ah, find the company a wee bit over-childish too.'

McLean shouted, 'Jesus H. *Christ*!' and stormed from the table, pursued by a tight-lipped Janey Menzies who, before that moment, had not been able to decide whose side she would take.

Alec Bell, left sitting alone and hugging a Coca-Cola can, blinked uncertainly in part-relief, part-disappointment through orb-like spectacles.

'I suppose that means it's off then?'

'What's off?'

'Tomorrow night. He's awfy mad.'

Caird hesitated, presented with a perfect opportunity for himself – and McLean too, for that matter – to withdraw with honour. Maybe, on reflection, he *had* got a bit carried away by bravado when he'd first proposed the idea, to say nothing of later when, during the planning stages, he'd allowed himself to be backed even further into a corner by challenging for the leadership. Undoubtedly there'd be hell to pay for him too, student or no student, once Vaila woke up to the grey dawn light of Sunday morning and looked out over the terminal . . .

'Or looking for any excuse to get out of it,' Shona snapped acidly, peeved that John McLean hadn't tried a little harder to re-engage her affections.

Her timing was, as it had been in the whole sequence of impending catastrophe, impeccable.

First, she'd effectively closed the door on any thoughts Peter Caird might have had of dropping the whole thing there and then and, second, that callow young man had become acutely aware of the pressure of the girl's arm so unexpectedly linked with his. Amply swelling breasts stimulated ambitions previously considered attainable only during his early and most optimistic schoolboy fantasies – to whit, entering into carnal bliss with Shona Simpson!

He shrugged deprecatingly, playing on the fact that Specky would be after John as soon as they left; emphasizing Shona's displeasure; taking a vicarious delight in McLean's obvious unease by reinforcing the challenge yet again.

'Yeah, well . . . he's probably too scared to actually do anything. There's aye those who talk big. Only a few of us have the guts to really stand and be counted.'

Alec had already scuttled off to find Big John by the time Peter Caird and Shona lifted their raincoats from the cloakroom and stepped out into the hush of night-time Vaila. It was cold and shiny wet, the rain now carrying more than a hint of sleet and dropping sullenly from a leaden black sky, broken only by the pallid snowy crags which enclosed the place of their birth. After buying chips at the Golden Fry up from the Cross they walked slowly down the main street, past dim-lit windows and tightly drawn curtains until the terminal itself came into view.

The arc lamps at the gate threw circular pools of orange light around the four fishermen whose turn it was to forgo the lure of the Stag in order to make up Councillor Mrs McLeish's duty-protest group. The gates themselves were firmly shut, with only one security man to be seen through the brighter windows of the small lodge. Constable Hamish Lawson had departed gratefully for a hot bath and a great drying-out of soggy boots; now an older policeman, whom neither Peter nor Shona recognized as being locally stationed, paced stoically in the middle of the slip road.

'Probably from Oban,' Caird grinned sarcastically. 'They're bringing up the reserves to discourage a total breakdown of law and order in Vaila.'

Shona looked doubtful about a *total* breakdown. 'But there's only four of them over there: wee Kennerty and the others.'

He opened his mouth to make a suitably devastating retort, then remembered the way he felt about Shona's breasts and just laughed indulgently instead. Privately Peter resigned himself to the fact that, while there might be grounds to hope for a conjoining of bodies, any meeting of minds was obviously out of the question.

'Come on, then,' he said, looking roguish. Daring her.

She giggled a bit doubtfully as he turned off to the right, heading for the point. Once it had been a wild and pretty area known as Sròine Rora, before the oilmen came to

69

Quarsdale, shut a large part of it off and covered most of that with steel. The student moved briskly, boyishly thoughtless, with the girl hopping and stepping gingerly an ever-growing distance behind him on her stiletto heels, following the curve of the chain-link perimeter fencing down a little-used track which rapidly deteriorated into wet grass. Even now this provided a discreet place by common municipal consent; inhabited largely by Vaila's courting couples in summer and the rabbits and few things else in winter. Certainly there were lights at intervals all the way down to where the fence met the lochside but they were placed to shine inwards, illuminating the Panoco compound and dazzling anyone within the boundaries who chanced to look out.

It may have been the stalag-like ambiance of the high wire or the harsh revealing luminescence of institutionalized power contrasting with such dark secrecy outside, but Caird began to feel quite stimulated at the prospects for tomorrow. He was now not so much captivated by lust for Shona Simpson's flesh as by celluloid-engendered visions of derring-do and SAS men in action, with purposeful, highly-trained silhouettes – all looking remarkably like himself – flitting like avenging shadows through the enemy night.

Once they'd traced the perimeter enclosing Rora's geometrically-precise entrails of valves and pipework, and skirted the vast crude oil storage tanks, each gleaming in grey and yellow, its individual Panoco logo spotlit with arrogant disregard for an environment which hadn't changed all that much otherwise in a hundred thousand years, they came to a part where the cold reach of Quarsdale opened before them. It faded three miles out to its meeting with the Atlantic Ocean; a maelstrom rendezvous in winter, marked against the blackness only by white breakers under the re-volving loom of a beacon perched in the shadow of lofty fortress Dùin Feadda well to the north, and the lower spark-ing flash of Riddock Skerries buoy two miles southwards. It represented the last romantic panorama glimpsed by many illicit lovers in Vaila in the second before their pulses quickened to the point of wild abandonment and the long grasses closed above them in rhythmically swaying discretion.

But it was the middle distance which was engaging Peter Caird's attention by the time a wet and slightly raddled Shona Simpson came panting to catch up with him.

Far out in the loch the riding lights of a small craft, a tug or something, moved in eccentric circles as she rode uneasily to the dim-crested seas. Slightly closer, though still some considerable distance from their windblown vantage point on what was now the beach, the giant tanker lay moored to the skeleton of piles which formed the offshore jetty; its soaring after accommodation a mass of yellow light suspended, or so it seemed at first glance, above the surface of the loch itself. Then the eye detected the unlit mass of the hull which supported that alien tower, still laden and low in the water, punctuated along its ruler-straight and unbeautiful deck-line only by the pallid flare of cargo lamps.

Between supership and terminal, sometimes lost in the intermittent reflections shredded and glittering on the backs of the waves, one green and one white navigation light marked the closing passage of a personnel launch inbound for Rora landing stage some two hundred yards to their right.

Peter Caird noted the way those lights tipped and veered and sometimes gyrated crazily under the scend of the following sea; thought of tomorrow and, just for a minute, regretted the bravado which had led him to insist on leading the seaborne prong of the scheme. But then Caird who, like many youngsters of Vaila had spent hours exploring the broad reaches of Quarsdale by sail and oar, set his jaw in an expression of quiet courage and dismissed such apprehension forthwith.

The girl dug him in the ribs, reminding him she was there.

'Now what? Because ah'm bluidy *soaked*, Peter Caird?' she snapped accusingly.

He turned away from the tanker and even in the darkness she could sense his nervous energy, his mounting excitement. 'By God but I'm ready for anything now, Shona,' Peter whispered, and took her by the hand. 'Please . . . The old salmon bothie's only a wee bit further.'

Shona knew her mother would half kill her when she finally arrived home; the mess she'd got both herself and her best

71

clothes into. Yet that acceptance encouraged her to be led further along the beach, stumbling through the coarse sand hollows and going over on her heels between the polished granite pebbles. John McLean would also assume the worst whatever she said – and if by chance he didn't, then her intuition told her she should still drop hints to make damn sure he did – while Peter Caird was obviously psyching himself up for something pretty way out. As well as being the doctor's son and thus possessing a bit of social class, he wasn't an entirely unattractive boy from a physical point of view.

Anyway, apart from having developed a leaning towards promiscuous experiment, Shona Simpson had always been a somewhat strong-headed lassie. She'd believed if she was goin' tae be hanged, then it might just as well be for the whole bluidy sheep!

The last of the old Vaila salmon netters had forsaken the cottage half a century before the oilmen came to Quarsdale. Now it only boasted half a roof and three quarters of a floor, but it was still dry in parts, and offered a place for couples to linger more comfortably.

The girl sensed again the pent-up excitement within Peter and felt herself quickening too as he rearranged the straw piled in one corner. She moved closer, fondling his shoulders, running her fingers through the back of his thick black hair. Making sure he understood her willingness.

Peter gave a sudden grunt of satisfaction and stood up, holding one of the torches he'd hidden under the straw with all the other things on the previous day. The yellow circle of light showed up the heavy-duty wire cutters, the cartons of red and white paint spray cans, the black boot polish for their faces, and the rolled-up sketch plan of the terminal.

'*Told* you I was ready for anything!' Caird declared, with the pride of a conspirator supreme.

He was never quite able to understand why Shona Simpson called him a 'Poofy wee bastard!' without even drawing so much as a breath before she stalked out and left him frowning blankly.

He never would. Not until the moment he died.

*

Fran Herschell had waited near the terminal gate rather longer than the specified hour for Duggan to return from his visit to the offshore jetty and *Calauria*. She didn't mind though, it gave her the opportunity to walk a little way up the main street and think, to feel the Highland winter astringent on her face and to sense the somehow still-dignified remoteness of Vaila which – with its granite houses in their centuries-old beds at the foot of the mountains and its silence broken only by the distant beat of less ancient music from somewhere up near the church – still seemed indifferent to the changing face of the rest of the world.

Only it wasn't, it couldn't afford to be any longer. The twentieth century had discovered Quarsdale and decided to use it; had sent the technicians and planners first, and then the construction crews and, finally, the giant ships trundling their poisonous cargoes. And Fran felt sad because she knew they would never go away again, no matter how hard people tried to make their voices heard. Industry dictated the extent of a nation's influence. Oil provided the life blood of that industry. The Rora Terminal thus represented a major investment in Britain; the implantation of a vital organ within the arterial structure of power.

Councillor Mrs McLeish and a few fishermen couldn't hope to challenge that. No more than the rabbits and the mountain stags, and the seabirds of Quarsdale, which had already been sacrificed in their hundreds, could. All protest might achieve now was to ensure that safety standards were constantly improved; that the local inhabitants were insulated as efficiently as possible from hazard, and that the fish and crustacea might be permitted to survive the chemical age in quantities enough to provide for those who surely possessed the right, should they still so choose, to glean their small livings from a wild and beautiful heritage more ancient than oil itself.

And Fran Herschell could at least aid in that rearguard action. If she did succeed in confirming what she already had reason to suspect was happening or, more pertinently, was *not* happening, behind the high wire of Panoco's Vaila complex, then perhaps she could convince the British press to shout loud enough even to force Government to take heed.

So it was strange how apprehension, not hope, took root in her usually well-ordered mind from that point on; kept niggling with ever-growing concern for those folk living quietly in Vaila, long after an apologetic and somewhat wet Duggan had finally collected and taken her back to Mrs McAllister's cosy Meall Ness Hotel.

Even over the neatly laid supper of cold venison and pink fresh salmon, made even more delicious by its subtle hint of illicit taking from some Highland river in the middle of the night, the anxiety continued to rise within her. So much so that she listened with half her attention as Duggan offered the Panoco public relations line: maintaining that great international corporates had only the good of the local people at heart; how very much the environment of those who lived in Scotland meant to a jet-weary board of directors who lived in Dallas; and how little did showing a profit matter when set against the need for absolute safety of operation.

As well as the even less subtle Duggan line; his awkward compliments; how terrific it had been to find someone like Fran waiting at the Vaila bus stop; what a fantastic boost to find any reporter could look like her. And the hints – dropped with a modest diffidence, to give Duggan credit. How a guy could feel kind of left out of . . . well, the *sophisticated* swim of life, marooned here in the middle of bagpipe land. Oh, and would she like another drink before she . . . ah . . . went up to her room?

Fran parried it all with easy grace. Her questions on the real state of safety on Rora she would ask tomorrow, after she had marshalled her facts and checked her other sources as carefully as she could. And the slightly embarrassed attempts to create a less formal relationship . . .

She'd been to bed with other men before she met John Herschell. The episodes had taken place during a part of her life before she fell in love, and she'd since learned they had meant little. But Fran was equally aware that she'd enjoyed those adventures, and that the temptation to continue with them was still a force within her. She wryly accepted that she found herself pleasantly susceptible to Duggan's flattery, intrigued by his boyish enthusiasm, his almost naïve anxiety to please, and she suspected that those same qualities would be reflected in his physical approach to sex.

But Fran didn't want that tonight; the apprehension had grown too strong within her. It wasn't as if she believed she was what the Scots call 'Fey', that she possessed any sixth sense, any real power to see into the future. So why *was* it that she couldn't rid her mind of the fear that, should that letter sent by some seemingly well-informed resident of Vaila hold any real substance, then the circumstances surrounding the great floodlit tanker out on Quarsdale could already be building to an unthinkable climax? That, just conceivably, disaster might already be brewing but a superheated flash away?

Pollution Control Officer Captain Mike Trelawney gave a relieved Chief Officer Spedini the final sanction to begin pumping the first of *Calauria*'s one hundred and seventeen thousand metric tonnes of Arabian Crude just before twenty past eleven on that Friday night.

After notifying Pilot McDonald and the foreman of the offshore jetty crew, he relayed his consent over VHF Channel 90, both to the stand-by tug *William Wallace* anchored some four cables to the west and to Expediter Blair in the Rora Terminal control room.

Reg Blair, in turn, called his two duty PPOs and Ollie the shoreside Pumpman over their personal pocketphones, then leaned forward to watch the flow gauges slowly begin to register on the console before him.

Finally he pulled the Log with its already exploded blob of a supership's name towards him and made the entry:

2328 hrs: Discharge of Arabian Heavy commenced.

While most of the rest of Vaila went to sleep.

The Ship

Catastrophe, in *Calauria's* case, still required the skein of incidents to unwind and create a specific situation at a specific time, and under specific conditions.

Many of those incidents would be occasioned by minor matters. All of them would coincide by sheer chance.

Take the unquestionably minor matter of Chief Engineer Borga's sluice valves, for instance. Not that it's easy to think about sluice valves at any time. Sluice valves, or sluice valves *per se*, don't exactly represent the sort of subject which concentrates the mind or grips the imagination. Certainly they don't, when reflected upon in isolation, suggest themselves as being parties to great and dreadful happenings in the middle of a black cold Scottish sea loch.

In fact it's so difficult to get passionate about sluice valves that really, to make them even remotely exciting, they have to be examined in the context of the part they played in the drama as a whole. To do that properly, Chief Moreno Borga and his cut-to-the-bone complement of six engineer officers and five ratings must also be considered, combined with the problems which beset them on that Friday night while *Calauria* lay outwardly passive to the offshore jetty.

The first impression a stranger might have formed when invited aboard was of simplicity. For a start the Liberian supership's main propulsion unit consisted of only one engine, and that a rather large and well-proven one: a Burmeister & Wain

23,000 horse power diesel which drove her single gigantic propeller and, simultaneously, provided steam by means of a linked Spanner exhaust-gas boiler. This steam in turn drove a main turbo alternator which supplied most of the on-passage power to operate everything from Captain Bisaglia's electric shaver to Chief Officer Spedini's computerized load stress calculator – or would have done had the bloody thing been working in the first place – as well as units such as her air conditioning, her accommodation elevators, her galley range and the heating coils located within her vast fuel bunkers.

But to imagine, because the basic concept of a Very Large Crude Carrier may seem straightforward, that all other aspects of its design and operation must prove equally simple, would be quite wrong. By only providing one single source of locomotive power for your average VLCC, for instance, the designers have saved shipowners a considerable capital expenditure – but they have also, in the event of a major breakdown, caused considerably greater hazard to everybody else who uses the seas or goes bathing from any beach near intercontinental tanker lanes. And they still haven't reduced the seagoing engineers' maintenance to a one-job-and-finish routine. Specialized ancillary systems also have to be incorporated within a VLCC. It demands, for a start, an incredible variety of highly sophisticated equipment to make your gargantuan egg crate capable of doing anything with its oil once it arrives at the end of what would otherwise prove a thoroughly pointless voyage.

Thus it was that *Calauria*'s engine room, though getting a bit old by supership standards, still presented an Aladdin's Cave of high-tech challenge to the oily-rag initiated; an ingeniously installed collage of secondary mechanical, electrical and hydraulic machinery which roared and hissed and whined and chattered, and forced the unwary who entered to clutch for a set of ear defenders before proceeding one step further.

Within that cathedral-like space Chief Engineer Borga bore responsibility for – apart from his main engine – two oil-fired Foster Wheeler boilers needed to provide for *Calauria*'s steam requirements while in port, plus two further diesel alternators supplying additional power for peak-load demands at sea, not forgetting the ability to look like an illuminated block of flats in harbour. Oh, and an emergency alternator. Just in case Chief Borga's lads slipped up and none of the other spark-producing gear worked.

And then there were *Calauria*'s pumps. Borga and his team had to worry about the readiness of four general service fire pumps, two foam pumps, the bilge pumps, the fresh water pumps, the fuel oil systems pumps, the hydraulic oil systems pumps, the deck wash pumps, the heating pumps, the cooling pumps, the stripping pumps, the life- boat's manually operated bloody bilge pumps . . . and, possibly most critical of all, those cargo pumps which provided the whole massive structure with its reason for being – the two steam turbine driven monsters capable of delivering four thousand cubic metres of Arabian Crude per hour when running at one thousand, one hundred and ninety revolu- tions a minute.

But even after checking all that moving and oil- shiny metal, it would be optimistic to believe that Chief Engineer Moreno Borga and his already sweating crowd might be able to relax awhile once they did step from thundering cavern into peaceful light of day.

Because the first items which would confront them would be a pair of twenty-ton steam-powered mooring winches sitting waiting for their attention at the after end of the main deck. Then, when they glanced round, they would see another two winches situated at the forward end of the main deck, and two more giant windlasses dimly detectable on the far-away fo'c'sle head; as well as one last brace located on the poop behind them – not to mention the five-tonners under the cargo hose handling derricks amidships of course, as well as their own engine-room stores winch: all demanding routine maintenance if not the outright repair which tends to be demanded by ageing mechanical objects on ill-financed ships like *Calauria*.

And then there would be the fire fighting monitors to service, and the miles of deck lines and steam lines and exhaust lines which were also Chief Engineer Borga's responsibility. As was all the ship's navigational equipment – her two obsolescent radars which never seemed to function at the same time; the echo sounder; the auto pilot; the gyro compass and the automatic siren; the rudder angle indicator; the engine revolution counter . . . each item a piece of vital equipment without which, particularly in narrow waters, the passage of monsters such as *Calauria* offered even greater hazard to other mariners than it already did. Yet the continuing serviceability of all these necessary devices depended on the uncertain skills of Borga's Liberian-certificated Electronics Officer, one Gianfranco Priori, a young Neapolitan ex-television repairman who'd so far failed dismally not only to fix Spedini's loading computer but who also appeared to have difficulty replacing a blown light bulb.

However, no navigational aid, serviceable or not, could have been deemed a criticial element in *Calauria*'s progress towards extinction during that particular weekend. As long as Captain Bisaglia's ship remained securely harnessed to an object as unyielding as the Rora Terminal jetty the loss of some, or even all her bridge instrumentation could never affect her prospects for survival.

But there again, a few tons – or more specifically,

the disappearance of a few tons – of perfectly ordinary hydraulic oil could hardly have been expected to present a potentially lethal deficiency either. Certainly not as a shortfall which might soon help a floating city along the road to extinction.

Which was where the otherwise rather dull subject of Chief Engineer Borga's sluice valves assumed considerable significance once again.

It all came back to the myriad auxiliary systems which make a VLCC a formidable maintenance task, linked with the Chief's understandable anxiety to hold on to a job which, at the age of sixty-two, was hardly likely to be available in any other ship. In this attitude Borga's insecurity paralleled the concerns of both Captain Bisaglia and Chief Officer Spedini – all three senior officers conscious of the need to save time and money for owners who would otherwise dismiss them without compunction.

The Chief's responsibilities didn't even end with the already complex mass of machinery and electrical equipment. *Calauria*'s massive carcass also incorporated the web of interconnecting pipework necessary to move the crude oil or sea-water ballast within the egg-crate sections that formed her tanks. Each strand of that web was controlled by a valve; so that each time the Mate wished to transfer cargo from one tank to another, either to stabilize the ship or to commence discharging from another area, he ordered the opening or closing of the appropriate sequence of valves. There were literally scores of valves to open or close aboard *Calauria*: sea valves and ballast valves, crossover valves and suction valves, discharge valves, filling valves, free-flow valves . . .

. . . and every last one of them demanding repair and maintenance by an engineer.

Most of them were fairly basic – manually operated from deck level and with little complicated

81

mechanism to go wrong – but certain systems, notably the sluice valves situated in the bottom of each tank – which, when opened, allowed free passage of cargo within the ship's compartments – were remotely controlled from the pump room. In effect these valves consisted of heavy steel covers kept continuously pressed down by hydraulic jacks in order to prevent an unintentional transfer of cargo while at sea.

And it was the sluice valves located in number six centre and both wing tanks – *Calauria*'s aftermost cargo compartments and next to the engine room itself – which were causing Chief Engineer Borga such anxiety that Friday night.

He had reached the conclusion that joints in the hydraulic lines supplying those particular control jacks must have been leaking constantly during the tanker's recent passage from Mina al-Ahmadi in the Gulf. In fact the only way he'd been able to maintain the integrity of the system had been by continuously topping it up with fresh hydraulic oil from his penuriously allocated reserve.

The owners would demand to know *why* such an expensive medium had been so carelessly wasted when the Chief could have carried out repairs to the jacks immediately. He anticipated with gloomy foreboding that they would still be critical, even when he respectfully pointed out that, during the passage, the jacks in question happened to be sub-merged under three thousand tons of cargo and it wasn't easy for an engineer to fix joints without being able to breathe for an hour or two because there were twenty-odd metres of Arabian bloody Crude above the level of his hat.

He didn't need to guess – he damn well *knew* – that they would prove totally unforgiving if he failed to effect repairs once number six tanks were discharged, and before they were re-filled with ballast for the voyage back to the Gulf. For such a gross dereliction of duty they would simply dismiss him.

So Chief Engineer Borga decided he had no alternative but to request Chief Officer Spedini to leave empty all three tanks extending the full width of the ship – numbers six wings and centre – in order to give his plumbers access as soon as they could wash and gas-free them after sailing from Rora Terminal.

It would prove a most fateful decision.

CHAPTER FIVE

Morning:
SATURDAY

The night went away more with a whimper than a roar. The sun even peeped briefly over Quarsdale early on that last Saturday morning, dawn-pink like watered blood staining the snow of the high peaks while the granite town stirred and the weary men who'd stood by during the small hours handed over to their reliefs.

The fisherman protesters exchanged good-natured banter with the going-off Panoco employees as they dispersed from the terminal gates: the oilmen to their beds; most of them straight down to the harbour and back to their boats, for it was the fishing, not the protesting, that provided their bread and butter and it took either a very lazy or a very tired man to ignore the need to work for the few extra pounds his labours would scratch from the loch.

Tomorrow – Sunday – they would rest; hae a long lie-in; eat a cooked breakfast; and maybe, if the need was pressing, surreptitiously mend a torn net out of sight of the neighbours, for no man on Quarsdale apart from the minister and the Panoco people would ever be seen to work on the Sabbath.

At eight a.m. Skipper Menzies' brand new *Robert The Bruce* took over as duty fire and safety tug off the big ship lying on the offshore berth, thereby allowing the *William Wallace* to make her twenty-minute run back into Neackie Harbour in order to refuel and take water for the following night. Wullie Gibb helped Engineer Burns with the heavy diesel hose passed down from the stone pier, then struggled out of his seaboots and the oiled wool jersey that had once been white but now presented more the colour of a Fair Isle sweater knitted by a drunken Shetland grannie, what with splashes of three-week-old supper from the galley range mixed in with sludge-brown streaks of rust from the towing wires and grease from handling deck gear. After that he went away home to his bed for a while, until Mum cooked a proper dinner on a stove that – as Wullie reflected morosely – didnae dae the bluidy rhumba while you wis fryin' onnit.

He passed the *Black Watch* and *Seaforth Highlander*, Panoco's other two somewhat older fire-fighting-capable tugs, as he walked by the waterborne plant dock. They sat quiet in the grey water, commissioned only when a VLCC was scheduled to move. Theoretically they were on fifteen minutes' notice to sail in an emergency . . . but everybody in Vaila knew the truth about *that*!

He just caught the hourly bus which ran around the shore of the loch and ultimately into the town. It took another twenty minutes to cover the few miles home, the way the road followed the contours formed by the lower slopes of the mountains and the jagged inlets gouged into them over centuries by the greedy seas of Quarsdale.

Wullie Gibb was tired when he finally clambered into bed. He was glad that tonight would be their last night as safety boat for another two weeks. Winter gave the tug crews a hard time, with its sharp teeth and its violent temper. He kind of hoped it might blow up a wee bit more by the time they were back on station.

Just so's Skipper McFadyen would be forced to run back into Neackie, even for a part of the night. Preferably about the time when it came to dicing wi' the mysterious explosive qualities o' Butcher Haig's best port sausigis.

Expediter Blair phoned through for the 0800 weather forecast and entered it in the Log before he went off duty. It promised intermittent breaks in cloud, giving 30 km visibility during the afternoon, but that winds would back sou' west rising force 5 to occasional 7 by nightfall. Daytime air temperature would only touch 8 degrees centigrade. The Atlantic low was still on the move.

He called Pilot McDonald out on the ship and warned

him. Archie said, 'It looks like we're in for a bit of a blow right enough, Reg. I'll pass it on to the Mate.'

Blair rubbed his chin. The bristles felt rough on the un-shaven skin. 'I'll need to brief the day man when he comes on. You planning to discharge all the heavy first, or ballast partway through?'

Looking out of the big window before the console, he eyed the vast shape of *Calauria* a quarter of a mile away, clearly visible now with her white-painted superstructure pink-soft under the watery sun. She was a lot higher in the water than she'd been when she arrived yesterday; trimmed bow high with the flat deck sloping aft to encourage the cargo to sluice through the length of her and increase suction to the pumps. He wondered where on that distant deck Archie McDonald was located. VHF conversations gave you a strange sense of remote intimacy; you talked as familiarly as if you were seated next to each other, yet you could never quite visualize your opposite number's situation.

'Original schedule proposed all the heavy but I'm on the bridge, haven't got the latest figures,' the Pilot returned as though reading his mind. 'How much ashore now?'

Reg glanced over his console gauges. 'About three two thousand metric. Not halfway through the heavy parcel yet.'

'Wait one. The Mate's just come up from the pump room.'

There was a short break with only the hiss of static whisper-ing through the Control Room speaker. Then Archie's dis-embodied voice came back.

'Chief Officer says he'd like to stick to his arrival plan; intermediate ballasting only after the heavy's completed discharging. That should be around half past six, say seven this evening. There'll still be more than enough weight in her to stop her ranging, even if we get a puff or two of force eight.'

'Affirmative. Thomson's the day man. I'll pass it on an' he'll keep you advised of any change in forecast.'

'Roger,' Pilot McDonald said cheerfully from the distant bridge. 'Speak to you again tonight then, Reg. Sleep well; give my regards to Ella when you get home.'

'Aye,' Blair acknowledged shortly and switched back to

his listening channel. He sat thinking about himself and Ella, and what they could do to resolve her disenchantment with Vaila, until Bill Thomson came in and said sourly, 'Mornin', Reg. Christ, but d'you know that bloody woman McLeish is out there picketing the gate already? Even said, "Mornin', Mister Thomson", to me, nice as you like, yet it's our bloody jobs she's after doing away with. You know that, don't you? *Our* bloody jobs!'

'They'd get on well together then; striving towards a common aim,' Expediter Blair reflected bitterly, forgetting for the moment what he himself had done to lay his own job prospect on the chopping block as he slipped on his bicycle clips and shrugged into his heavy Panoco anorak.

'. . . my wife and District Councillor Jesse McLeish.'

Chief Officer Spedini had felt increasingly confident as he entered *Calauria*'s dining saloon for breakfast at ten past eight that morning. Offloading had gone well overnight following a slight delay in accommodating the whims of Panoco's somewhat humourless Plant Protection Officer, *Capitano* Trelawney. An acceptable replacement for the condemned fire wire had taken some time to find from the ship's minimal complement of spare gear – but other than that they'd met no unforeseen delays. He'd even managed to grab a few hours' sleep before four a.m.; Second Officer De Mita was proving a reliable backup as officer of the harbour watch. •

And then there was the Captain, of course. One couldn't help but feel that *Capitano* Bisaglia was always there to offer a tolerant word of criticism, a gentle lead whenever his young Chief Officer's inexperience revealed itself. Spedini knew he would never be allowed to make a serious mistake so long as he kept the master fully informed of his intentions which, in the case of the present discharging plan, he had indeed done before they'd berthed at Rora. Bisaglia had nodded, and said, 'You are quite happy that this is the way according to your best calculations, *signore*?'

'*Si, Capitano!*' Spedini had answered, projecting rather more confidence than he'd felt. 'In the absence of the loading computer I have double-checked the stress factors at each stage, as well as our trim and stability figures.'

He hadn't known whether to feel complimented or apprehensive when Bisaglia barely glanced at his proffered calculations, representing sleepless nights before his desk. The little master had simply shrugged before commenting, with a trace of bitterness, 'Our Electronics Officer Priori does leave a little to be desired. He must have come very cheaply for our employers, eh?'

It had been the only time Chief Officer Spedini had heard his Captain speak disparagingly of the owners. The same could hardly be said of Chief Engineer Borga, though. Even as the Mate helped himself to bread, apricot preserve and coffee from the servery he could hear the familiar plaintive growl from the Chief's table.

'Cut this; dispense with that; save a little here; trim back a little there . . . Shit they give us, Visentini. Shit to maintain corroding shit. We spend our miserable lives perched on whole lakes, seas – positive *oceans* of oil! Yet the products from them, the fruits of our own extorted labour, they deny us as if it was some kind of elixir of power.'

The Chief took a deep breath while Spedini settled at the deck officers' table, picking a slot between the Captain's still vacant chair and twenty-year-old Third Officer Marcora. There were surreptitious grins on the faces of the few engineers listening to their senior; it was old ground, a joke, a daily harangue from the man who performed miracles as routine, drove himself harder than any in the service of those same owners whom he so vehemently condemned.

Borga waved a bread stick violently at Second Engineer Visentini. 'I tell you, young Cirlaco; lube oil they expect me to dispense in little glasses like Scottish whisky; hydraulic they demand should be doled out by the millilitre; shims I have to cut myself from tin cans; gaskets from bloody salvage . . .'

The bread stick stopped in mid-flourish as Borga caught the Mate's eye, then homed in on him like a compass needle on a magnet.

'Your tank numbers six across, *signore*? While I curse our

bosses it is you to whom I have to break the news that I have a real problem . . .'

Even before Borga began to detail the intimate technicalities of sluice valves and hydraulic leaks Chief Officer Spedini had already lost his appetite. In his view it wasn't so much Chief Engineer Borga who had a real problem: it was he – Chief Officer Spedini. The young Mate anticipated immediately that, whatever repairs the Chief wished to effect within *Calauria*'s aftermost tanks, he would require empty, washed and gas-free spaces in which his engineers could work with safety. Yet Spedini's meticulous calculations had depended on the immediate refilling of those same cargo compartments with sea-water ballast before discharge of his forty-one thousand tonne parcel of Arabian Light: an operation vital to compensate for the constantly varying forces which would be imposed on the hull throughout the day as the tanker rose higher from the loch.

Yet now he'd been caught by a change in circumstance. Re-distribute the load remaining within the ship as Chief Borga demanded he should and, by definition, he would incur a whole new series of potential dangers; of trim and stability alterations and bending moments quite unknown until such time as he'd re-calculated their effect upon the floating structure that was *Calauria*.

Any other VLCC mate, thought Spedini, would have displayed high dudgeon for the sake of his image, cursed all engineers for the improvident creatures they were, then simply gone back to the ship's office, flashed up his computerized Loadicator, and called for an effortless revision of his original scenario.

But not Mario Spedini. Oh, no! For poor bloody Chief Officer Spedini, already a martyr to accounting avarice and the inadequacies of low-priced electrical officers, would have to wrestle with pencil on prehistoric paper over columns of hogging factors and sagging numerals and stress tables and mathematical equations which had already taken hours to produce and which he suspected, when tackled under pressure, would take even longer to reappraise. It could prove that, by having to repeat such time-consuming labour, he might be forced to delay the unloading operation itself; might even be forced to consult Captain Bisaglia for advice which would seem elementary to any truly seasoned mate, thereby incurring not only the displeasure of the owners but also his respected master's shocked disillusionment.

Breakfast time on that last Saturday hardly promised to be a carefree event for everybody in the vicinity of the offshore jetty.

Certainly not for thirty-two-year-old Mario Spedini.

By the time he'd replaced the telephone receiver at much the same moment as Chief Officer Spedini lost his appetite, twenty-year-old Police Constable Hamish Lawson of the Highland Force wasn't too damn thrilled either at the way fate was screwing his plans for that day.

He'd intended to drive the considerable distance down to Oban, buy a stereo radio he'd had his eye on for some time and eventually, perchance, call upon a certain young nursing sister over whom he'd cast a similarly covetous eye for even longer; ever since, in fact, he'd met her at the last Highland police ball.

But because, like ordinary members of the public, policemen catch colds and flu, have close relatives die on them, or break ankles ski-ing as one young bobby had done on the previous Thursday, it had come to pass that there was a shortage of available men to patrol the Quarsdale area. Accordingly his Divisional Chief Superintendent had asked his Superintendent, his Super had requested his Inspector, and his Inspector had duly ordered his Sergeant to seek out volunteers for overtime on that coming night.

So instead of a fondly anticipated weekend free of duty, which should have been his infrequent right by rota, Hamish had just been told that he'd volunteered to work an extra shift starting from eleven p.m. Mobile this time, admittedly – it seemed that the powers that be had decided the threat to the terminal wasn't so grave as to justify a policeman's overtime in averting it. Tonight he would be able to travel his beat in one of the station's blue and white pandas; covering Vaila town centre but with special emphasis on the

Rora Terminal. Defending it from the nocturnal depredations of those led by the arch anarchist, District Councillor
Auntie bloody Jesse.

Gloomily prodding a plate of bacon, egg and fried bread
he decided to forgo the lure of National Health flesh, watch
a bit of Saturday afternoon sport on TV, then go back to
bed. It promised to be a long and boring night.

Constable Lawson's prediction, as things turned out,
proved to be only half correct.

Duggan was in his office by half past eight on that morning,
meticulously checking out the paperwork involved at terminal level when a hundred and seventeen thousand metric
tonnes of crude oil passes from custody of ship's master
to storage depot. *Calauria*'s arrival at Rora had placed a
considerable strain on him too, in that the Liberian VLCC
represented the first big consignment to be his sole responsibility. He knew that Charlie would expect him, as Deputy
Superintendent, to have everything squared away on his
return from Panoco's Dallas head office; no unresolved dis-
putes relating to manifests and bills of lading, demurrages,
laytimes or what the hell ever.

Charlie would also be looking for Duggan's implementation of the last round of cost-cutting exercises in the terminal's operation; worse still, he'd probably be bringing back
a further series of brand new Stateside-dictated economy
measures. The days of oil companies being carefree spenders
were long gone: perpetual Middle Eastern wars allied with
the ever-escalating costs of exploration and recession in the
industrial world had caused savage competition between the
multinational fuel corporations. Now management either
achieved their financial targets or were out on their butts;
them and most of their staffs.

Trouble was, Duggan couldn't avoid thinking about the
reporter when he should've been concentrating on ullage and
deadweight reports: she was so goddamn unsettling, that
Herschell woman. Her company last night as they talked in
the Meall Ness had both frustrated and strangely excited him
– her cool sophistication, so unexpected in one associated

91

with a small provincial newspaper; the curve of her throat; the turn of her perfect ankles; the velvet waterfall of her hair; the way she moved – hell, even the way she'd simply sat and smiled provocatively yet at the same time parried his attempts to establish a more personal relationship.

But it wasn't just that – the physical side – which so disturbed him. Duggan would cheerfully admit that he possessed a healthy young man's libido, still sweated over erotic fantasies in which strikingly beautiful women hurled themselves upon him with writhing abandon . . . women not unlike Fran Herschell, come to that.

But he sensed a threat from her as well. A threat, and a hint of determination. She hadn't asked many questions, yet he suspected she was seeking many answers. She hadn't dug too deeply, yet she'd left him with a feeling of unease when they'd parted, of apprehension almost. That feeling wasn't what he'd anticipated after being interviewed by a small-time woman journalist either.

They were due to talk again over dinner tonight; tomorrow he would show her round the terminal; maybe even take her aboard the Liberian VLCC before she sailed, if the master was agreeable. Or maybe not. Mrs Herschell knew too much about ships and possessed an unhealthy curiosity. Duggan might have been susceptible to feminine charms, but he wasn't stupid. The conversation he'd had with Trelawney when the night-shift PCO was going off watch a few minutes before had left him in no doubt that the Italian-manned supership presently berthed on the offshore jetty was anything but super.

'She's a bad one, Duggan,' Trelawney had said bleakly. 'I feel it in my gut. The quicker she goes the better; she's a wicked bastard.'

No, Duggan didn't think, on reflection, that it would be a very bright idea to show Mrs Herschell over *Calauria*.

He leaned forward with a sigh and pulled Rora Terminal's current storage tank distribution sheet towards him. He still had to decide where Expediter Blair was to stack seventy-six thousand tonnes of Arabian Heavy and, at the same time, avoid mixing it with the Light when they began to pump it ashore in the early hours of tomorrow morning. Making an error of that magnitude wouldn't be a very bright idea, either.

He noted from the chit left on his desk that the Liberian's master proposed to take on intermediate ballast around midnight, before Heavy Crude unloading commenced.

Duggan hoped to Christ the tanker's crew knew which valves to open and close before they started. The last accidental pollution of Quarsdale, fortunately before his time, had occurred when a Jap Flag ULCC had taken on bunker fuel from the terminal – and pumped it straight through the bloody ship and out the other side!

Shona Simpson, when she awakened around ten, was still simmering with the humiliation of her cross-country safari with Peter Caird the previous evening. Her indignation was fuelled by resentment over what had inevitably developed into yet another blazing row with Mum, who'd waited up until she'd finally arrived home well after midnight.

Some mornings, if the room wasn't too cold when she climbed out of bed, she'd slip off her nightdress before padding to the mirror to gaze with a certain pride at the reflected nude before her. Today, sexuality flouted, she just flopped in front of her tiny dressing table to glower through black-ringed shadows of hastily removed mascara at the image of a girl with petulant lips and a score to settle.

Big John McLean *had* been right after all – Cairdy hadn't changed a bit, he was still the same colourless nancy boy he'd aye been at school. University life hadn't made him one wee bit more mature; all it seemed to have achieved was to make him even more full of himself.

Moodily she prodded at her tangled blonde hair, then began to brush it with short, vicious tugs. Gradually, indignation smoothed with every stroke, she started to plot retribution. Him, the great local doctor's bairn wi' the big dramatic way he was planning to upstage all the other geriatric lunatic protesters here in Vaila – well, now was the time for him to learn it took mair than a superior air and a plum-in-the-mouth accent to get away with insulting Shona Simpson.

Some might have judged Shona's resentment to be some-what excessive; certainly more bitterly felt than might have been expected from a normal nineteen year old. In fact some might have considered her a very disturbed young woman indeed. Still, she was almost in a good mood by the time she'd slipped into jeans and a T-shirt before going downstairs to the kitchen. Her father was there, looking pointedly at the clock before eyeing her with weary reproach over his morning copy of the *Northern Citizen*.

'Your mother's away to the shops,' he said. 'You could have helped her carry the messages.'

'And so could you,' Shona snapped, reaching for the milk.

Apart from that brief exchange she ignored him. Jimmy Simpson was a man who had meekly acquiesced in the slow economic murder of the Highlands; unemployed now for more than four years since they'd moved the fish processing plant down to Oban, he'd long conceded all responsibility for his family's maintenance to the State. Mister McReady behind the counter in the Social Security office had become the bread provider; Shona's older brother Alistair – who, having left home at eighteen to become a corporal in the Argyles, had already proved himself a man of great good sense – fulfilled the role of family councillor during his infrequent leaves; while Mum, an unsympathetic woman of bleak aspect, had gradually embraced the duties of accoun-tant, domestic manager and disciplinarian while displaying an ever-more open contempt for the husband she'd once loved but now simply dominated.

It hardly provided the environment for a happy upbringing. Perhaps it was inevitable that Shona, not exactly bright but nevertheless every bit as strong-willed as her mother, had been destined to become a rebel. Ever since she'd left school her sole ambition had been to break her links with Vaila, move to Glasgow and seek independence in the form of a job and her own flat.

Until last night, anyway. Now she'd found a new and more pressing determination – to get her own back on Peter Caird. And Shona Simpson, who conceded even to herself that she might not have displayed academic brilliance but still considered she possessed the cunning of a female Machiavelli, had not the slightest doubt she was capable of devising some brilliant strategy for accomplishing precisely that. Just as she'd previously played Caird's conceit against John McLean's egotism at the disco, then surely, tonight, the same petty jealousies could provide the means by which she could bring Cairdy's plan crashing in ruins about his head.

Gradually the seed of an idea began to take root. She could maybe press them to go a wee bit further than was proposed; to escalate the affair far enough beyond what would be considered an ordinary student prank so that official retribution on the ringleader would be sure to follow. Doctor Caird had a position in the town, was conscious of image – directing the public spotlight on his son could well turn what had been devised as a brave gesture into total disaster . . . but *only* for Peter Caird, of course. Nobody else. And just enough to get her own back for the slight he'd offered her.

Or at least that was Shona's vague intention as she ate her breakfast porridge while, at the same time, ignoring her father.

Mrs McAllister brought Fran a cup of tea and a sliver of shortcake at nine, then drew the curtains to allow the watery sun to light on the warm bed before she finally bustled away with a kindly smile and a promise of breakfast in the residents' dining room at any time before ten o'clock.

The girl lay for a long time, unwilling to face the morning chill not unfamiliar in Scottish country houses as old as the Meall Ness. Finally she did summon the courage to prop herself on one arm and, pulling the blankets tightly across bare shoulders, gratefully sipped her tea.

She hadn't slept well. Several times during the night she'd found herself snapping wide awake to sense that same unease; an anticipation, almost, of grave events already in the making.

Fran nibbled the shortbread and tried hard to shake the sensation off, to concentrate on something else. That merely brought to mind a second quite unexpected factor which had prolonged her periods of wakefulness through the small

95

hours – the existence of Duggan. The more her thoughts dwelt on the terminal executive, the more Fran Herschell found herself conceding that he had made a greater impression on her than she'd first admitted. Physically she'd never considered him anything other than attractive but, until Duggan had actually left the Meall Ness last evening, she hadn't seriously considered the alternative of his staying overnight. Only after his departure did she become aware of stirrings of regret for opportunity dismissed.

Fran knew going to bed with Duggan wouldn't have diminished her love for John. She'd always possessed an unashamed inclination towards selective promiscuity – John had been only too aware of that himself before he married her. But any adventures in the future would remain strictly physical; she neither wanted nor intended to enter into some deep-rooted and enduring affair.

Fran Herschell found herself smiling wryly. Sheer practicality would, at the end of the day, have decreed frustration. For one thing, the brisk Mrs McAllister seemed unlikely to be indulgent towards free love under her own roof; the Meall Ness was hardly a discreet *rendezvous d'amour*. It was improbable that her hostess would cheerfully have volunteered to bring a second cup of tea once she'd opened the bedroom door . . .

Breakfast was a homely business of porridge and bannocks still warm from the griddle, of smoked Quarsdale haddock yellow-streaming with farmyard butter followed by tea, toast and Dundee marmalade from a stone jar. It seemed the hotel was full; there were others still in the dining room even at that late hour. A young couple with English accents and a penchant for the surreptitious touching of hands across the table, who might well have been honeymooners; an elderly lady over in the corner, who demolished everything laid before her with the gusto of someone treating herself to a break from being old and lonely; two middle-aged men at the table beside the fire who cast covertly wishful glances in Fran's direction – speculating, probably, on what an attractive sophisticate like her was doing in a dull, dull place like this.

'Just following my trade as always,' Fran reflected sardonically. 'Even now I'm prying – no, spying really, when you
get down to it. Watching, probing; straining for snippets of
random conversation; trying to collate an identikit picture of
what I'm really looking for.'

Which would turn out to be what? She remembered sitting
with Duggan in the Panoco Rover after his meeting her off the
bus. When Loch Quarsdale first came in view, breathtaking in
its reach and majesty, yet despite that wealth of natural
wonder her eyes had still focused instantly on the one
man-made object in sight – the VLCC, the supertanker,
Calauria. Clean enough looking from a distance; not the
worst FOC hull she'd seen by any means, yet . . . yet there
had been an aura of, well, almost of *sadness* about that ship;
as if, deprived of loving care in her advancing years, she lay
to her wire and nylon fetters reflecting wistfully on what
might have been . . .

Fran shook herself. It was an improper flight of fancy for
a fact-conscious journalist – to credit a ship with the capacity
for feeling sad. Her husband was the one who thought like
that. John sincerely believed that ships possessed souls, felt
pain and elation, sighed wearily and stumbled when the great
global rollers caught helmsmen unaware to thunder green
and spiteful across their decks, yet tossed their heads with
sheer euphoria when coasting those same giant seas under
the hands of a truly skilled pilot.

Almost unconsciously she'd begun to register intriguing
strands of oil-related conversation from the two men by the
fire just as Mrs McAllister came to the table.

'Anything more, lass? Toast, a wee extra pot of tea
maybe?'

'No thank you, Mrs McAllister; that was lovely. By far the
nicest breakfast I've had for a long time.'

Mrs McAllister looked pleased. 'I take a pride in seeing
all my guests comfortable. I hope both yourself and Mister
Duggan found the supper I'd left for you last night to your
liking?'

'The nicest supper too, without a doubt. Thank you
again.'

'Och, I was pleased to do it. He is a very acceptable young gentleman is Mister Duggan.'

The two men rose from their table. One sighed, then joked, 'It's climbing those bloody boarding ladders after a meal like that which gets me. Why don't they make VLCCs sit lower in the water, Ed?'

'S'obvious. Because they'd have had to call 'em VSCCs then,' the other grinned. 'Very *Small* Crude Carriers, Roger!'

'Panoco people, Mrs McAllister?' Fran asked curiously after they'd gone. Her hostess shook her head.

'From some big company in London, Mrs Herschell. I believe they're interested in the quality of the oil the big ships bring to Quarsdale. There are always a few of them booked into the Meall Ness.'

'Cargo assessors,' Fran nodded. 'Independent specialists.'

'You know about oil tankers then?' Mrs McAllister looked surprised that any guid Scots lass should display interest in such a male-dominated subject.

'Not really,' Fran said hurriedly. 'But my husband's in the merchant navy. He sometimes talks about them.'

Her hostess picked up the teapot, then hesitated, obviously intrigued. 'Mister Duggan tells me you are a newspaper writer. Do you have some . . .' Mrs McAllister looked around surreptitiously then lowered her voice to a conspiratorial whisper, '. . . some unusual bit of news to investigate then, Mrs Herschell? Some doings which might be considered as, ah, *unconventional* within our wee local family?'

'. . . and that, Mrs McAllister, slots you right into place,' Fran thought. But she hadn't found the flaw in Mrs McAllister until now and, fortunately for Fran, most people had some flaw. If they hadn't, then people wouldn't be people and journalists would produce very boring newspapers.

'Unfortunately, no,' she returned gently. 'My editor only wants me to produce an article describing Panoco's impact on the community. How, seven years after the oil began to arrive, the terminal has affected all of you here on Quarsdale.'

Just for a minute the slightly flawed and much more human

Mrs McAllister looked faintly disappointed. But then she brightened.

'Och, bless you, lass,' she said with transparent sincerity. 'There can hardly be a soul within twenty miles who doesnae thank the guid Lord every day for the bounty He bestowed when He gave us yon unloading platform out there in the loch.'

It took Fran Herschell a few minutes and another cigarette to really digest what Mrs McAllister had claimed.

And to wonder yet again who in Vaila, whether intentionally or not, was clouding the real truth about the Rora Terminal.

And, for that matter, what the real truth *was*.

When the noon weather forecast was received at Panoco Control, day-shift Expediter Thomson logged it in as anticipating a sudden drop in air temperature by midnight; precipitation giving not more than 18 km visibility during sunny afternoon periods and, more significantly for Pilot McDonald aboard the VLCC on the jetty, winds backing sou' westerly 6 gusting to occasional 8.

Idly flipping back through the pages he shook his head once again with mild irritation at his night oppo's ink blotch. Reg could be bloody careless sometimes. Also an ex-Navyman, Bill Thomson ran a taut operation during his shift; for one thing he insisted on keeping a legible Log. The way Blair had left it, you couldn't even decipher the name *Calauria*.

One might almost think that the ship that had berthed port-side to on the offshore jetty at 1856 yesterday, had suddenly taken it in mind to . . . well – suddenly to obliterate itself!

The Ship

Ironically, of the many varieties of ship which exist to serve man, the type at least risk from the sea's violence because of the buoyant nature of its cargo also happens to be the one at greatest risk from salt water's corrosive attack – again because of the nature of that same cargo. Any derivative of oil is a subtle fifth columnist in chemical terms; an enemy within; a staunch and reliable ally of corrosion in a war of attrition against steel.

Tankships, then, are doomed to live short lives even when their seaworthy defences are maintained, their rust-resistant armours regularly revitalized, their ever-weakening members surgically replaced. They die very quickly indeed once such protective measures are withdrawn. Death sentence is passed in the moment when their owners decide they have become unviable; that support in return for loyal service is no longer a profitable commitment.

Calauria was just such a tanker; already weak with cancer, though not eleven years old. Certainly she'd continued to work well enough, despite having been diagnosed as terminally sick over two years before she berthed at Rora, but VLCCs have a remarkable resilience by virtue of their massive scantlings – the dimensions of their bones. That skeleton can waste considerably yet still hold together; it is the safety margin which steadily reduces in the first phase of mortal illness, not the ship's ability to function.

Calauria's sickness had not been due to any callousness on the part of her first owners. They had, in fact, been quite loyal to her, had looked after her well-being with genuine pride when she was young and handsome, but she had never proved a really healthy ship. Corrosion had infiltrated her early in life and had been expensive to retard; she had suffered vibration problems; her frames – the bones of her – had showed signs of distortion for no apparent reason, as had sections of her tank bulkheads. After eight years of costly service, matters had come to a head. Further structural weaknesses causing grave concern were discovered during a routine docking and ultrasonic hull inspection in Singapore. The surveyors advised her already disenchanted owners that she had become a critical case; needed major surgery, in fact.

That prospect of prolonging her safe life was denied her. It was considered at board level that enough was enough in *Calauria*'s case, that it was commercially prudent to cut losses, and dispose of what could well prove a financially embarrassing corpse by offering her for sale 'without warranty, and as inspected'.

She would have to pass into hands operating under some appropriate Flag of Convenience, of course. Under British maritime regulations, by Dutch, Danish, Norwegian or any other responsible maritime nation's classification standards, she could never have passed a governmental condition survey to certify she *was* a safe and well-found vessel.

Some Liberian surveyor must still have considered she was though. He *must* have done, because some other official in Africa immediately issued *Calauria* with a certificate of seaworthiness indicating she was most unlikely to founder or fall apart or . . . well, simply blow up or whatever under normal operating conditions.

And to be fair, she probably still was.

Just as long as she wasn't abused. As long as

those still massive steel bones wouldn't be called upon to provide one extra kilogramme of resistance to stress, because her reserves of strength were exhausted. It wouldn't be possible to rely on her designed safety margins any longer.

She didn't have any left.

CHAPTER SIX

━━◆◆━━

Afternoon:
SATURDAY

The sun still gleamed a watery winter satisfaction while lunchtime came and went on that last Saturday before Vaila became famous for a brief, headlined moment throughout the rest of the world.

A few people stopped in Reform Street to comment on what a braw day it was; cheering to catch even a glimpse of the sun after such a dreich and dismal time over the New Year. Jeemie Fairbairn the postie even suggested that, 'Wan mair morning like this an' a' they Spanish people fae Marbella will want to be flying intae Quarsdale fur their winter holidays!'

Most of those who had been working overnight were still sleeping. Some, perhaps, a little more easily than others.

Deckhand Wullie Gibb slept, much as usual, like a baby; curled up in his mother's back bedroom with his thumb in his mouth, and her frightened to hoover the living room carpet in case the noise wakened him.

Mrs Gibb was always glad when the *William Wallace* finished its fortnightly stint as overnight safety vessel out in the loch. It was difficult enough trying to run a house without having to tiptoe from room to room during daytime hours as well as looking after three young men and a daughter – two sons plus the *Wallace*'s first and only Mate, Eck Dawson, who spent so much time now hanging around the little council house at 27 Blantyre Place in pursuit of her lass, Katrina, that he might just as well have been one more laddie of her own.

There wasn't any Mister Gibb senior. There hadn't been

since a tramp steamer out of Glasgow called the *Brackenbrae* met with an East German cargo liner called the *Gutermann* in the middle of one foggy night off the Newfoundland Banks in December 1971. When the *Gutermann*'s bow cut through the *Brackenbrae* petty officers' accommodation it also decapitated her lamptrimmer, ground her donkeyman into a bloody smear all mixed up with her chief cook and the second steward, and snipped both of ship's carpenter Gibb's legs off neat as if he'd trimmed them himself with his own cross-cut saw.

He'd probably bled to death still trapped in the remains of his bunk, or maybe the shock alone had been enough to kill him. At least he couldn't have felt anything more awful than he'd already suffered by the time the sea finally roared into what was left of the *Brackenbrae*, and took her down to lie not too far from what had once been a truly elegant Italian liner called the *Andrea Doria*, an aristocrat of the seas which would never, in her days of pride, have wished to be associated with such an undistinguished British tramp. But the bottom of the ocean is a very cosmopolitan place and a great leveller of national pride.

Little Wullie was only nine years old when that happened. The *Brackenbrae* survivors sent nearly twenty-three pounds they'd collected between them for the widowed Mrs Gibb, who cried quite a lot for a week, then went down to the Post Office and bought twenty-three pounds' worth of National Savings Stamps to divide equally among her children, keeping nothing for herself.

Chippie Gibb's fuzzy snapshot still took pride of place in a tortoiseshell frame on the dresser. He'd sported a fine nautical beard and it must have been raining when the picture was taken, because Mister Gibb was wearing a sou'wester. Wullie couldn't but be reminded of a well-known advertisement for tinned sardines in olive oil every time he happened to notice his late Daddy's portrait.

Pilot McDonald slept during the afternoon as well, but only in brief snatches and to make up for what he'd lost overnight. Job and finish aboard the VLCCs was attractive enough, generally affording the compensation of equally long duty-free periods whereupon Archie – who loved trout fishing and snatched every chance on offer to gather his rod, his flies and his flask of hot coffee – would clamber briskly up the slopes to any one of half a hundred rarely-visited lochans in which the water was clear as diamond ice and near enough as cold. There, with fingers as delicate as any surgeon's, just feeling the water through the fine thread of gut, he would tempt the fat brown fish with Jock's Petard or McIntosh's Pride or some other Judas-feathered delicacy supposedly irresistible to the finny palate, until the same split cane tip that had given so much pleasure to his father and his grandfather before him tugged, almost imperceptibly at first, as the least wary trout of all rose lazily to the fly.

Or maybe didn't. Quite often Archie McDonald would return home with nothing at all in his bag to show for all that effort. But that was the excitement of fishing; the lure which attracted him and many like him just as surely as a Black Butcher skilfully laid across a breeze-ruffled surface will eventually take some record lochan brown's fancy.

On that Saturday afternoon Pilot McDonald felt something less than enthusiasm for the prospect of dozing intermittently through yet another night. It would be late tomorrow, Sunday, before *Calauria* completed discharging and he returned her again to the pilot's debarkation point south of Sgeir Garth where the cutter would be waiting. Then, and not before, would he restore to Captain Bisaglia undisputed control of his own ship, clamber down one of the longest pilot ladders in the world, and head at last for home and bed.

Unless he was really unlucky. If the weather blew up as it very well could at this time of year, and the great Atlantic seas came sweeping in between the Heads after breaking clear over the black pinnacles of Garth then, even with the cutter afforded a lee by a hull as vast as *Calauria*'s, Pilot McDonald might find it impossible to leave the ship and would have to travel with her until such time as she could put him ashore elsewhere. Last year Duguid was taken way down to Cardigan Bay before they could land him; the winter before Archie McDonald himself had finished up in Rotterdam. Twice. Six years ago Captain Denby, Panoco's senior Rora pilot, was virtually kidnapped; a tanker-happy Greek master had bluntly refused either to stop his ship or allow a helicopter to approach before he reached his next destination. The ULCC had sailed empty as a matelot's rum bottle and with nothing more to deliver in Europe. Denby ended up flying home from Ras al Tanura in the Gulf twenty days later, bronzed, full of stuffed vine leaves and ouzo, and with a penchant for playing and replaying Zorba's Dance. It seemed the crazy Greek had simply decided his Scottish pilot badly needed a holiday in the sun.

As he slipped into his anorak and prepared to go down to the pumproom for a routine check on progress, McDonald hoped to Christ the weather would hold until he left *Calauria*. Her intermediate outward destination was Europoort for minor repairs which, presumably, her owners couldn't put off any longer.

And the last place Pilot McDonald wanted to be marooned in was Rotterdam again. Well, not in winter anyway.

Expediter Reg Blair didn't sleep at all easily through that Saturday lunchtime. Normally when working nights he – who, as an ex-Navyman, thought nothing of watchkeeping in odd hours – would sleep soundly through until fiveish, when Ella would come into the bedroom with two cups of tea and sit on the bed while they talked. Sometimes, if there wasn't much to say, they'd just sit and hold hands in silence because a simple act of affection like that had been until recently – again because of Reg having spent the first nineteen years of their married life in the Service – a most exceptional thing for them to do.

Unless she'd been going through one of her unsettled periods over being confined in Vaila, that was. As soon as Reg sensed the signs of discontent in Ella he seemed to tighten up inside, to withdraw from her. And she – because she really did love him, and was acutely conscious of her own selfishness – would know with a surge of guilt that it signalled a few more days before they would hold hands again.

107

This day he woke before two, still tired after only five hours' sleep, and lay staring up at the ceiling – which the ex-Chief PO in him still couldn't help thinking of as a deck-head – with his hands behind his head, listening to the mutter of voices from the kitchen. Ella would, as usual, be hurrying to do all the things like clean football boots and find the school strip that should've been washed after Ken's match last Saturday and which seventeen-year-old Ken should bloody well have looked out for himself before the last minute anyway! Reg had been in the Navy at seventeen. He'd washed his own gear an' by God, if he hadn't reported precisely on time, and properly kitted out in the rig of the day to boot, then the Buffer would've been down on Very Ordinary Seaman Blair like a ton o' gunmetal shackles.

He muttered 'Shit!' out loud and turned on one elbow to stare out of the scuttle . . . the bloody *window*! He'd have to get the Navy out of his system: he was plain Mister Blair now and had been for long enough; not Chief Gunnery Instructor Reginald, Be Bloody Respectful If You're A Rating an' Still Treat Courteously Even If You're An Admiral, Blair.

Above PCO Trelawney's house across the road, provided by the company as was Blair's itself, the sun was attempting to struggle from behind its grey filter while the raindrops dried in random patterns on the glass for the first time in weeks. It reminded him yet again of last night's bitter reference by Ella to their living in Vaila as opposed to Saudi Arabia. The only difference apparently being that, 'It didn't rain all the time in Saudi!'

It seemed she didn't like sun an' didn't like rain, and didn't like oil because it made him work nights, but sure as hell didn't like being bloody poor either. So what *was* the way out of their situation?

The frustration rising within him made him clench his fists. His concern for Ella's happiness had already been instrumental in his decision to leave the Navy at the peak of his career instead of signing on for a further Five, and he'd never really managed to break the bonds cleanly. Now she was subtly pressuring him into abandoning a well-paid job with Panoco, and for what? The bloody dole?

Panoco's duty Expediter for that last Saturday night shift at Rora Terminal turned over in bed and stared unseeingly at the bulkhead . . . at the bloody WALL!

Maybe he already was doing what Ella wanted, but unconsciously this time. Jesus Christ, but she couldn't have done a better job – even if she'd tackled it herself an' that was f'r sure – of screwing things up for any future he might have had with Panoco.

He wished he hadn't been so impulsive now. At best it wouldn't change anything; at worst – for Reg, anyway – if his action *was* about to precipitate some probably quite minor official storm then the cause would almost certainly be traced back to him. And employers, especially multinational employers, didn't tolerate disloyalty: not even when it only expressed itself as one very small voice of concern for, well . . . simply for people.

He hadn't had the guts to sign it at the time. Now Expediter Blair was sincerely wishing he hadn't had the guts even to write it.

That *bloody* letter to the *Northern Citizen*!

Captain Bisaglia went ashore for lunch on Saturday.

He felt quite brisk; much more at ease with the world. Though the harbour standing orders he'd prepared insisted that he be called at any time a problem arose, his officers of the watch had found no cause to. He'd slept soundly overnight, awakening through sheer habit only once at four in the morning for a quick turn around the deck followed by a visit to the pumproom and a brief chat with Second Officer de Mita; just to satisfy himself that *Calauria*'s discharge was still going well.

It had largely been due to his growing confidence in Chief Officer Spedini's capability. Now *there* was a young man with a considerable future. Even the temporary loss of the ship's Loadicator facility hadn't seemed to perturb the lad as it would many others. Such additional calculations as were required to produce a Rora plan for discharge had been submitted by Spedini with a quiet efficiency that even Captain Bisaglia, who had prided himself during his own days as Chief Officer in possessing an evenness of temperament untypical of most of his Italian maritime colleagues, would have found difficult to emulate.

Not that Bisaglia would ever have expected to undertake such complex load planning aboard an unsophisticated old Type T2. His generation hadn't been pampered by – certainly weren't educated to – such unseamanlike gadgets as on-board computers, but then they hadn't required them. They'd sailed in ships which really could absorb punishment, which would hog or sag like a sausage in brine if you were careless, but still never fail to recover. In the old days, when ships were fashioned to last and were crewed by sailors instead of academics, your tanker was built to massive scantlings; you could juggle your parcels of crude without the preparatory finesse demanded of an Einstein. Oh, you did your calculations – simple calculations from tables and standard conditions of loading already provided by the designers – but you could also draw from experience; you flew your tanker by the seat of your pants, so to speak. And almost invariably your tanker forgave you if you were, on occasions, a little less than brilliant.

Captain Bisaglia did feel a minor twinge of guilt about his Chief Officer's recent efforts though. He really should have looked more closely at Spedini's preparation for the Rora arrival, even if only as a gesture. Admittedly he would have found great difficulty in understanding the finer points as they affected *Calauria*'s stability, but it might have pleased the young man, compensated slightly for his inconvenience.

Many ship's masters would have just shrugged and growled, 'Tough salami! So the Mate's had to work as hard as I did when I was his age. So the guy gets paid for it anyway.'

Bisaglia didn't think like that. He was a considerate man, Captain Tommaso Bisaglia. A kindly, well-meant man who would never have caused intentional harm to anybody.

It would be nice to think that he spent that last Saturday in a pleasurable manner, and most probably he did. Even his habitual anxieties had diminished considerably by then – his unhappy and sadly justifiable concern about his own competence. Particularly once the strain of berthing his ship had been eased by that copybook docking on the offshore jetty.

He thoroughly enjoyed his luncheon ashore with Duggan. They ate at the Meall Ness, but the fare bore little resemblance to that eaten somewhat unenthusiastically by the POW Guardia Marina Bisaglia forty years before, especially Mrs McAllister's Cockaleekie, a modest Scottish offering yet with the vegetables swimming in such a delicate broth that the Captain considered it his duty to savour every spoonful; to record each sip indelibly on his mind. It was a sincere tribute from a man who had eaten in almost every country of the world. Even the braised venison which had followed, as tender as any cut of veal and moistened deliciously by a sauce just hinting at its whisky content, had been forced into gastronomic second place. As for the pudding . . . There had been no room for pudding within Tommaso Bisaglia on Saturday, and perhaps just as well. Had he been tempted to the Atholl Brose, then his appreciation of Mrs McAllister's kitchen craftsmanship might well have exploded, betraying forever that temperamentally placid image of which he was so proud.

Duggan had, in turn, enjoyed lunching with the Captain. It had followed from a spontaneous invitation on his part, extended during late morning on completion of *Calauria*'s documentation because, by then, not only had Duggan found time dragging prior to his scheduled dinner date with Fran, but the Rora Deputy also considered himself entitled to a modest expense-account celebration. His Saturday hosting of Tommaso Bisaglia actually marked quite an important milestone in Duggan's own career representing, as it did, the first occasion on which he'd been entrusted with sole responsibility for the distribution of an inbound parcel within the tank farm's massive storage complex. And Duggan had worked hard to earn that confidence; had proved himself a thrusting, sometimes even ruthless challenger in the Panoco executive stakes despite Fran Herschell's initial assessment.

They talked of many things over that pleasant meal, the elderly Captain and the young aspiring executive, though never of imprisonment nor of a war which had ended before Duggan had even been born. The Captain's command of English, halting at first through lack of practice, became more fluent as the coffee – and the Drambuie – flowed with only modest self-denial.

It was well into the afternoon, when the sun had almost given up its one-sided battle with the winter's grey, before they finally made their slightly unsteady farewell to Mrs McAllister and the Meall Ness. Duggan, like General Mac-Arthur, promised solemnly to return, then wondered vaguely how the hell he'd ever manage to eat another of Mrs McAllister's meals in the company of Fran Herschell later that night, while the Captain – ever mindful of the needs of others – wandered among the souvenir shops in Reform Street with an amiable though glazed eye: a man with a mission.

Chief Borga had, it appeared, developed a hydraulic problem – or at least the ship, as opposed to Chief Engineer Borga himself, had – which now required the Mate to prepare further modifications to the unloading schedule currently in progress. The unfortunate Spedini, doubly overworked in view of his lack of computer facilities and finding himself with no spare time for window shopping, had accordingly requested his Captain to make two purchases on his behalf while in Vaila.

Now the order for tartan cloth the Captain could understand. And of course he, as a man of the world, still respected the boy. But . . .

Well, to be perfectly frank – it *did* seem a little odd to the Drambuie-hazed Bisaglia. That an otherwise refreshingly normal young man like his Chief Officer should express a curious desire to own . . . well, to own a Scottish dolly.

Female it had to be, according to Spedini. With long black hair . . . and a *kilt*?

When Davie Coull's taxi – one of the only two surviving in Vaila because who needs a taxi to the station when there isn't a station left within forty miles? – dropped Fran Herschell at the big house over on Fariskay she stood for a minute gazing back over Quarsdale towards the town.

Even as she watched, the sun forced a dying shaft of light through a momentary breach in the overcast's defence. It lit Vaila like some fairyland village, speckled by glittering windows, with the suddenly bright spire of the church a golden wand defying the dark wilderness of the mountains. Fran thought how beautiful it was, and how nice it would be to live there all the time.

But then she saw that the sun had not touched upon the loch; that the vast silhouette of the visiting tankship lying to the offshore jetty was still dense-black as the tongue of any demon, and that it soared even higher above the beautiful town than the spire of the church itself and thus appeared to dominate, almost to feed on the ancient place which played host to it.

The reporter shivered again, and knew that her forebodings could never be properly calmed simply by thinking of Duggan.

'Aye, you're right. And it was such a bonnie, safe wee town before the vandals came, Mrs Hirsel,' a voice commented briskly from behind.

She turned. Councillor Mrs McLeish stood with folded arms at the door. 'Herschell,' Fran corrected automatically. 'Fran Herschell, Mrs McLeish.'

'Come away in, lass. The pot is ready for the kettle and I might find a scone or a cake if you're of a mind to spoil that lovely figure of yours.'

'Newspaper people punish their bodies all the time.' Fran smiled as she followed, first into a hall with oak-panelled walls and a magnificently carved staircase, and from there into a drawing room so big and yet so warm that the two didn't seem possible together. 'It's all fast food and midnight snacks.'

'It's called "progress",' Mrs McLeish commented drily before she disappeared into the kitchen. 'But then so is pop music, germ warfare – and yon powder kegs some call superships.'

She returned in moments with a tray containing enough

home baking to satisfy a regiment. 'You must try my gooseberry jelly,' she urged, more a command than an invitation. 'You'll taste last year's summer with every mouthful, I promise.'

'How do you do it all?' Fran asked with genuine admiration. 'District Councillor, local organizer for half a dozen committees and housewife all in one.'

'I use the time God gives me,' Mrs McLeish retorted matter-of-factly. 'Chinese Gordon used to say that every minute was precious; waste one and it's lost for ever.'

'Chinese Gordon?'

'You would know of him better as General Gordon of Khartoum. A Scot, of course. And a great one at that.'

'You really are a surprising lady, Mrs McLeish. Why *are* you so against the Rora Terminal?'

'You're very direct, Mrs Herschell.'

Fran looked innocent. 'Didn't you say minutes were precious?'

Her hostess eyed her for a moment, a hint of wary amusement in the look. 'Why don't you work for a proper newspaper like the *Scottish Daily Express*? I've the feeling you could if you set your mind to it.'

'Perhaps for much the same reason as you have for not becoming a Member of Parliament as opposed to a District Councillor, Mrs McLeish. The SNP are well established here. I'm sure you would be elected if you set your mind to it.'

Councillor Mrs McLeish smiled openly then, for the first time. She didn't look half so fearsome when she did. 'You're telling me politely that I'm too parochial?'

'We're both contented in our own ways. Contentment is the death of ambition.'

'I only want to see Vaila and Quarsdale prosper again,' the Councillor said. 'I was a Dewar before I married. My father and grandfather were Provosts here, and Dewars have been public servants ever since the clans gave up settling our civic affairs with claymores. I'm a seventh generation busybody. I don't want to be remembered as the one who presided over the death of this community.'

'Then why *are* you so against the terminal?' Fran reiterated. 'Doesn't Panoco's investment represent the salvation you're searching for? The economic miracle so many other Scottish regions would welcome.'

Suddenly there was a sardonic twinkle in the eye of Mrs McLeish. 'You're staying with Maggie McAllister at the Meall Ness, I see.'

Fran flushed. 'Why do you say that?'

'You're practically quoting her, lassie. Do you know how many guests are booked into the Meall Ness by Panoco every week? The surveyors and the cargo assessors and the oil company representatives and the marine superintendents fae different tanker companies?'

'Oh!' Fran muttered, feeling angry with herself for not having recognized the good Mrs McAllister's vested interest in oil.

'Aye!' The throaty chuckle covered thinly veiled criticism. 'There's no denying that the big ships represent Maggie McAllister's economic miracle right enough. Seven years ago she bedded and breakfasted a few commercial travellers plus a tourist or two each week in the summer. Now she's a hotelier no less, and with the business up for sale at over a hundred thousand pounds.'

'But there must be others who've benefited? Every rate-payer for a start. The shopkeepers; other service industries; certainly those local people employed by Panoco . . .'

'I maintain that it's fools' gold, girl. And it comes at a very high premium. Och, I don't just mean the environmental ugliness: the fences and the steel cylinders and the miles of pipe like the entrails of some gutted stag savaging the beauty of Sròine Rora. I don't even mean the danger to Quarsdale's ancient fishing grounds – the hundred thousand tons of black poison that could spill tomorrow; tonight . . . maybe during the next second as we sit here, and destroy them for genera-tions to come.'

Mrs McLeish rose then, and walked over to the great bay window overlooking the loch. 'You see, when I referred to "the death of a community" earlier, Mrs Herschell, I meant it. Quite literally!'

She gestured towards the ship as Fran came and stood

beside her. 'They say there is the destructive power of an atomic bomb stored inside some of those monstrous machines. That one there, now. See? Swollen-bellied with the potential for disaster? And yet they allow it to lie less than half a mile from where two thousand people live.'

The reporter looked. *Calauria* still lay oppressive in the shadow; silent and menacing and vast against the offshore jetty. Still causing her to shudder inwardly for whatever reason.

'Does it not frighten you a wee bit too, lass?' the older woman asked quietly. 'Does it not make you wonder? Does it not raise some doubt in your mind as to whether Quarsdale might or might not *have* any long term future in which to prosper?'

Fran started to get irritated. Instead of conducting an interview she found herself on the defensive; arguing in favour of logic, of normality, of what she wanted to believe for Vaila's sake, and she didn't like it. She was quite capable of taking a balanced journalistic view without attending to some abstract unease within herself. And certainly without being subjected to the subtle dramatics of a local politician.

'As far as pollution of the loch is concerned, any reasonable person would have to admit you have a point. It does give ground for anxiety. But as for your other fears; the threats of death and destruction. VLCCs are being discharged every day without incident, Mrs McLeish. All over the world. And it *is* crude oil coming ashore, not liquid gas or benzine or petroleum spirit which carry a much higher risk of explosion. Admittedly no source of energy can be considered one hundred per cent safe, but we can't survive in a contemporary world without those sources either. Surely it has to be a question of balancing industrial risk against national need?'

Mrs McLeish tried to appear humble; she only succeeded in looking challenging. 'You think I'm just a foolish old woman, don't you?'

'I don't think you're old at all,' Fran rejoined tartly. 'And I certainly don't think you're foolish.'

'Aye?' The voice was dry again: slightly sardonic. 'Well, I'll lay myself open to a further charge of being considered

116

parochial. It does seem a somewhat uneven distribution of economic miracles, when Vaila takes the risk while the rest of the nation – including England, mind – benefits by the results.'

'You identified the culprit yourself – you called it Progress. I can scream outrage as much as I like through the columns of the *Citizen* but I can't reverse it. I can't even do all that much to make it safer for those of you who are genuinely concerned. Not unless . . .'

She hesitated, thinking of the letter.

'Unless what, Mrs Herschell?'

'When you invited me over here last night, you said you would tell me the real truth of what people should know. And you gave me a hint about certain shortcomings in the terminal operating procedures. What are they, Mrs McLeish? And how serious are they?'

'I thought,' Councillor Mrs McLeish said with enormous patience, 'that you were never going to ask!'

Chief Officer Spedini, unlike his Captain, had not recovered his spirits by mid-afternoon.

Immediately after Chief Engineer Borga's bombshell at breakfast the VLCC's Mate had laboriously consulted his ship's copy of the *Conditions de Chargement* – a booklet illustrating as many as thirty-eight appropriate loading conditions as calculated by *Calauria*'s French designers; obligingly translated into English, though unfortunately not into the mother tongue of her present crew. He discovered nothing of value. It offered no useful guide to redistributing the amounts of cargo still on board at that stage; only a somewhat unsettling and red-printed warning advising Masters and Chief Officers, 'Not to depart from the recommendations herein contained.' Ever since then he'd huddled in his office up on the boat deck while the ship grew lighter and lighter and rose higher and higher out of Quarsdale, poring over an ever-growing mountain of stress tables and weight factors as well as producing reams of discarded figures – and got nowhere.

It underlined the fact that Mario Spedini was too inexperienced an executive officer to cope with a situation which would, to a more seasoned VLCC mate, still have presented an aggravating exercise in hard-sweat mathematics but certainly no crisis. Spedini, quite simply, had neither the background nor the ability to handle the current problem.

And so it was, by three o'clock on that Saturday afternoon with over three-quarters of *Calauria*'s Arabian Heavy parcel – then something in the order of sixty thousand tonnes – already discharged from both wings, that Chief Officer Spedini was finally forced to face his inability to resolve, by traditional calculation, the problem of how to leave Number Six centre and both wing tanks empty in order to allow Borga's engineers access. Or rather, he knew how to leave them empty but could not establish precisely what critical alterations in trim would then occur; what still water bending moments might be envisaged over the weight-vulnerable length of *Calauria*, and – the most vital forecast of all – what additional stresses and strains would be imposed on the supership's hull.

Spedini, however, did still have some options open to him even then.

He could have called in the admittedly even less experienced Second Officer de Mita for discussion, for a mutual brainstorming session drawing on their combined knowledge. Between them they might just have worked it out.

But he didn't. Because Spedini, with three gold rings on each epaulette, was far too proud, too conscious of his position to admit fallibility to any more junior officer.

He could have consulted his Captain before Tommaso Bisaglia had taken passage ashore to keep his luncheon appointment with Duggan. He certainly should have done, even at that early stage; it was both prudent and his statutory duty to advise the master of any uncertainty which might affect the safety of the ship.

But he didn't do that either. Because Spedini was too career hungry; too anxious to be seen as a model chief officer and thus earn, on completion of his contract, the meritorious discharge so necessary to attain command in better ships.

He could even – had he been half as apprehensive for the

118

immediate future as any more knowledgeable tankerman would have been by then – have cabled the owners in Hong Kong and requested their assistance. *Calauria* had a nearly identical twin; a sister ship under the same house flag currently loading at Kharg for Rotterdam. They could have instructed *Pharenia*'s Spanish Chief Officer to programme *Calauria*'s base data into her hopefully still-operational Loadicator and cable back the guidance so desperately required – always assuming that particular Liberian-certificated Spaniard didn't happen to prove as inadequate in crisis as Spedini.

But he never even considered doing *that*! Because not only was Spedini determined to avoid any hint of official criticism, but he was also far too complacent; he really hadn't learned his lesson yet. He still believed he could – well, put quite bluntly – flannel his way through the current embarrassment as he'd successfully managed to do, thanks to the tolerance of the elderly Captain Bisaglia, on several previous occasions.

Chief Officer Mario Spedini didn't take up any of the options he might have done to protect his ship from himself.

It was to prove the final, the most catastrophic ingredient of all in the alchemy of total disaster.

The Ship

Her losing battle against corrosion meant that, after only eleven years of operation, *Calauria* had reached the point at which every frame, every longitudinal, every shell plate, stiffener and girder forming her hull should have been considered suspect.

To be fair, they probably had been. As Chief Officer Spedini had earlier informed Pollution Control Officer Trelawney, the ship had indeed been dry-docked at Chusan and subjected to a special hull survey during the previous year. Certain areas of concern were noted, and recommendations for repair duly passed to her new Flag of Convenience owners.

> 'Corrosion in advanced state in both fore deep tanks, No 1 starboard cargo tank, No 2 port and starboard cargo tanks, No 4 port and starboard ballast tanks, No 5 port and starboard. Recommend repairs be effected by plate or section renewal as the case may be . . .'

Some of the repairs were carried out immediately – the most vital ones necessary if *Calauria* was to stay afloat. The less pressing ones were tacitly ignored on the principle that, assuming wastage was to progress at an equivalent rate over each individual part of her, collectively those parts would still be able to withstand all but the most unusual stresses placed upon the giant ship by sea and man's demands – or at least they would for as long as it would take to grab a profit before selling on yet again to even more unscrupulous operators.

But rust doesn't work that way. Rust is rather more subtle in its assault.

And rust is very difficult to deceive, too. Being clever with rust can rebound on the deceiver; can lull him into a sense of complacency which might very well kill him – or, rather more likely, kill his trusting maritime contemporaries – in the end.

They use things like anodes to try to deceive rust; to lure it from its intended victim. Sacrificial anodes, they call them; and the clever ploy itself is known as cathodic protection. Chief Engineer Borga would have known all about sacrificial anodes, as would Captain Bisaglia and even Chief Officer Spedini for that matter, because they're one of the few defences man has yet devised in his attempt to divert the full onslaught of rust.

They're tolerably effective. Usually. And they had been incorporated within *Calauria* from the day she was first launched. Her new owners, uncomfortably aware of the disease already rife within her bowels, had even continued the cathodic protection game at considerable cost when they effected the other minimal repairs, on the grudging premise that a stitch in time should hopefully save a bloody expensive sinking.

An anode is such a simple idea. It's based largely on the theory that if rust is hungry, then feed it. But don't feed it with the stuff and substance of your ship – with the structure itself. No! You tempt it, entice it, offer it nourishment by providing it with a morsel even more succulent, more easily digested. Like a nugget of magnesium or, equally suited to rust's palate, zinc.

Not that it's quite that straightforward – just feeding rust with soft junk, then replacing the junk as soon as it's been consumed with more junk, while your steel stays shiny bright and strong as the day it was rolled in the mill.

For a start it's salt water, not the rust itself, which

eats the nugget. What actually happens is that a quantity of anodes are welded within the ship's hull, usually located in areas most prone to corrosive onslaught, namely those tanks most regularly filled as part of the vessel's salt-water ballast pattern. While full, that salt water then acts as an electrolyte, setting up a galvanic couple which, in turn, deposits a thin protective coating to the steelwork. Within maybe two or three years each sacrificial anode has been . . . well, sacrificed; and so has to be replaced by yet another tasty morsel.

But as with most clever ideas, there is a snag. And those who attempt to deceive by offering a miserly zinc and salt-water cocktail as bait for rust can never afford to overlook it.

Make a hole in the lid of a tin can, then fill the tin can with water – any kind of water. It doesn't matter. You'll discover there is a minute air space still remaining at the top of your can, an air space which is practically impossible to top up.

Now go down to your nearest oil terminal and borrow one of their Very Large Crude Carriers, and try filling *that* up with water. Salt water this time, as would be used for ballast, just to be scientifically precise. And you'll find you have much the same difficulty as you did with your tin can airspace; it simply refuses to go away. Furthermore – because now you're talking about a few hundred tonnes of water instead of a dribble or two from a jug – the air space will extend to several centimetres below the level of the tin lid.

Which is the underside of the steel deck, in a VLCC. Tankermen call that gap between contents and tank top the 'ullage space', and it can prove lethal to the unwary.

For it means that the galvanic coating swishing about in the salt water ballast of that monster VLCC doesn't get much opportunity to transfer itself to the underside of the deck because it hardly ever reaches and immerses it. So corrosion will leap joyfully to the attack yet again unless you can do something else to protect that last remaining and singularly exposed area.

If you're a responsible VLCC owner you will probably treat it with a semi-permanent coating of tar epoxy, or maybe some organic zinc compound guaranteed to send rust away for a few more months or years. If you're very responsible indeed, and truly concerned for the security of your crew and the environment, then you might well have treated the tank internals of the whole vessel from her inception, and maintained the coatings according to the demands of wear and tear. But not many owners would have gone to that length, because the process is very expensive and there has to be an economic ceiling on safety.

The ullage spaces in *Calauria* had been so treated in the golden years of her career, when there was a pride and a profit in her. Eventually, when she began to ail and support had been withdrawn, that critical shielding had been discontinued. Her new owners had failed to compensate for the accelerated decline in the condition of her deck by prudent replacement of its most seriously corroded members.

This meant, as she lay alongside the offshore jetty at Rora Terminal on that sun-dappled Saturday afternoon, that some structural members, particularly certain longitudinal girders strengthening the main deck of the Very Large Crude Carrier *Calauria*, had wasted to less than forty per cent of their original dimensions.

Particularly those in way of No 79 transverse bulkhead separating Number Three tanks across, and Numbers Four Permanent Ballast Tanks.

A point located almost midway between bow and stern.

Her PBTs were still empty at that stage of unloading, affording a considerable amount of free space. Many hundreds of cubic metres of empty space, in fact.

And, under certain atmospheric conditions, empty tank space in any variety of oil or petroleum vessel, whether giant ULCC or mini-coaster, can kill in the blink of a tiny little spark you wouldn't even see with the naked eye.

CHAPTER SEVEN

Early Evening:
SATURDAY

Peter Caird began to get the boat ready as soon as dusk fell and there were few people walking by the yacht club hard to start conversation. Vaila was still very much a village entertained by the business of others; there would be many who'd like to know why it was that the doctor's son was readying a wee scrap of a dinghy in this, the most dreich and unlikely sailing season of the year.

It was largely for that same reason that he hadn't taken the mast and sails from the club store. What was needed tonight was a platform for artistry, not a vehicle of pleasure, and anyway, when high adventure in its most clandestine form was proposed, you hardly wanted to drawn attention to your presence out on Quarsdale by a great white Terylene arrow bobbing in the blackness screaming 'Look!'

He'd finished his single-handed struggle to turn the boat from its inverted winter position, and had secured the bottom boards in place, when he felt a momentary twinge of unease as a figure approached through the gloom.

'Thanks!' he snapped as he recognized Alec Bell. 'All the hard work's done now.'

'It's no' very big,' Specky said uneasily. 'I'm no' a good sailor.'

'You don't have to be,' Peter retorted. 'It's Shona who's going with me. You're with the land party.'

'Not any more. I've just left them. She says she's changed her mind an' that she's staying ashore with us . . . She's no' too thrilled with you just now.'

'Christ almighty,' Caird muttered. 'I knew I should never have let women in on it. Especially Shona Simpson.'

'She seems tae think you're a poofter,' Specky volunteered slyly, always quick to stir things up. It made him feel more secure somehow, less of a target for jibes himself. Peter Caird didn't pay much attention, suddenly concerned as he was with this new threat both to his authority and to the project in hand. It called for two of them out there tonight and, whatever else, Shona did know a lot about boats. She never ran short of offers to sail as crew from the younger club members as well as having the necessary flare for adventure; the devilment to have a go and damn the consequences.

'Well, *you're* not coming out with me, if that's what the rest of you are suggesting,' he stated positively.

Specky said, 'That's fine,' with obvious relief, and turned to leave.

Caird called hurriedly, 'Where're *you* going, then?'

'Home. For tea.'

'But you're not a good sailor,' Peter insisted somewhat pointlessly, as if Bell had shown a desperate desire to accompany him. 'You get seasick f'r a start.'

'That's what I just said,' Specky agreed happily. 'Cheerio then.'

'Oh f'r *Christ's* sake!' Cairdy snarled, beginning to see his whole operation fall apart at the eleventh hour. 'What about McLean? Would he not come?'

'Only if you chlorophylled him.'

'Chloroformed,' Caird muttered absently.

'Aye, well, he says he's a professional seaman while you're just an amateur.'

'Professional *seaman*?' Peter jeered. 'He's only been out a couple of hundred yards to Calf Skerry in his dad's boat, and that because he's more fitted to using muscle than brain f'r a living.'

'He says you'll want to be captain 'cause you're a snob.'

'It's my idea an' *my* bloody BOAT! Cairdy started to shout, then got a grip on himself. If he allowed pride to rule his head then the scheme would be off altogether and, anyway, the chances were that if Big John McLean went out with him in the middle of the night only one of them would come back. It also occurred to him in passing – not that he was

127

scared of McLean, mind – that which one of them did come back might be slightly open to doubt.

'Look, Alec: this is stupid. We're behaving like wee kids.'

'You an' Big John are,' Specky reminded him virtuously. 'And Shona. Not that there's anything unusual in that.'

'All right, you've convinced me,' Peter sighed, clinging desperately to the illusion of command. 'Seeing you're so keen you can go with me in the boat after all.'

Specky Bell's brows furrowed with concentration as he thought about this for a minute. Not exactly bright at the best of times, he still sensed that somewhere along the line he'd lost the drift of the discussion. And enthusiastic he was not. Not one wee bit!

'You sure I've got to?'

'Change of plan. Operational necessity.' Caird shrugged matter-of-factly, fully in control again. 'Unless you're scared, that is?'

'Ah'm NO' scared!' Bell blinked owlish denial.

He turned to peer nervously down the hard to where the loch broke in rumbling white scallops sharply luminescent in the falling darkness. From this low vantage point the funnel of the tanker, lying as it did a full quarter of a mile out, appeared to reach up to and support a scud of black cloud which, even to Alec's unseamanlike eye, suggested the coming of a wild and stormy night.

'Ah'm bluidy terrified!' he added. But only in a whisper of course. So's Cairdy wouldn't hear, and make fun of him again.

Reg Blair flushed the toilet then rinsed his hands and stood leaning on the washbasin, staring at himself in the mirror. His stomach was churning with apprehension; facing up to the prospect of being fired had only made him feel worse.

Ella's voice called, 'That you in there, Reg?'

'Even your having to ask makes me wonder!' he retorted. He dried his hands, then went out into the hall. 'You're up early,' she said.

'Couldn't sleep.'

He didn't tell her he'd been lying awake for nearly two

128

hours already. Or that he didn't feel too good. He was beginning to withdraw from her again, and that in its turn increased his resentment.

'D'you fancy tea or coffee just now?' Ella went into the kitchen. 'Ken's still out playing football. I'll make the meal when he comes in.'

'Before or after you've cleaned the mud off his bloody boots for him?' Reg muttered.

'Mmm?'

'Tea, please,' the Expediter said. He followed her in and sat down, prodding at the sugar in the bowl while she made it.

'You'll spill it on the table next,' she cautioned automatically.

Reg stabbed the spoon back in the bowl and flared, 'Jesus Christ, Ella! Any more complaints?'

Ever so deliberately she placed the cosy over the teapot then turned to face him. 'I didn't *make* you write that letter, you know.'

'Didn't you?' he queried enigmatically.

'And what does that mean?'

He didn't answer. It sounded silly on reflection.

She waited a moment, watching him appealingly for a response, but it didn't come. Eventually she sat down at the table and placed her hand over his. At least he didn't withdraw.

'Do I make you very unhappy, Reg?'

'No! Christ, of course you don't!'

'Then what's wrong? *Is* it the letter? Because if it is, then I don't think you've got all that much to worry about. I can't see newspapers paying much attention to something that wasn't even signed.'

He wriggled his hand from under hers. 'I notice you say *I* don't have much to worry about. If I get the bullet, you go on social security too, Ella. It's both of us looking for another job, another house.'

'You know what I meant.'

'Yeah.'

Cynical again, even resentful of her, and perhaps with

129

some justification. She felt her eyes blink involuntarily. She couldn't help it. She couldn't help being miserable in Vaila; or conceal her dislike of its isolation through every single minute of every day. As far as Reg and herself were concerned, for as long as he continued to work in the more remote backwaters of the oil business, it seemed that tears would be an inevitable adjunct to love.

He looked at her and saw her unhappiness; rain drops seen through the windows of her eyes: tears seen through the windows of Panoco Control . . . the world was crying for them both because they already had the one thing that mattered and yet they still continued to hurt each other.

'I'm sorry!' he muttered, sliding his hand back under hers. 'I just happen to love you. Probably too much, and that's half the trouble.'

Ken barged in through the back door, dropped his bag of football gear in the middle of the floor and headed for the fridge and a whole pint of milk.

Automatically Reg withdrew his hand again but, for Ella's sake, fought the impulse to pick the muddy bag up and throw it back out in the garden. And Ken along with it. 'Win, did you?' he asked with forced interest.

'Three, two the School!' Ken panted off-handedly, already halfway through the bottle.

'That's nice,' Ella sniffed.

Reg got up from the table. 'I'll go an' get dressed,' he said, then smiled reassuringly at her. 'And as far as the other thing's concerned; so the worst happens and they pay me off. So what? We'll manage. But you're probably right anyway. Who's going to pay attention to some nit-picking anonymous letter?'

'See you might be famous soon, Dad,' Ken called as he began to lay a trail of discarded clothing for Mum to retrieve along the hall and into the bathroom.

'You disappoint me,' Reg retorted absently, feeling a lot happier. 'Always assumed I already was. Anyway – why?'

'Eddie McAllister's Grannie owns the Meall Ness. He says she's got a reporter staying with her jus' now, from the *Northern Citizen* . . .'

130

The sick feeling was back in his gut even before his son had finished.

'. . . come all the way up fae Glasgow, Eddie says: to do some kind of article on where you work.'

Pilot McDonald went for an evening constitutional along the offshore jetty just before it got dark. It wasn't his part of ship so to speak, being a safety area clearly defined as the responsibility of whichever Pollution Control Officer happened to have the duty watch, but what with ring bolts and stray gear and pipework and mooring lines a tanker's deck, even the vast main deck of a U or a VLCC, tends to present an ocean-going obstacle course. Archie preferred to stretch his legs with a brisk walk along the comparatively uncluttered length of the island structure.

The offshore jetty consisted of five concrete-piled and quite separate islands, interconnected only by a slender steel-spanned and boarded catwalk. The centre island was the largest, providing a platform for the cargo handling facilities with their crane-like Chiksan arms, a two-storeyed personnel building and a fire control tower. Extending north and south from that central platform were four further concrete mini-islands known as Dolphins which acted primarily as strong-points for the mooring lines of visiting ships.

Huge though the tankers were, the offshore jetty was still twice as long, nearly one third of a mile. *Calauria* lay port side to against its westerly, seaward face, which placed her roughly at right angles to the loch's entrance some four miles away.

On that particular Saturday Pilot McDonald decided to turn right once he had climbed to the higher catwalk from the centre platform and *Calauria*'s gangway, thus taking him in the direction of the personnel landing stage, public telephone box and rest hut situated on the jetty's southern extremity, the mini-island known as Dolphin 24. It meant he could look forward to a bracing stride into the snap of the freshening wind.

Before he left the ship he called Panoco Control on VHF.

'Off for a gallop down to Twenty-Four, Bill. Half an hour or so.'

Even from a quarter of a mile away Thomson's retort held a note of mystification. 'You mus' be bloody mad. It's got to be freezing out there.'

'I'm healthy,' Archie grinned into his handset. 'Healthy, good-living and pure of mind. You ought to try it.'

Lights were sparkling over in Vaila as he walked, heralding the coming of the second night of *Calauria*'s stay. By God but it *was* cold, at that; especially exposed to the cut of the wind as he was on that man-made island in the loch. Gratefully he hugged his flotation jacket around him, seeking its added warmth. The Quarsdale pilots always wore them when boarding; fleece-lined anoraks with inbuilt buoyancy to aid survival during the first shock of an accidental ditching while also incorporating a small gas cylinder which – by triggering automatically on immersion – inflated further air pockets within the collar to hold nose and mouth above the surface until its wearer could be recovered.

Or that was the theory anyway. Fortunately McDonald, in common with the other Panoco pilots, had so far never had the need to experiment. He never wanted to either, and certainly not now. The latest wave of head-office-dictated economy measures currently being implemented by Duggan decreed that the pilot cutter be reduced to operating with a two-man crew. Even under calm conditions, hauling the weight of a waterlogged – and very possibly unconscious – body aboard would prove a Herculean task; in any degree of seaway, it would be nearly impossible.

The narrow catwalk along which he strode so briskly was constructed a dizzy forty feet above the loch's surface. Even so, when compared with the Liberian's current freeboard – the height to which his massive charge had risen from the water during this interim stage of her unloading – Pilot McDonald still only found himself walking more or less on a level with *Calauria*'s main deck as he headed towards her bows. Acres and acres of rusted steel plate which hadn't smelled paint for years spread to his right as he passed; seemingly miles and miles of pipework which hadn't felt the

132

rasp of a crewman's wire brush since scale had first gained a foothold a hundred thousand nautical steaming miles before. It was curious how he hadn't been quite so aware of her poor condition from his loftier station on her bridge. Or was it because he'd seen much the same thing so many times before? Had his capacity for concern been neutralized by familiarity? This VLCC wasn't exceptional; there were many sailing into Rora in an equally poor state of maintenance, particularly those Flags of Convenience vessels which now made up the bulk of the world's crude tanker fleet. But this near view was educational. McDonald began to appreciate the private comments made all too regularly by PCO Trelawney on completion of his pre-discharge safety checks. He began to feel a fellow mariner's sympathy for Captain Bisaglia too; a pleasant and still capable seaman from what little he'd seen of him. The elderly Italian master had obviously, in common with his exhausted command, seen better days.

When he finally reached the end of the catwalk McDonald lingered a moment, gazing westwards and out towards the Heads. Three cables off the VLCC berth, the tethered form of the duty tug *Robert The Bruce* traced elliptical images with its single white anchor light against the falling night. More distant still the stark silhouette of ancient fortress Dùin Feadda showed arrogant above Roinn Tain and, less discernible to any but an experienced eye, the two-mile line of restless whitecaps marking its separation from Riddock Skerries: the waveforms of the Atlantic jostling for position before sweeping into Quarsdale.

Assuming everything went according to plan he'd have that corroding monster well clear of them again by this time tomorrow. But that was only assuming . . . Pilot McDonald, being human and possessing a natural impatience, was anxious to see the stern of her. It was out of season for fishing, but he was nevertheless anxious to climb up to the lochans, even without his rod, for a relaxing Sunday afternoon. He was hoping that the next forecast, due on the change of terminal shift at 8 p.m., wouldn't indicate a further deterioration of the weather. It could lead to delay, necessitate an alteration to the VLCC Mate's proposals for taking on only

133

a minimum of intermediate ballast between parcels. If the already ominously freshening wind rose a further couple of notches up the Beaufort Scale then unless – Spedini, was it? – well, unless Chief Officer Spedini agreed to pump some additional weight into her belly before she discharged the second half of her cargo, *Calauria* could well become unmanageable as she lay pinned against the jetty under the press of a sou' westerly gale by then screeching down the unencumbered length of Quarsdale. The tugs would never be able to pull her off the berth and turn her bows seawards; not until the winds died once more. But that was where taking a decision became a risky commercial gamble on the part of both pilot and shipmaster. For if, on the other hand, the wind didn't materialize after all, then the extra ballasting operation would have created roughly one hour's expensive and unnecessary delay for every additional eight thousand cubic metres taken on.

'God rot the planners who hadn't foreseen these problems,' Archie reflected irritably, much as he'd done on many previous walks into the wind. 'An' I bet they gave the buggers an award for industrial bloody achievement once they'd finished!'

There was no one in sight on the personnel landing stage of Dolphin 24 as he turned back towards the ship and the homeward tramp along the catwalk. It was hardly surprising; the manpower cuts had bitten into every part of Panoco's Vaila operation. The offshore jetty's shift complement had recently been reduced from its originally designated eight man team to only six: the duty PCO, a jetty foreman, three jettymen – and one solitary Plant Protection Officer trained in basic fire-fighting.

'Every cloud has a silver lining. It'll leave more room in the escape rafts for the rest of us,' had been the laconic if somewhat defeatist reaction from staff. But a crisis of confidence was building at Rora. Though few were yet prepared to challenge the economy measures openly for fear of management retaliation they were, nevertheless, becoming a matter for concern; particularly to the Pilots, Expediters and Control Officers such as Trelawney.

'It's a bloody sad state of affairs,' Archie McDonald reflected bitterly as he headed back; not invigorated as he should have been, but suddenly depressed by rusted ships and the raising of spectres better avoided.

There was no doubt about it; morale around the terminal was plummeting, loyalty corroding as surely as some of the big ships that visited it. Secretly none of them – McDonald included – harboured any intention of hanging around their charge should the nightmare of fire ever become reality. The general consensus of opinion was: the way Panoco had downgraded the system out here in the middle of nowhere, it wouldn't make much odds whether they had one, two or twenty hands immediately available should a hundred thousand tonnes-plus of crude oil really make up its mind to burn. Hell, you needed a little more going for your prospects of survival than the selfless resolution of a few fire-fighters, however highly trained.

'Like being a good swimmer.' Pilot McDonald's sombre deliberations took on a savage humour. 'As well as being bloody fireproof.'

Nothing particularly exciting or unusual happened to anyone in Vaila during the early part of that last evening. Or only to Mrs Leachan up in Craigie Drive behind the Church. She'd boiled eggs for Mr Leachan's tea and taken them into the sitting room to where he was watching the Grampian Television news, snapping rather unfairly, 'If you'd get off've thon chair and get yoursel' a job, Jimmie Leachan, we could've been supping the chicken instead o' just its eggs!' Then she noticed Mr Leachan had gone a rather odd colour, very grey indeed. And then he slowly slipped off his chair and died with a rattle and a rasp on the carpet in front of her . . .

It *was* quite an exciting and unusual event for Mrs Leachan – and probably for Mr Leachan too, for that matter, though nobody could be quite certain of that – but it didn't have the slightest bearing on what was to take place on Loch Quarsdale later that same night.

. . . other than that it made Mr Leachan one of the few

135

people in Vaila who didn't get out of bed to see what was happening when it eventually did, of course.

No bearing at all. It simply illustrates what an ordinary, even somewhat dull place the Scottish burgh of Vaila usually managed to be. Particularly on a Saturday evening in winter.

By eight o'clock on that evening in which Mr Leachan didn't quite manage to eat his boiled eggs, Police Constable Lawson – who hardly needed Vaila's lack of excitement illustrated because he'd spent enough Saturday nights tramping about the place to learn about it at first hand – had survived the fickle dagger of fate, at least for as long as it took to finish *his* tea, and had begun to polish his boots and press his black uniform trousers in preparation for the involuntary extra night shift which he had, it seemed, volunteered for anyway.

He couldn't help wondering what the nursing sister down in Oban was doing right at that moment, and with whom she was doing it; though it *was* still a bit early for that sort of thing. But when you're only twenty years old and as disappointed as Hamish was at seeing the promise of a golden weekend erased from your diary at the whim of some unsympathetic Inspector, then you tend to take a morose view of things in general.

There was a film on TV which he half watched while standing before the ironing board. It was about a remote scientific station stricken by a plague of giant wriggling caterpillars in which more or less everybody died with bulging eyes and enormous Thespian enthusiasm. Hamish couldn't help wishing the giant caterpillars could perform an emergency encore on the demonstrators at Panoço's gates before he was due on duty at eleven; particularly on Councillor Auntie Jesse.

Not that even gruesome massacre would retrieve his thwarted romantic foray now. If it was left to his Inspector, he'd have to spend an extra shift hunting the giant caterpillars and, once he'd arrested them, write a report for the Procurator Fiscal . . . but policemen, particularly twenty-year-old policemen, are human too and given to flights of fancy just like everyone else.

Police Constable Lawson was going to have a very long incident report to write before he cleaned his boots again, and would have to face duties that night which he would find not only hateful but violently distressing. And would discover all too brutally that true horror can never be emulated on celluloid.

The militants ate their Saturday teas separately in their respective homes.

Well, it was dinner really, in Dr Caird's house. Peter's father and mother always sat down to lunch, followed by dinner at eight; not dinner at midday followed by tea on your knee whenever the good programmes on the telly started. Though on that particular evening there was a slight delay because Dr Caird had been called away to Mrs Leachan's up on Craigie Drive in order to diagnose precisely *why* Mr Leachan hadn't been able to eat his boiled eggs. Which didn't take very long, but meant the soup had to be re-heated by the time he'd written out the death certificate and given Mrs Leachan either blue or green pills to stupefy if not console her, and finally telephoned Geordie McGruar the undertaker – who, on reflection, must have been a tea rather than a dinner man seeing he'd finished eating and was immediately available for business before a quarter to eight.

Peter Caird didn't mind waiting. He wasn't due to rendezvous with the reluctant Alec Bell until the operational countdown began at half-past eleven. Also it would be gey chill out there on the loch, so a recent hot meal inside him wouldn't go amiss.

Specky Bell, for his part, didn't eat anything, tea nor dinner. His mum got quite concerned in fact, because Alec usually had such a healthy appetite and it was only after he'd made the excuse that soup and stovies were to be served at the late party he'd been invited to that she finally accepted that her son wasn't hovering on the brink of some serious ailment. He didn't elaborate on whose late party it was, and fortunately his mum didn't ask.

The reason Alec Bell wasn't hungry was partly because he was so apprehensive of going out in yon stupid wee dinghy thing of Cairdy's that his mouth was dry as the bottom of the budgie's cage, and partly because logic suggested that the less he had in his stomach, the less time he'd spend disposing of it over the side of the bluidy boat!

Shona Simpson didn't have to make any excuses about being out late after her tea – not that she'd have bothered to anyway – because her mother specifically forbade her to go out at all that evening after the way she'd carried on last night.

She was very quick to forbid, Shona's mother. Just as Jimmie Simpson was very quick to hide his head behind his paper and pretend not to notice when family conflict threatened.

But this time Shona didn't mind. She just flounced up to her bedroom for the sake of appearances, slammed the door and locked it pointedly. Then got from her wardrobe the rope she'd used often enough already on such occasions and lay back on her bed with her arms behind her head, the radio blaring pop, waiting. And fondly imagining the look on Peter Caird's face when he found things getting way out of hand with his precious plan.

Janey Menzies ate her tea just as she'd always done, and hardly gave the coming night a thought. But Janey wasn't particularly bright, and as long as she was out with John McLean it didn't really matter what they were doing.

John McLean, on the other hand, was thinking of little but the night ahead. Still secretly torn between apprehension over the consequences of what they were proposing to do and reluctance to lose further face in front of both Shona and, more particularly, Peter Caird, he got into trouble not only from *his* mother for being morose and poking at his food, but also from his father, who loudly criticized him for no' having ony go in him; nae interest in the *Vian*'s future. But that was largely because McLean senior was shortly due down at the gates for another weary night of daft protest along wi' the rest of the inshore men where, no doubt, they'd all be bullied like recalcitrant bairns by thon virago District Councillor Mrs McLeish into believing they were getting somewhere wi' the oil barons.

138

'Aye. Well you just see,' John had flared back at his dad. 'If I set my mind tae it, I could dae more to attract public attention to the terminal than ony of you old yins.'

'*That'll* be bluidy right, laddie,' had been his father's parting shot as he slammed out of the house just before eight. 'You couldnae do onything worthwhile if you tried!'

It was that last remark which finally cemented Big John McLean's wavering resolution.

It was also to cost the lives of a great number of men before many more hours had passed.

Wullie Gibb met Engineer Burns for a pint in the Stag before they caught the half-past-seven bus out to Neackie Plant Harbour. Wullie's prospective brother-in-law wandered into the public bar a few minutes later, accompanied by the *Wallace*'s Skipper McFadyen; then Auld Phimister the night shift gateman turned up, along with Plant Protection Officer Downie. It was a meeting in which the conversation inevitably turned to Panoco matters and – just as inevitably because Tam Burns was in on it – Panoco matters with a tendency towards doom and gloom.

'Ah'm tellin' you,' Tam predicted with relish between sips from his export, 'the way the bosses have cut back, wan wee spark out there on thon platform and we're all on oor way up in the world.'

'You said that yesterday,' Wullie reminded him reasonably. 'You say it every day f'r that matter.'

'They'll put it on your tombstone,' Phimister chuckled wheezily. 'Here lies Tam Burns, wan spark gave him back intae the hands o' God.'

'There'll probably no' be enough of me left tae make up a decent coffin-full,' Engineer Burns speculated, thrilled at the prospect.

'It's the truth, man. They'll not know whether tae scrape you up or paint you over,' Eck the Mate encouraged.

'They'd have tae put me inna bucket.' Tam Burns was in full masochistic flow by then and Wullie couldn't stand it any longer. He dissolved into fits of giggling while Eck began to make curious noises into his pint.

'It's not so funny as all *that*, you lads,' the Skipper protested mildly. But Jimmie McFadyen had sailed in petroleum tankers when he was a deep sea man, and never showed any sense of humour when it came to being blown up. The others doubled up anyway. All except Tam Burns, of course; he just stood with his glass in his hand and a faraway expression in his eyes.

'The chances o' fire are minimal and you know it, Tam Burns,' McFadyen persisted. 'Yon are crude carriers we're handling. Crude's got a pretty high flash point, it'll no' ignite from just a spark.'

'Ahhh, but it's the gas that'll get us,' Burns insisted anxiously, worried now lest there might be some hope of his surviving to die of old age. 'Wan spark an' thon gas clouds hanging ower they VLCCs is a flamer, ah'm tellin' you.'

'No it's bloody NOT!' The Skipper was getting irritated now. 'You're always on that bloody hobbyhorse o' yours as if just mixing air and hydrocarbon vapour's enough tae blow us all off the perch. Christ but you're an engineer, man! You know fine that specific conditions are needed. There are flammable ranges; it's only a narrow ratio of gas in proportion to atmosphere that's explosive – somethin' between two and eight per cent gas in the air forms the only combination that'll blow.'

'Plus the fact that you've got to have a source of ignition, Tam,' the Mate added hurriedly, reading McFadyen's mood and sensing the advisability of being seen to know everything a responsible Chief Officer ought to. 'And where d'you get ignition in a safety area like we got out there? Nae ciggies or matches allowed past Pheemister here on the gates; pressurized personnel spaces anyroad, so's the gas cannae find its way in; flameproof electrical equipment on the jetty itself; tank lids kept closed; flame screens or whatever fitted over the ships' ullage ports . . .'

'Do we have to go through all this?' Wullie interjected. 'I dinnae get paid till eight o'clock. Ah'm no' wanting tae listen tae some Panoco Muppet's security lecture.'

'You shut your face, Deckhand Gibb!' Eck rejoined, needled at being cut short in full flow of knowledge.

'. . . and Ship's Cook!' Wullie retorted unabashed. 'Though I dinnae get paid f'r *that*, either. And you weren't so high and mighty yesterday, Eck Dawson, when you wis wanting me tae fix you up again wi' mah sister, Katrina.'

'D'you lads fancy another before the bus comes?' Downie asked diplomatically, well aware that the crew of the *William Wallace* spent most of their time together in heated argument.

'Mine's a nip and a pint,' Gateman Phimister specified instantly, betraying a speed of reaction disproportionate to his advancing years. 'Seein' I've got a whole mob tae control once I clock on.'

'He means he'll have tae keep the gates locked on Jesse McLeish so's he can still watch his television,' Wullie interpreted cruelly.

'They even carry safety approved torches, so where's your sources of ignition?' It didn't seem to matter to Eck Dawson that no one was listening any longer.

Or to Engineer Burns, but he was used to being ignored. Quite enjoyed it really.

'Wan spark,' he persisted mournfully. 'Ah'm still tellin' you lads, all it needs in the middle o' the night when a'thing's quiet is jist wan tiny wee spark.'

'Don't,' Skipper McFadyen snapped, 'be sae *bluidy* ridiculous!'

By the time she'd returned to the Meall Ness Hotel from the grand house on Fariskay, Fran Herschell had conceded at least that Quarsdale might well provide the setting for an industrial disaster of major proportions.

She considered the implications of what she'd learned from Mrs McLeish while trying to relax in a hot bath; difficult, because of the growing sense of urgency within her. Usually Fran managed to remain detached from her work, never became involved on a personal level, but on this occasion she couldn't; her earlier unease was becoming stronger with every hour that passed. Even while getting ready for her dinner date with Duggan she made occasional notes on the pad lying beside her bed.

She was also aware of a sense of anticlimax. She knew

there could be nothing between her and Duggan now, and the realization disappointed her more than a little. Fran was sure that once she'd raised the questions she had in her mind, her interview with Deputy Terminal Superintendent Duggan would become just that – an interview, and a stiff one at that. In fact their evening together would, probably, be cut frustratingly short.

Duggan, on the other hand, forced himself into a very cold shower; not only in anticipation of *his* long awaited dinner date but also to help him recover from his marathon lunch with Captain Bisaglia. Even after calling into the terminal during late afternoon to check everything was going okay with the *Calauria* discharge he'd still felt the subtle betrayal of Drambuie dulling his physical edge.

Duggan didn't suspect, of course, that it wasn't so much a glowing, well honed body he'd need for his pending assignation with the desirable Mrs Herschell, as a razor-sharp mind.

Expediter Blair left the house at 7.36 p.m., much the same time as usual. Even though Ella had pecked his cheek at the door and pressed his hand reassuringly Reg still felt ill over the news that the press apparently *had* taken his letter seriously. When you really got down to it, it wasn't simply because his action threatened their future prospects; Reg was also an ex-serviceman; a man trained in duty and responsibility, who took loyalty to heart. Yet here he was, suffering the pangs of conscience of the betrayer.

'A Judas,' he reflected bitterly as he wheeled his bike down the garden path. 'That's what I am. Just a bloody Judas to the guys who pay me; to managers like Duggan.'

Pollution Control Officer Michael Trelawney left his company-provided home en route for work at about the same time; in fact he met Blair in the middle of the street and they cycled the half-mile down to the terminal together. Reg couldn't help feeling a bit envious of the PCO; it was simply a routine night shift for him – no drama; no trauma; no fear of losing his job. It was curious though; the way Trelawney swivelled in his saddle to wave goodbye to his wife Madge who was still watching them go as they turned the corner. He didn't often think of doing that, while Madge didn't often brave the doorstep's winter chill for quite so long either.

Of course Captain Mike Trelawney couldn't possibly have suspected that he might never wave to Madge again.

Could he . . .?

Chief Officer Spedini had barely completed his alterations to the load distribution plan in time. The hours of mental callisthenics had left his brain numb; he wasn't capable of taking a balanced view any more. He did feel confident, however, that he'd finally produced a safe compromise, allowing the ship to work uninterrupted yet leaving Numbers Six across empty for Chief Borga.

And to give Spedini his due, that could well have been the case – had *Calauria* been a supple, shiny-new ship conforming to the scantlings on which her builders' *Conditions de Chargement* had been based.

At twenty to eight he hurried to the master's cabin, knowing they had almost finished discharge of the first Heavy parcel. He feared Bisaglia's displeasure at his having left vital decisions affecting the subsequent ballasting stage until the last moment – for only God and the piles of discarded figures on his desk would have confirmed that Mario Spedini, a tankerman supposed to be worth the three gold rings on his epaulettes, had required as much time as any first year apprentice to complete his task.

But Tommaso Bisaglia, who had prudently kept a low profile in his cabin since his return from the Drambuie-fuelled Vaila shopping expedition, was only relieved to find the problem had been solved.

And no doubt brilliantly. The Captain still sincerely believed he could not do better than entrust the harbour working of his ship to his Mate – as a great majority of masters are, in fact, inclined to do despite their ultimate responsibility. Certainly young Spedini had always overcome previous difficulties in a most competent manner.

'On this occasion I must accept your recommendations, *signore*,' Bisaglia ruled for the second time on that voyage.

'Time is pressing. I leave it to you to implement the ballast procedures, after advising the terminal's PCO and the Pilot, naturally.'

It was only when Spedini had opened the door of the cabin that the little master's voice took on a rather more stern note.

'You will perhaps take your parcel with you when you go, Chief Officer. Over there, on the chair.'

Spedini halted abruptly, confused and still geared only to stress factors and shearing moments. 'Parcel, sir?'

'Your, ah . . . dolly, Spedini,' the Captain said through pursed and disapproving lips. 'Your plastic Scottish lady. With the kilt!'

It was nearly 8.00 p.m.

On the offshore jetty the supership *Calauria* had completed discharge of her seventy-six thousand tonne parcel of Arabian Heavy.

In a short time she would commence taking on ballast.

The Ship

So within less than twenty-four hours the larger
part of her cargo was already gone into the terminal's care; safely stored in the great shiny structures marking Sròine Rora. Only forty-one thousand tonnes of Arabian Light remained aboard – a
modest burden in VLCC terms; less than one third
of *Calauria*'s total carrying capacity. It created a
curious illusion. Like an iceberg melting below sea
level there was less of her, yet, at that state of part
unloading, she revealed a mass much greater than
on her arrival; even more breathtaking than before
to the unfamiliar eye; rising sheer and blockish from
the loch with a rusted girdle, usually submerged,
topping her underbelly; dripping and blinking in
the harsh glare of jetty lights. If – because there
was no costly anti-fouling left on the acres of her
bottom – you ventured very close to the great cliff
which only a few hours previously had hung suspended below *Calauria*'s laden waterline, you
would have seen the darting tongues of countless
fellow-travelling barnacles fumbling and feeling
uncertainly for molecules of food, slowly drying
and dying in the alien air.

The bow sections of the ship were now quite
empty. Her forepeak and deep tanks had carried
no cargo anyway on this last voyage, while Numbers One Centre and Wings retained only a few
tons of slop and the gloss of mineral black together
with – or until such time as they could be vented
and freed of gas after sailing at least – an atmosphere heavy with risk. Her aftermost payload
spaces – those three cathedral-like compartments

immediately forward of the engine room, containing Chief Officer Spedini's current *bête noir* of the leaky sluice valves – had also been discharged and they, in particular, would require voiding of any suspicion of lethal contamination before Borga's repairmen dared enter.

The Heavy carried in her remaining centre compartments had also been drained by then, while the PBTs – those Permanent Ballast Tanks situated roughly midway between bow and stern and shortly to assume such apocalyptic significance – were still empty of sea water. *Calauria* was, therefore, floating comparatively high and light during that early Saturday evening, with the final element of her cargo – the second and much smaller parcel of Arabian Light – spread along both sides of her mid section only, confined within Numbers Two to Five starboard wings.

Looking down into the egg-crate VLCC at that particular moment it would have been clear that, despite its concentration amidships, such oil as did remain was still evenly distributed along almost half of the Liberian tanker's length. Certainly no critic of Chief Officer Spedini could have claimed that *Calauria*'s state of loading, at the time of the shift change within the terminal, was placing excessive stress on her hull.

Which was just as well for those fortunate day workers currently departing, because Rust was poised to launch its most massive strike yet against the already reeling forces of Steel.

Having been permitted to accelerate its offensive by her owners' parsimonious withdrawal of cathodic protection from Captain Bisaglia's command, Rust had already succeeded in wasting many deck and upper side plate members in the region of the critically situated Permanent Ballast Tanks. Now it simply required one further push, one Hell-sent tactical opportunity, to achieve complete victory.

On that Saturday evening – because it is the men who control ships rather than the ships themselves who are more often prone to failure – such additional support was already in the offing. During the coming night Rust would enlist the aid of an unwitting but nevertheless thoroughly co-operative saboteur.

An agent with impeccable credentials; a most strategically placed fifth columnist.

He had, in fact, already achieved the greater part of his mission as an enemy within. He had done that the moment he rose confident from his desk aboard *Calauria*.

Chief Officer Spedini himself.

CHAPTER EIGHT

Late Evening:
SATURDAY

The black-restless stage of gigantic Quarsdale was almost set.

The anticipated wind had increased only slightly by eight o'clock on Saturday evening much to Pilot McDonald's satisfaction, but had veered to westerly again until it was now blowing almost directly down the loch towards the offshore jetty.

Much to Wullie Gibb's dissatisfaction; him being aboard the *William Wallace* and halfway out to the duty tug anchorage by then. But Pilot McDonald would soon be dining posh – nae doubt on somethin' or other wi' spaghetti – inna bluidy palace a hundred feet above the loch's surface, while Wullie could only anticipate cooking supper f'r a bunch o' thankless gannets aboard a wave-banjoed yo-yo that mair often than not felt like it wis six feet below it! Unless the weather blew up more of course, and the Skipper was forced to run for shelter to Neackie.

By 8.00 p.m. Police Constable Lawson had completed the task of ironing his white uniform shirt and polishing his black boots; had laid out his handcuffs, his baton and his warrant card in preparation for the coming battle with the Quarsdale Mafia; and had settled in front of the fire to watch the giant wriggling caterpillars devour the remainder of those scientists in remote Alaska or wherever. By then he'd decided that if they did descend on what often seemed an even more remote Vaila, then rather than eat the protest committee they'd be more usefully employed in consuming either his Sergeant or his Inspector. Better still, both his Sergeant *and* his Inspector.

By 8.00 p.m. the night shift of the fishermen's protest

148

committee, which included Big John McLean's dad, had assembled *en* grudging *masse* outside the main terminal gate where a stony-eyed and unsympathetic Gateman Phimister watched them from his warm buckie.

At precisely eight o'clock Fran Herschell left her Meall Ness bedroom and walked downstairs to meet Duggan, already waiting pink-scrubbed and carefully languid for her in the residents' lounge. She read an appreciation of her appearance in grey eyes which both gave the lie to her first impression of immaturity and rekindled the attraction she still felt towards him. That excitement was immediately displaced by frustration at being torn between professionalism and fleshly self-indulgence.

At eight o'clock Peter Caird began to help his mother set the table for dinner, still delayed due to the unexpected pre-boiled-egg decease of Mr Leachan.

At 8.00 p.m. a Mrs Annie Clunie, who hadn't meant to cause any trouble and had really only borrowed her husband's Datsun to drive round and see Auntie Isobel for a minute, ran over a black cat called Thomas. That was in Reform Street.

Now Thomas' death was obviously suicide; he was well known as a mentally retarded cat who regularly belted across the road at precisely the wrong moment. Yet there were those in Vaila who later claimed that the squashing of Thomas had been a portent of events to come. There were others – particularly the older Highland folk still inclined towards believing in the power of the Evil Eye and convinced that the Meenister should never set foot on a boat – who even hinted openly that the motorized massacre of Thomas had cast a spell of ill fortune over Quarsdale for the rest of that night, and that anything going wrong had been Annie Clunie's fault.

It wasn't, of course. A scientific appraisal of the events subsequent to Thomas' extinction would demonstrate that – other than having proved bloody bad luck for the cat – corrosion combined with human error had been responsible for the nightmare which followed. Not poor Annie Clunie at all.

At 8.00 p.m. it began to rain on Vaila again.

At precisely eight o'clock on that last Saturday evening, Terminal Night Expediter Blair relieved day shift Expediter Thomson.

No one was in the control room when Reg entered, hopping on one leg while trying at the same time to remove his bicycle clips. The extension speaker of the VHF was turned up to full volume though, hissing and crackling irritatingly with static from Channel 16. Blair adjusted the *squelch* control until the hissing died away, then walked through to the tiny kitchen and mess room running off the corridor. Bill Thomson was washing his lunch-time plates at the sink.

'I *like* to hear a bit of static when I'm through here,' the day man said, slightly nettled. 'Comms is what we're all about, Reg. Static in the background lets me know I'm still receiving: otherwise I begin to worry the set's gone U/S.'

Blair secretly wished that was all *he* had to worry about, but conceded Thomson's point. 'Sorry, mate,' he shrugged, then went back to the console and turned the *squelch* up just enough to detect its sibilant reassurance.

'Ready to take over when you are,' he called over his shoulder as he sat down. 'An' it's bloody raining again.'

Reg didn't look at the Log. Bill Thomson was a bit of an old woman – didn't like him peeking at the Log until he was ready formally to hand over the watch . . . well, the shift really, if you cut out the fancy Navy terminology. Anyway, obviously nothing was coming from the VLCC on the offshore jetty right then; all flow gauges registered a zero discharge rate which suggested she was probably ballasting from sea. He leaned his chin on his hand and waited, gazing reflectively at the familiar lay-out of the Expediter's console. Reg Blair felt secure in that seat, properly at home. Much as he'd felt when he *was* in ships, cocooned somehow from external domestic pressures.

Bill had been right about one thing. Communication really was the name of the game in the Control Room. The whole terminal depended on its comms links – particularly on its

Very High Frequency radio net – to operate efficiently. To operate at all, for that matter . . . Rora Terminal to Neackie Harbour; Crude Carrier to duty tug; tug to jetty; jetty to personnel launch; launch to shore – the airborne permutations were endless. Handheld sets enabled pilots a mile out to sea, the duty Pollution Control Officers, PPOs on their security rounds within the complex, even key management like Duggan sometimes far afield in the company transport, to call into the Expediter at the squeeze of a pressel switch. To receive instructions; pass information; respond immediately to routine or – God forbid in view of the bomb they'd built around themselves – emergency summonses . . .

And he, ex-Chief Gunnery Instructor Reginald Blair, worked at the heart of it; was the nerve centre through which all operations were channelled while he was on duty. The Expediter was Number One Boy; nothing could pump or pass or move within the terminal perimeter – and that included the offshore jetty – without some action, some authorization, some implementation through the flick of a switch by him. *Panoco Control* was even his call sign. Absently Blair ran his hands over the shiny-grey metallic surface of the panel before him, sensing the pride he always felt in the responsibility he carried.

At least he did until Thomson came through from the galley – the 'kitchen', dammit! – and tried to make up for his earlier sharpness by asking brightly, 'How's Ella then?' Whereupon Reg immediately remembered the letter, lost all feeling of well-being, and became thoroughly irritated.

'Look, let's just get on with the hand-over, eh?'

Thomson looked a bit hurt. He thought Blair was showing resentment over his good-natured reminder that keeping alert for incoming VHF traffic was all-important; particularly when you were absent from the Control Room, like in the toilet or kitchen. Mind you, Reg always had been a thin-skinned bugger, even in the Navy; and especially where Ella was concerned.

'Suit yourself, mate. So the forecast's much the same, westerly six to seven with rain – McDonald's still swithering out there about whether or not to recommend an increase in

151

interim ballast. High water jetty due at zero two sixteen zulu. Your Duty PCO's Cap'n Trelawney again, if he's arrived.'

'He's already on his way out in the launch, Bill,' Reg offered, trying to sound apologetic without actually apologizing. His apprehension for the future wasn't anything of Thomson's doing, just his own. 'We cycled down in company.'

'Good. So you're in for a quiet few hours. Our Liberian friend completed her Heavy Crude discharge a few minutes ago, now she's preparing to ballast. No further transfer operations scheduled till early morning, though her Chief's warned he needs around two hundred tons of bunker fuel before they sail. You'll find it all in the Log.'

'Right,' Reg nodded. 'If that's all, I have the watch.'

'You always was more Navy than Nelson, Reg,' Thomson grinned, mollified now. 'Try and keep awake.'

'So's I c'n listen for the VHF as responsibly as Uncle Bill, eh?' Blair couldn't help needling his friend. Thomson had the grace to look penitent.

'Sorry about that. Kind of teaching my granny to suck eggs, wasn't it?'

''Night, Bill. Say hello to your hammock f'r me.'

Day Expediter Thomson turned with his coat half on at the door. 'Oh, and Duggan's left word he'll be at the Meall Ness all evening by the way. Call him if there's any problem. Right?'

'Affirmative. See you in the morning,' Reg said.

The giant floodlit tanker out at the jetty was all blurred once more; exploding in a fuzzy halo as it were, like yesterday's ink blot in the Log. But that was simply an optical illusion, seeing it through the raindrops trickling down the window.

The night was crying again.

It wasn't a leisurely beginning for all the Panoco key men following the turn-over of that Saturday shift. After boarding *Calauria* and relieving his predecessor, Pollution Control Officer Trelawney was almost immediately approached by Chief Officer Spedini who announced, somewhat off-handedly to Trelawney's mind, that he was ready to begin ballasting.

The PCO assumed the Mate's nonchalance was typical of the man, in character with his lack of concern during the pre-discharge safety checks. He didn't read any lack of confidence into the young Italian's attitude but then, few of those who knew him ever did. Including Captain Bisaglia.

He thought wryly, 'Shit! Course you couldn't have managed it a bit earlier, before Harry signed off an' went shoreside, could you?' All he actually *said* was: 'I'd like to confirm the procedure in consultation with the Pilot, then break the safety seals myself if you don't mind, *signore*.'

Spedini shrugged agreement; not that he had any choice. When it came to double checking on anti-pollution measures within the Rora sphere of operations, the company had the last word. The last major spillage had occurred when the wrong valves were opened, because her British Old Man had been paralytic in his bunk at the time, her Greek First Mate was too bloody lazy to go down to the pump room, her Chinese Second wasn't qualified to fill a teapot without close supervision. Yet a later abruptly-fired Panoco Pollution Control Officer had still been naïve enough to presume that *someone* in her crew must've known what the hell he was doing. It had been a warning of the risks of complacency, and the consequences of that accident were still uppermost in every current PCO's mind.

But there would always be certain facts – or educated assumptions, really – which had to be taken on trust in respect of each and every inward-bound VLCC. The most vital were her own officers' forecasts of the trim and stress factors affecting that particular vessel throughout the unloading process. Practically every arrival was in some way unique, either in its voyage cargo distribution or by virtue of its design. The economic necessity for fast turnarounds made it impossible for any transient shore official, not even tanker-experienced seamen such as PCO Trelawney or Pilot McDonald, to evaluate a resident Chief Officer's calculations. Only he and the master had time to prepare for cargo movements in advance; held the builder's data essential for

153

safe planning and, hopefully at least, an intimate knowledge of his own vessel.

From the main deck PCO Trelawney called McDonald to meet him in the ship's cargo control room. There, in company with Spedini, they briefly ran over the Chief Officer's proposals for the interim ballast phase. While it would be wrong to claim that Spedini was unco-operative, the two Panoco men found him less than keen to discuss details, but attributed that to his unfamiliarity with the language. Neither was entirely happy with his proposal to confine ballast to Numbers Two to Five centre tanks and both PBTs, while leaving Six across empty for repairs. They both foresaw that *Calauria* would sag considerably amidships, particularly towards the completion of ballasting, as an additional forty-two thousand tonnes of sea water more than doubled the existing weight of Crude still aboard.

But equally, they both understood Spedini's dilemma. The only way to spread the load over a greater length and thus to reduce the stress at any single point on the hull would be to ballast her bow spaces as well – particularly those comprising her deep tanks and Numbers One across. But further weighting of her forepart while still leaving her after end light would mean *Calauria*'s floating head down, stern up in effect and thus making it impossible to drain her of the final part of her cargo.

Trelawney even suggested they compromised by restricting the volume of ballast. He didn't have figures to go on, though – it was more the gut feeling of a seasoned tankerman – and he was only too aware, as was Captain Bisaglia who'd diplomatically avoided any involvement in the discussion, preferring to leave the high-tech talk to his thoroughly modern switched-on Mate Spedini, that you couldn't fly Very Large Crude Carriers by the seat of your pants.

He didn't press the point, but then, PCO Trelawney was conscious of the vulnerability of his position. It wasn't part of his brief to over-rule a VLCC officer unless he was absolutely certain that some grave error was being made, and not even Trelawney believed that was the case in this instance. Tankers were still tolerant within wide safety limits. He didn't consider she would be under greater stress than would normally apply in a heavy seaway.

Besides, though Captain Mike Trelawney was an honourable man who would always place duty before career if he felt the need to stand firm, he could not ignore the fact that any interference on his part in ship's matters outside his terms of reference must automatically involve him in sharing the blame if anything went wrong later.

And compromise could very well invite precisely such a disaster. As a seaman Trelawney also knew that Archie McDonald might very well need that additional ballast. The berth Pilot was as professionally accountable as PCO Trelawney, but for entirely different reasons. His primary responsibility was to ensure that every VLCC in his temporary charge was ready at all times to slip the berth in emergency, the offshore jetty being exposed as it was to the effects of wind and sea. To be able to do that, experience told him she would require a minimum loading amounting to some thirty per cent of her deadweight in order to keep her both in manoeuvring trim and with her propeller submerged – meaning, in *Calauria*'s case, Spedini's recommended forty thousand-plus tonnes. Before they could discharge her final parcel of cargo, therefore, Pilot McDonald had to be satisfied that it was to be replaced by a similar weight of sea water or his charge would rise from the loch like a gigantic windsail; a particularly alarming prospect on this Saturday evening when they were faced with a forecasted gale.

So while McDonald also saw that considerable stress would be created at the centre of the ship on conclusion of ballasting, he could only assume – as PCO Trelawney had – that it had been calculated as being within *Calauria*'s safe design limits. Neither Panoco representative had been made aware of the failure of Spedini's Loadicator and it never occurred to either of them to question whether or not the discharging plan had indeed been computer-analysed; they simply took it for granted that it must have been. They further presumed that *Calauria*'s master, Captain Bisaglia, would have been consulted and thus would have vetted his Chief Officer's procedure.

155

Both were to prove fatal assumptions.

During the entire period in *Calauria*'s cargo control room her even younger Second Officer De Mita hovered attentively in the background awaiting instructions, but was never invited by Spedini to take part in the discussion itself. Ironically Archie McDonald was reassured by that; forming the totally wrong impression – as had many others before him – that, in Spedini, they were dealing with a Mate so quietly self-assured and competent that he needed to concede no part of the VLCC's planning to his subordinates.

It was finally agreed to ballast Numbers Two to Five centres leaving one metre of ullage space. In order to save time *Calauria*'s own pumps would be used to speed the operation. The Permanent Ballast Tanks would simply be allowed to flood to sea level, then topped up with hose lines from deck.

At 20.28 GMT on Saturday evening, Pollution Control Officer Trelawney satisfied himself that there was suction on the pumps, then broke the seals on the valves which admitted sea water into the relevant systems. Before he left the compartment he also watched intently to ensure that De Mita *did* activate the correct valve controls from the console.

Sea water began to roar into *Calauria*'s gas-laden tank spaces. For every 98 tons taken aboard she would settle one centimetre deeper in the water; at a filling rate approaching some 7,000 metric tonnes per hour it was anticipated that ballasting would be completed within six hours – by approximately 2.30 in the morning.

Accompanied by Archie McDonald, Trelawney then went topside and, with the aid of a powerful torch, carefully inspected the loch surface in the region of each sea valve to make certain no oil was being accidentally discharged. Finally he walked round the exposed and rain-swept expanse of deck to confirm that air was being displaced only from the nominated tanks.

It all underlined the fact that PCO Trelawney was a thorough and conscientious man. But then, so were Pilot McDonald and Expediter Blair thorough and conscientious men. And Captain Bisaglia and Second Officer De Mita . . .

they were both conscientious men within the limits of their cheaply purchased abilities. Even Chief Officer Mario Spedini was a conscientious young man trying very hard to succeed.

Though tragically, in his case, without any ability. Other than, of course, the ability to exude a spurious air of confidence.

By 9.00 p.m. the somewhat capricious wind had increased slightly in strength once again. Anchored some half-mile to seaward of the offshore jetty the duty fire tug *William Wallace* began to snub uneasily at her cable.

At nine oh six the first sausage shot out of Wullie Gibb's frying pan. He stormed up to see the Skipper and told him that if he wanted any supper, then either he went back tae the sanity o' Neackie or made do wi' a jam sannie, or got some other bluidy mug tae do the cooking!

The Skipper told Deckhand Gibb to bugger off his bridge and carry on wi' cremating the sausisgis or get clapped in irons for mutiny. As soon as Wullie had trailed back down to the galley, muttering veiled threats of resignation, Skipper McFadyen cast a well-experienced eye around the shore lights to satisfy himself that his modest command wasn't actually dragging – which it wasn't as yet – and determined to stay on station just as long as he could, because that was what they were paid to do whatever yon cocky wee bastard Gibby thought. But Skipper McFadyen, too, was a conscientious man.

He did begin to wonder, though, if he was being unreasonable with Wullie. The other Skippers did withdraw on occasions, every crew had limits of endurance . . . and it would be hard to find another chef with quite Wullie's touch for the galley.

It wasn't only the seas of Quarsdale which were becoming unsettled by then. Expediter Blair began to feel really rough at about the same time. His stomach hadn't ceased to churn with apprehension ever since son Ken had dropped his bombshell. After a whole hour with little to do other than let

157

pessimism run riot, largely because no transfer operations were taking place which would otherwise have occupied his mind, Reg was on pins; waiting for Duggan to come through the Control Room door and snap: 'You, ex-Chief Petty Officer – ex-*Expediter* Blair – are goddamned fired!'

Even his last entry in the Log had been made over half an hour before; dictated by a laconic report from Pilot McDonald.

2030: Jetty gate valves closed. Commenced to take on ballast

He sat for a few minutes longer, staring unseeingly through the rain on the window out towards the floodlit supership; then his bowel discomfort became so intense that he felt obliged to go to the toilet.

The staff toilet ran off the kitchen passage at the back of the Control Room. Its door opened outwards, neatly blocking the passage. Once or twice the Expediters had complained about that and had asked for it to be rehung the other way – occasionally someone would leave it ajar and, for such was the way of the world, it always happened when you were carrying a brim-full mug of tea and not really concentrating on where you were going.

Before Reg Blair left the console temporarily unmanned he adjusted the *squelch* and ensured the volume of the VHF was fully turned up so that the hiss of static filled the air again. It wasn't possible to monitor an incoming call from the toilet otherwise; a weakness in the system already pointed out by the somewhat hypercritical Bill Thomson, and for about the thousandth bloody time. Though actually it *was* one of the points Reg had made in his now bitterly regretted letter – that management had never seen fit to approve the installation of extension speakers throughout the Control Building despite the fact they were clearly essential.

Mind you, considering they'd built the whole bloody terminal in the wrong part of the loch it was hardly surprising they failed to appreciate the importance of a detail such as that.

Anyway, Reg turned the VHF fully up as usual to ensure he would hear if needed. Judas or not, he was far too

158

conscientious an employee to ignore such a vital responsibility.

Police Constable Lawson, being every bit as conscientious as anyone else, had checked into the Vaila Station well ahead of his duty period. By ten to eleven he'd changed from the grey civvie anorak he wore while walking to work into his tunic, and had carefully read the incident telexes and crime bulletins which testified to the existence of a whole exciting world of villainy out there in the rest of Scotland.

He wasn't exactly surprised to learn that not one solitary citizen or liege of their own borough was recorded as having been robbed, mugged, assassinated, raped or even gently molested within the last twenty-four hours. Certainly one unfortunate resident *had* died in exceptional circumstances – a Mr Leachan out on Craigie Drive, an individual not known personally to Hamish. It seemed, however, that event had been precipitated more by a boiled egg or heart attack – the sudden death report appeared a little ambiguous as to which – than criminal violence. No doubt the postmortem down in Oban on Monday or Tuesday would reveal all.

Oh, and someone had reported finding the corpse of a black cat in the gutter in Reform Street – probably Thomas, a vicious animal well known to police throughout Vaila for its lunatic predilection towards unexpectedly darting across the road inches in front of motor cars and thereby acquiring the status of suspect in several unsolved concertina accidents. Constable Lawson darkly deduced a case of premeditated murder by insurance men unknown, rather than a purely haphazard squashing, but it seemed unlikely that justice would ever be done to the killer. The day sergeant had already passed the incident to higher authority for action; not to the Inter-City Homicide Squad but the District Council's Refuse Department.

Slightly cheered by the prospect of a future minus both Thomas and the regular traffic accident reports his activities entailed, Hamish put the kettle on before wandering over to the desk where Sergeant Robertson was moodily flicking through the pages of the Station Book. At least, Lawson

159

reflected, he could look forward to being warm and slothfully mobile.

He signed out the Panda and took the keys from the hook. Now, Batmobile on stand-by – tuned like a fiddle an' ready to jet anywhere in Gotham City – Constable Lawson was ready to battle with Crime wherever it lurked.

'Where d'you want me then, Sarn't?' he asked.

Dugie Robertson bore the jaundiced look of one about to commence an eight-hour graveyard shift.

'The wash bed oot the back,' he growled without even glancing up. 'Hose down the motor, it's mair like a tractor fresh fae a midden-moving than a polis vehicle. Then away down to the terminal and see if any of the fisher lads are still hanging around. Oh, an' while you're in Reform Street – pick up yon deid bluidy cat!'

Fran Herschell noted Duggan's apparent lack of appetite during the progress of their meal. She couldn't help wondering if he detected some change in her; whether she was betraying the distaste she felt for performing her professional function under the guise of social intercourse. She should have found some excuse to call off this dinner. It would have been much more honest to have conducted the interview across a desk with some unknown company representative politely on guard against loaded questions, than to have allowed a personal relationship to develop between them, however tenuous.

Duggan's malaise wasn't due to that, of course. He simply felt a disinclination for more rich food following so closely upon his luncheon with Captain Bisaglia. As far as Reporter Herschell was concerned, he was even less wary of her than during their first meeting. To him she was still only a journalist from the woman's page of the local rag, despite her surprising knowledge of maritime affairs. Furthermore he found himself increasingly fascinated by her: by the tumble of her hair; the slight hardness of lines cornering perfectly groomed eyes which hinted tantalizingly at an experience of life at its fullest; even the soft, yet at the same time so provocative amusement occasionally lighting within them in reaction to what Duggan himself suspected were ingenuous and fumbling compliments. To him, her womanhood seemed to mock what he interpreted as his own lack of *savoir faire*.

So conversation had proved difficult at the start. But the excellence of the meal helped; that and the crackling fire and the comfortable tick of Mrs McAllister's many clocks and the occasional spatter of raindrops against thickly muffled window panes all created, briefly at least, the illusion of intimacy.

So much so, in fact, that by the time they'd finished eating and Mrs McAllister had bustled in to clear the last of the dishes, even Fran was surprised to find that the dining room had long since emptied. Their hostess had waved away their apologies along with Duggan's proffered American Express card.

'I have laid out your coffee in the lounge along with a wee selection of liqueurs,' she'd insisted. 'You help yourselves and I can always have a wee word with Mister Duggan about the settling sometime later.'

Fran stood for some time before the windows overlooking Ouarsdale. Only the black-threshing silhouettes of wind-tortured broom marked the existence of any foreground; the middle distance seemed entirely dominated by the glare from the ship on the offshore jetty, a seascape of reflected light tossing and twinkling and multiplied a hundredfold through the optics of clinging raindrops.

'Come and sit beside the fire,' Duggan finally called in a low voice. She could sense his nervousness; the urgency which suggested he was steeling himself to proposition her before his courage failed. She kept her reply to a gentle reproach.

'My interview? I have to get *some* facts together, Duggan. It's why I came up here, remember.'

'Later,' he said. 'First thing tomorrow morning.' It was almost an appeal.

'Now,' she insisted. 'Please, Duggan?'

He wriggled in his seat and looked crestfallen. Well, more petulant really. For the first time that evening his macho image was slipping.

'It seems you're determined. So let's get it over with.'

'Thanks.'

She walked over to sit opposite him by the fire, conscious of his eyes narrowing in almost comical frustration as she tried, unsuccessfully, to cross her long elegant legs unobtrusively. Taking out the small personal tape recorder she always carried in her bag she triggered it, laying it on the coffee table. 'Do you mind? It's easier than taking notes.'

He eyed it, frowning.

'You won't need that. I can always give you menus or whatever you want to take back.'

'Menus?'

'Canteen menus. All wholesome chow and company subsidized. Presumably that's the sort of background material you're looking for? The way the guys eat; the recreational facilities; the standard of housing we . . .'

'Why are the offshore jetty escape rafts four months overdue for their annual service and certification, Duggan?'

He blinked. 'Huh?'

'Why are the offsho . . .'

Duggan said, 'I heard the question, Fran. I just don't see what interest it can possibly hold for women.'

'I don't write for women; I write for readers. Broadly speaking I'm here to report on the demo, if you remember?'

'The demo's about pollution and the environment. Life rafts have nothing to do with it.'

She shook her head. 'Everything about Rora's a matter for public concern. Those people standing in the rain down there are scared, Duggan. I'd hazard a guess that most of them don't even know what they're frightened of, it's just a feeling they have. And perhaps, by explaining, you could help dispel that anxiety.'

'Or land myself in big trouble with the company if I say the wrong things.'

'Why should you?' she probed quickly. 'Are you implying that, simply by telling the truth, you might be saying the wrong things as far as Panoco's concerned?'

Duggan stood up abruptly. He wasn't looking petulant any

162

more; he was beginning to look angry. 'It seems my only answer can be "No comment", *Mrs* Herschell!'

She shrugged. 'All right! Then let me ask you another. The automatic fire-fighting systems servicing the Rora Terminal and the offshore jetty? Are they still being maintained in the state of readiness prescribed by your original planning consent?'

'Where the hell are you getting these questions from?' Duggan snapped. 'Okay: so you'll tell me a journalist's sources are confidential. But it's the same reply – no comment!'

She leaned forward and switched the tape recorder off, keeping her gaze impassive with an effort. 'A different kind of question, Duggan – off the record this time. Are you really sure you want me to report this interview in that way?'

'Meaning?'

'Meaning Panoco Oil Terminals PLC were asked by my editor if they would grant an in-depth interview to the *Northern Citizen*. They agreed, and made no restrictions as to content; nor, incidentally, would we have accepted any had they attempted to do so.'

'Then Charlie got recalled to the States leaving me to fill in as whipping boy,' Duggan supplemented bitterly.

'As an official spokesman for your company, certainly,' Fran said. 'And I'm sorry it's you, I really am, Duggan. But I'm still duty-bound to put further important questions to you. I promise your responses will be reported faithfully and in context – so do you *really* want people to read: "A company spokesman declined to comment"?'

Duggan sat down again, staring grimly at the fire. He knew what the public's reaction would be, all right. It would be like handing a full belt of ammunition to crusaders like Jesse McLeish. Ironically the young executive looked more attractive than ever right then; all pretence at smoothness discarded.

'Okay. Then let's try your goddam questions for size,' he growled eventually. 'It looks like you've really planned to grab me by the balls tonight, lady!'

Fran couldn't help smiling wryly to herself. But it was

163

understandable that she should. After all, Duggan wasn't *that* far from the truth . . . other than in one small detail.

Peter Caird was late; nearly five minutes late for the eleven-thirty rendezvous at the derelict salmon fishers' bothie. The first they knew of him was a furtive 'Pssst!', then a movement in the bracken and he'd arrived in a camouflaged combat jacket and looking tremendously pleased with himself. He'd already recce'd the terminal gates and discovered they'd withdrawn the permanent police presence. It wouldn't make that much difference, the way he'd planned entry, but at least it showed that security was back to a minimal level.

Specky Bell sniggered nervously, trying to keep his mind off the boat. 'They see him here; they see him there . . .'

'. . . they see him *every* bluidy where!' McLean jeered spitefully. 'They'd hae a job not to, considerin' the noise he makes!'

Cairdy looked superior; he'd been anticipating an immediate challenge from John McLean. 'It's "seek". "We seek him here . . ." etcetera. *The Scarlet Pimpernel*: Baroness Orczy!'

'Scarlet Pimple, mair like,' Bell sniggered to the girls from behind his hand.

'Looking forward to your trip out to the tanker, Alec?' Caird counter-attacked. Specky Bell stopped sniggering and looked unhappy again.

'Hello, Peter,' Janey said hurriedly because she didn't like them sniping at each other, especially when John was about to engage in an uphill intellectual battle with Peter Caird.

'Hi there, Janey,' the student winked, carefully debonair. 'Hello, Shona. You ready for the big night?'

Shona Simpson ignored him, tight-lipped, and turned pointedly to John. 'What next then?'

'Well, we . . . um . . .'

'Personal camouflage,' Cairdy interjected, smoothly competent. He rummaged under the straw in the corner and produced a tin of black boot polish. In her new outrage Shona forgot she wasn't speaking to him. 'You can go stuff

164

yersel', Peter Caird, if you're expecting me tae smear that on *my* face!'

They eventually compromised with the boys using the polish and the two girls gingerly patting Janey Menzies' mascara, which would wash off a lot easier later, along cheekbones and across the bridges of their noses.

'Maaaaammy . . .' a shiny black Specky clowned, determined to be seen as imperturbable in the face of danger.

'Och, stop buggering about!' McLean snapped irritably. Putting Bell down was automatic with him, and easy to do. Caird was different. Cairdy was a sight mair intelligent than Alec. Possibly – a grudging concession – even than McLean himself in some ways. But John had discovered on the way to the beach that he had a more-than-vindictive ally now. Shona was with him it seemed, and between them they would hopefully find some way not only to screw things up for the Student Prince but also to show John McLean's own father just what a proper demonstration was.

So finally they were ready. All the brave talk was finished, now there could be no turning back. Each with spray can and torch in hand they filed, noticeably silent, from the desolate bothie into the wind and the rain. A quarter of a mile away the ship towered, not so much challenging as threatening it seemed at that moment, from its tossing bed of light, causing Alec Bell to shiver and even Peter Caird to frown a little anxiously at the risks they were about to invite.

But it was undeniable that he was a young man of resolution. That was why, unlike the others, he'd worked hard enough at school to get himself accepted by a leading university. It was also why he'd got himself into the corner he was now in, come to that; for resolution, without common sense, can sometimes become foolishly blinkered.

Getting a grip on himself he thrust the wire-cutters towards McLean. 'Give us forty minutes. You take your party through the wire at midnight plus thirty an' hit the installations at precisely zero one hundred. Check.'

'Och, f'r *fuck's* sake!' McLean ridiculed him, forgetting the girls were within earshot, though Shona sniggered anyway. 'You're off your heid, Cairdy – a bluidy nutter! You been

165

watching too much TV. We're only goin' tae paint them, no' blow them up.'

'I'm cold,' Janey urged diplomatically. 'Come *on*, John. Please.'

'I *wisnae* buggering about; ah wis doing mah Al Jolson bit,' a hurt Alec Bell protested somewhat tardily and to no one in particular. 'Ah wis just keeping morale up for you ones.'

'Ohhhh, shut *up*, Specky!' Caird snarled bad-temperedly, suddenly feeling lonely and a little frightened.

'That's right, Admiral; take it out on the wee lad!' McLean shouted triumphantly over his shoulder. It was his turn now to get Cairdy rattled.

'You keep your bloody VOICE down, McLean!' Peter bellowed after their disappearing figures. But only McLean's laughter supported by Shona Simpson's stupid giggling carried above the crash of waves along the shoreline.

It wouldn't have mattered to Big John if anyone *had* heard. The youth was careless of the consequences now; brooding resentfully at that paternal contempt shown him over teatime.

It was understandable perhaps, but nevertheless a dangerous frame of mind to be in. Especially for an irresponsible and rather slow-witted lad determined to show off.

At precisely one minute to midnight there came a faint rumble of thunder from somewhere out in the loch.

At least the few who detected it – mainly those located aboard the still-ballasting *Calauria* – *assumed* it was thunder. Which was odd.

Because no thunder had been predicted for Quarsdale over the next few hours, and weather forecasting – like the calculating of stresses as they affect Very Large Crude Carriers – has become a fairly precise science.

But nobody gave it too much thought. Mostly they'd forgotten it even by the time the church clock in Vaila began to strike twelve.

. . . and Sunday morning had begun.

The Ship

Considering the hog and sag syndrome again – that when a floating body is unevenly loaded along its length it will either droop at each end, which is known by seamen as 'hogging', or it will sag in the middle like . . . well, like Captain Bisaglia's salami in brine – then it was hardly surprising that *Calauria*, after four hours of ballasting only her midships tanks, was sagging badly.

In such a condition the forces acting upon the ship consist largely of either tensile or compressive stresses. Tensile stress is created when opposing collinear forces – those being applied in opposite directions along a straight line – cause a stretching moment; as happens, in fact, when one pulls a sheet of paper apart: when the inherent strength of the paper is overcome it will tear. Any steel plate or hull strengthening member will do exactly the same in a supertanker.

Compressive stress on the other hand occurs when, instead of pulling your sheet of paper apart, you push the ends towards each other. Collinear force again, but the other way round. So then it buckles. Just like those steel plates and strengtheners in the supership would do. Everything under compression – paper, steel, wood, human bones – will eventually bend once its point of critical buckling stress has been reached.

When a ship at sea is virtually suspended by bow and stern alone – bridging the trough, say, between two giant wavecrests – or, alternatively, is secure in harbour but sagging under a concentration of cargo amidships – then the tensile stresses are trying very hard to pull her keel apart while, simultaneously, the compressive stresses are beavering away in their determination to buckle her deck plating. Designers expect that sort of punishment to go on; they're acutely aware that the ocean produces an infinite variety of waveforms, while masters or chief officers can occasionally be a little less than infallible. Accordingly the men of the drawing boards allow ample safety margins, as well as warning everybody to be vigilant.

It was hardly surprising, then, that by midnight on Saturday, with some thirty thousand odd tonnes of sea-water ballast having been added to the weight of Light Crude still within her midships section, *Calauria* was sagging just as Spedini's copy of the *Conditions de Chargement* predicted that she would. But Chief Officer Spedini had taken a gamble on her builders having been over-cautious in their own interests. Contemptuous of ordinary prudence which suggested he seek more experienced counsel, he had dismissed their warnings, having concluded from his own calculations that, while the VLCC would indeed suffer greater than normal stresses, they would still not place his vessel at serious risk.

The irony was that Spedini, in his arrogance, had quite possibly been right. By responsibly maintained ship standards his distribution plan *should* still have kept the supership's burden within the limits of her tolerance.

Only *Calauria* had by then become an intolerant ship.

The first stage of hull failure was the compressive buckling of one longitudinal just below main deck level in the ullage space of Number Four Permanent Ballast Tank port side. That particular strengthening member had been permitted to waste to some thirty-eight per cent of its original dimensions. When it buckled the welding which stitched it to its strake – a continuous length of steel side plating – also disintegrated. Neither the stiffener nor the welding would from then on, play any further part in holding the ship together. She was still taking in ballast at a rate of some seven thousand metric tonnes per hour and thus the stresses were constantly increasing.

A few minutes later the first underwater hull plates suffered slight plastic deformation. Not to any great extent right then, but still enough to allow crude from some wing tanks to seep gently from the ship.

The evidence of that first breach was hardly noticeable; sounding exactly like a distant peal of thunder within the vast cathedral spaces of the ship. Nevertheless, progressive hull failure had to be the inevitable result as from one minute to midnight.

For Vaila it marked the precise moment when the nightmares of a few became reality for all.

For the rest of an unsuspecting world yet another major maritime disaster had begun.

CHAPTER NINE

◆▬◆

Disaster Sunday:
Phase One

PPO Downie, the senior security bloke, came into the Control Room shortly after midnight and began rummaging through the stationery cupboard just as Reg Blair was passing the current forecast to Pilot McDonald.

'So it looks like your blow's coming after all, Archie. Now they're predicting sou' westerly gale immediate. Heavy rain, continuous cloud, fifteen km visibility, air temperature dropping to two degrees . . . Look, hang on a minute – Wait one.'

Blair swivelled to eye Downie irritably. 'What're you poking around for now?'

'Torch batteries.'

'You already got new ones *last* night.'

Downie pointed the safety torch at him. It glimmered rather than dazzled. 'Someone must've left it switched on.'

'Oh, I wonder who?' Blair sniffed sarcastically and went back to the set. 'Sorry, Pilot. How's ballasting going?'

Archie sounded satisfied. 'We'll be completed in about an hour an' a half. The Mate estimates he'll begin discharging the Light Crude around zero two hundred, certainly before high water.'

'Affirmative. Anything further for now?'

'Negative, Reg. Out.'

'Listening on Sixteen and Ninety. Panoco Control out.'

'I can't *find* any spare batteries,' Downie grumbled in the background.

'No bloody wonder,' Reg retorted. 'Some careless bastard keeps using them. Try the next shelf down – behind the box of envelopes. I want to pass the weather to Jimmie McFadyen.'

He turned the VHF channel selector until the red Sixteen showed in the window. 'Watchdog, Watchdog . . . Panoco Control.'

Downie said, 'There's a box of pencils here. C'n I pinch a couple?'

Reg grunted 'No,' as a matter of course, then the *Wallace* came up through the speaker.

'Panoco – Watchdog.'

'Eleven, Jimmie.'

'Going down.'

Reg wasn't being brusque as he click-stopped the channel selector yet again. They didn't waste time on Sixteen. It's the international maritime VHF calling and distress frequency; the Coastguard listens on it; all ships at sea listen on it; constantly monitoring for emergency. It's strictly for making contact before shifting to a working channel. You abuse the system by chatting on Sixteen and your low priority transmission could be smothering some less fortunate seaman's cry for help from thirty miles away.

'Watchdog – Panoco Control.'

'Aye, Control: go ahead.'

'You get the weather, Jimmie?'

'Ay. More than I can say about mah supper.'

'Supper?'

'Yon wimp, Gibby. Put the halc lot ower the deck, all mixed up wi' the soup and the custard. And on purpose too, my guess.'

Blair had to smile. Even despite his worries he had to smile. Downie was grinning like Alice's Cheshire Cat in the background: the ongoing battle aboard the *William Wallace* provided a constant source of entertainment for the Panoco employees.

'Sorry about that, Skipper,' he commiserated gravely. 'How's things otherwise? What's the sea state like?'

'You're lucky ah'm no' allowed tae blaspheme over the radio,' McFadyen growled from the ether. 'It's uncomfortable and getting worse. She'll no' lie to her anchor much longer wi'out damage.'

'You going back into Neackie then?'

'I'll gie it a while more. I'll advise.'

'Roger,' Blair said. He was surprised McFadyen was still out there; with the westerlies building straight down Quarsdale over the past few days most of the skippers would have run for shelter long ago. Or had Jimmie been making a bloody-minded point with someone – like Wullie Gibb?

'Anything else, Skipper?'

'Only that if there's a body washed up on the beach by morning, there's nae need tae hae it identified – it'll be Gibb's!'

Downie started to guffaw whereupon Blair muffled the handset quickly. 'Shut up! He c'n maybe hear you.' He uncovered it again. 'Just advising you that the tanker expects to complete ballasting by zero one thuree zero, Skipper.'

'Roger. Watchdog out.' McFadyen went off abruptly and the steady hiss of static took over.

Downie had found the spare batteries. He began to button his oilskin. 'I'm starting my round from the canteen now. D'you want me to warn Ollie you'll need him around one-thirty?' Chic Oliver was the Duty Pumpman. There wasn't a lot for him to do while the VLCCs were ballasting from sea and he tended to nod off in a quiet corner.

'You can do.' Blair massaged his stomach abruptly and muttered, 'Christ!'

'You all right, Reg?' the PPO frowned. The Expediter shrugged.

'Gut's a bit queasy tonight. No sweat.'

'You worry too much, mate,' Downie chided. 'Just be glad you've got a job, there's plenty haven't.'

'Downie, I really don't know how you manage it, to say all the wrong bloody things at the wrong bloody time . . .' The pains came back and Reg blurted out, 'Look, hang on in here f'r me while I go to the heads, eh?'

Downie grinned. 'Still Pusser's Navy, eh Reg? Ordinary people like me use toilets or WCs or crappers, never heads.'

Blair got halfway down the passage when Pilot McDonald's voice sounded faintly from the Control Room. Reg had never realized quite how much sound *was* blanketed once you did leave the area without increasing the speaker volume. He hurried back despite his discomfort. Downie was already sitting in his swivel chair looking vaguely at the console.

'What do I do now?'

'You're a lot of help. Just move over, I'll take it!' Blair growled. He triggered the pressel. 'Pilot – This is Panoco Control.'

It was a call on Channel Ninety, the Rora inter-personnel frequency. No need to switch to a working band.

'Reg, did you pass the whole of the midnight forecast a few minutes back?' Archie McDonald queried, a bit sharply it seemed to Reg.

The Expediter frowned. 'Affirmative. Why?'

'No mention of electrical storms in the area?'

'Negative – but wait one . . .' Blair double-checked his latest sheet rapidly, feeling slightly peeved; any met prediction suggesting the possibility of atmospheric static would have held significance for him as it would to anyone involved in handling thousands of tonnes of potentially explosive material.

'Definitely negative. What makes you think there might have been?'

'Thought I heard thunder, around midnight,' McDonald echoed.

'That was some time back. You never mentioned it when we last talked.'

The Pilot a quarter of a mile away out in the loch sounded puzzled. Puzzled, but not particularly concerned.

'Sorry, Reg; only the jetty foreman thought he heard it again. Just a couple of minutes ago.'

For Peter Caird the commencement of his voyage should have persuaded him that the time had come to swallow his pride even at that late hour and abandon what any sensible person would have seen as a high risk – no! As a plain bloody reckless – adventure.

Both of them got themselves soaked even before they managed to launch the dinghy which, as soon as its bows tasted salt water, appeared to develop a bloody-minded perversity of its own. Every time they'd struggled to ease it from the yacht club hard into the steadily advancing ranks of breakers some particularly mischievous curler thumped icily against the bows, paying them off; causing the errant craft to broach and swirl back against the sand.

But eventually they were both aboard and Caird was fumbling to ship the oars in their crutches, with bottom boards floating and bumping noisly in the bilge. Alec Bell did sod all to help, of course; seated fearfully in the sternsheets, a dripping misery against the background wash from the terminal floodlights, clinging leech-like to the gunn'le on either side while peering apprehensively around through streaming spectacles.

'Bail,' Peter snarled ill-temperedly as he began to pull strongly at last, with the oncoming waves thumping and banging under the frail bow. 'Bloody bail, Specky, an' be of some use!'

'Mah wellie boots are full of water,' Specky moaned.

'*You'll* be full of water if you don't bail,' Cairdy retorted threateningly. 'I'll put you over the side even if we don't sink!'

He didn't really mean it though; the bit about sinking. The student had regained his confidence once they'd cleared the beach and the lines of breaking surf; he knew the boat intimately; the loch, even at night, had never held any fears for him, and he was an experienced enough small boat sailor to have taken what he'd considered to be every reasonable safety precaution. They both wore lifejackets; the buoyancy bags under the thwarts would keep her afloat even if she became, by some freak chance, totally waterlogged; they carried torches and whistles and even a few pencil flares as well as a pressurized fog siren that looked very much like a can of spray paint only it had a red plastic horn stuck on top of it.

Less helpfully, he'd also retained that sublime egotism which deprecated caution as a weakness of the old or the unintelligent. Deep down Caird might appreciate that embarking upon the black night bluster of winter Quarsdale in what was, by any standards, a cockleshell craft contravened

174

normal prudence, but in his youthful arrogance he believed himself more than capable to rise above the dangers.

Which suggested that, when it came to blind self-assurance, Peter Caird and a certain Chief Officer Mario Spedini had more than a little in common . . .

They had rowed a good way from the beach by the time Alec Bell finished bailing. By then the darkness seemed to swirl around them. Bell, in particular, gained the impression of having become detached from his familiar world; of having entered a violently gyrating limbo situated somewhere between the wet-glistening yellow lights of Vaila which were slowly drawing astern, spreading ever wider on either flank of silver-metallic Sròine Rora, and the elongated scatter of harsher luminescence which marked their destination, still a frighteningly long way ahead.

'Let's go back!' Alec Bell pleaded. 'Ah don't feel well and it's dangerous.'

A flurry of spray burst beneath the bows and immediately dissipated into horizontally-propelled needles, whirling astern and drenching them yet again under the press of the wind. Caird sensed then that the storm was upon them and for the first time felt a weakening of determination, but immediately that brief anxiety became overwhelmed by a new euphoria. Peter's over-fertile imagination had been weaned on boyhood devotion to the salt-encrusted works of Marryat, Conrad and C. S. Forester – most particularly Forester: for when had Horatio Hornblower RN *not* been plagued by uncertainty and self-doubt immediately prior to embarking on his duty of vanquishing Napoleon's ships of the Line or standing fast against the utmost furies of the sea? – Peter recalled those stirring pages and was fortified by resolution once again. The SAS scenario had been superseded: now he was heavy into the classic Man against the Elements bit . . .

'Just a squall,' he shouted, and pulled even more bravely, whereupon a cream-topped black wave reared beside them and gave a liquid chuckle as a little of it clambered inboard.

'Och, JEEEEZE!' Specky Bell squealed.

'Bail again,' Peter laughed – recklessly. 'Keep bailing, Mister Bell. We'll make a seaman of you yet.'

'You're a fuckin' NUTTER, Caird!' Mister Bell screamed back. Just before being sick all over everything.

But shortly after that a rather curious thing happened . . .

Once they'd reached about halfway – had gained perhaps two hundred metres from the now quite remote shoreline – the loch suddenly appeared to quieten; to become less . . . well, less violent altogether. Which really was very odd indeed, because the wind still snatched their hair into long wet fingers with as much spite as ever, and the sprawling golden lights of the town astern had begun to wear hazed concentric rings when observed through the curtains of driving rain, so *that* certainly hadn't eased one bit either. But more thought-provoking than anything else – the waves themselves were still getting bigger. Some, having once passed under and receded towards the shore, were actually masking the Vaila lights completely as the dinghy sank into their following troughs. Yet that hadn't been evident earlier, even though the Quarsdale seas themselves had sported many more white caps at that time.

'We're coming under the lee of the tanker,' Peter Caird explained knowledgeably. Which was a nonsense really, seeing they were still far too far down-wind, even of an object as massive as *Calauria*, to feel any real easement of the sea state.

But the waves, larger or no, *were* softening nevertheless. Undoubtedly becoming kinder. Even Specky sensed it and was eternally grateful.

Well: may be not quite 'eternally', as it turned out. More sort of . . . *temporarily* grateful.

It was then that he started sniffing. It showed he was feeling better certainly; up to that point the only senses Alec Bell had been able to pay attention to were those of sound, sight and equilibrium. Anyway, he suddenly began sniffing the air, like a fat, half-drowned pointer dog Caird thought maliciously, wearing glasses an' yellow wellies.

'C'n you no' smell onything, Cairdy?' Bell queried at last.

'Like *what*?' The embryonic Hornblower's tone was

brusque. He'd been rowing without being able to risk a breather for some time now; the only awareness *he* had was that of a steadily increasing strain on arm and shoulder muscles.

'I dunno,' Specky shrugged, frowning again. Now the worst seemed to be over he should have been feeling more confident by the minute – for surely the return passage would be smoother with the seas behind them – yet instead he was becoming conscious of a brand new apprehension; an unease occasioned, this time, by something rather less tangible than the simple fear of being seasick again. He sensed that it had its origin in whatever ominously cloying malodour was being carried towards them on the wind.

'It's a sort of *garagey* smell,' he persisted vaguely. Words never had been Alec Bell's strongpoint, even at school. 'If you ken what I mean.'

'No. Look, bail a BIT more f'r God's sake; it's not a bloody pleasure cruise we're on!'

While Alec leaned forward and dredged half-heartedly with the plastic scoop, he mentally thumbed through his limited vocabulary in search of a more specific description. It took a minute or two to find one.

'Yon smell, Cairdy. Is it not a bit like . . . well, like *engine* oil or somethin'?'

It wasn't only Specky's vocabulary that was limited. While Peter Caird navigated his roller-coasting scrap of dinghy just offshore, a long way further out in the loch – where the waves really were becoming sailor-sized – a strained and near-enough deathly silence held sway in the cramped mess-room of the stand-by tug *William Wallace* throughout the whole of supper-time.

At least there'd been a conversational silence. From outboard the sigh of the wind and the thresh of those steadily increasing seas invading Quarsdale through the two-mile entrance between the Heads had formed an eerie accompaniment to the boom of wave against hull and the metallic clatter and crash from the foredeck as the *Wallace* snubbed ever more savagely against the restriction of her cable.

177

Such familiar noises off were caused by what everybody knew to be the final coming of the long-expected westerly gale. The unusual silence within arose because nobody had ever before been forced to endure the misfortune of Skipper McFadyen's company at a time when bread, jam and margarine – not pan-fried sausisdgis or mince'n tatties or even a good fatty steaming-hot ship's stew wi' doughballs an' carrots innit – formed the major meal of the night.

. . . or no one had until tonight, at least.

And it had all been caused because a quite openly mutinous Wullie Gibb had finally managed – either by an Act of God or through the malignant perversity of one prepared to go even to the length of the ultimate ship-board blasphemy to make his point, no one had quite been able to suss out which – to let the whole of a three course bluidy dinner slide clear off the range and on to the filthy galley deck a' mixed up thegether.

Certainly nothing could be guessed by trying to read Wullie's eyes. He'd just sat there at his corner of the table all through that mute beggars' meal and chewed steadily through half a loaf and three quarters of a jar of strawberry preserve, with the mugs and plates and the aluminium sugar bowl and every other item of mess kit sliding haphazardly from side to side under the constant roll and plunge of the tug before bringing up with assorted rattles and tinkles and clatters against the chipped mahogany fiddles. Never once did the cocky wee bastard reveal as much as a self-satisfied gleam of triumph to any man aboard.

It was only after the Skipper had finally stumped up the companionway, still without having uttered a single word, to relieve the Mate from anchor watch in the wheelhouse, that anyone dared break the silence.

'The sugar content of a meal like yon has tae be lethal to a man wi' mah tendency towards diabetis,' the ship's Chief and only Engineer Burns pronounced; anxious that no one should think he might have gained any dietary benefit as a consequence of such culinary misfortune.

'Only yesterday you was sayin' sugar gave you furred-up arteries,' Wullie reminded him. 'Thon body of yours is like a steeplechase course – all your diseases racing nose to nose wi' each ither to see which wan can kill you first.'

A hissing purler rose black above the level of the starboard scuttle, then flung itself against the hull. This time the tug snubbed so viciously it sounded as if a giant had kicked at the bows with steel-tipped boots. The sugar bowl, goaded beyond reasonable limits, took off from the table and scattered a long white trail across the deck.

'I'm gettin' fed up wi' this. It's about time McFadyen gave in an' took us back into Neackie!' Deckhand McDade protested with more than a wee touch of exasperation.

'Aye? Well maybe one of you big brave sailormen should tell him. I mean, if he'd listened tae me an' gone in an hour ago you'd've all been eatin' sausisdgis,' Wullie pointed out to nobody in particular; eyes fixed innocently on some tremendously interesting detail of the deckhead. They watched him suspiciously to see if he was trying to stir things up, but he still gave nothing away. Eck Dawson, who hadn't heard yet about the death of the dinner, came down from the bridge and crunched through the sugar.

'Can't understand why *he's* in such a hell o' a mood,' he said, jerking his head back up the companionway. 'Whit's fur supper then, Wullie?'

'Bread an' marge.'

'And what else?'

'Jam! If there's ony left: an' if ye're prepared tae face diabetis wi' the courage of oor bionic Engineer here.'

The Mate looked uncertain. Nothing crucified on Wullie's griddle? It was either the wrong ship he'd boarded or Gibby playing anither o' his practical jokes.

'Very funny. So where's mah sausisdgis then?'

So the rest of them, with more than a little rancour, told him precisely which bucket of galley slops they were in, and why. Whereupon Eck, being a very large man who'd always thought far more of a substantial cooked supper in the middle watch than he did of Gibby's sister Katrina anyway, lifted Wullie by the throat and pinned him, threshing wildly, against the bulkhead.

'Ah once got a book out of the library called *The World's*

Great Disasters. You was innit,' he ground out. 'I got anither one called *Pests*. I read all aboot poisonous wee insects like you, Wullie bluidy Gibb . . .'

'Oh, you *can* read then,' a faintly purple Wullie choked, defiant to the end. 'You'll be tellin' us next you can dae joined-up writing.'

'Sssssssh!' Tam Burns hissed sharply. 'Stop stranglin' him. For a minute anyway.'

They listened attentively. The Skipper's voice carried clear from the wheelhouse. 'Panoco Control – this is Watchdog.'

Then Reg Blair's reply over VHF, 'Watchdog: Control. Eleven, Jimmie.'

And eventually, grudgingly: 'Ah'm abandoning station and going back into Neackie. It's bluidy impossible to lie out here.'

The messroom clock declared it was twenty minutes to one on Sunday morning. In that moment of executive surrender a close observer might just have perceived the first hint of a beatific smile touching the lips of Deckhand Wullie Gibb.

But a thoroughly inscrutable one, mind. No one would ever know f'r certain whether Skipper McFadyen's Sabbath supper really *had* been destroyed by freak of weather – or by sheer malice aforethought.

There had certainly been no malice in Fran Herschell from the beginning of her tension-fraught interview with Duggan. She'd had to force herself to do her job, because that was her reason for remaining in Vaila over Sunday night, in the homely comfort of the Meall Ness. Yet she had come to accept that she really didn't want, on that particular assignment, to discover what she'd been sent to find; she quite simply didn't want to hear the wrong sort of answers from Duggan even though she suspected they could form the basis for her most significant piece of investigative journalism yet.

And it wasn't because of what they could do to Duggan personally. She was very conscious, as no doubt the unfortunate Deputy himself was, that they might well destroy his prospects of advancement with Panoco. If half the allegations contained in that anonymous letter to her editor were justified, then the *Northern Citizen*'s headlines would certainly invite follow-up sensationalism from some national papers.

She could visualize the bill boards already: OIL GIANT IN TWO-THOUSAND-LIVES GAMBLE. ECONOMIES HIT SAFETY STANDARDS. MULTI-MILLION DOLLAR IRRESPONSIBILITY. SAVE A BUCK AT ANY COST. SCOTS COMMUNITY ON OILMENS' CHOPPING BLOCK . . .

Duggan, as spokesman no matter how reluctant, would be professionally marked. Any major international company forming the target of press criticism like that would discard the executive who hadn't been able to deflect it as being indiscreet if not totally inept.

No, Fran hated that prospect, yet it wasn't because her reporting could hurt Duggan that she was reluctant to succeed – she'd deliberately backed him into a corner in the full realization that a press witch-hunt might result. Should her suspicions prove founded, then her responsibility to expose the truth and pressurize the authorities was greater than any fleeting loyalty to an individual. But she still hoped that this truth would turn out to be one of dull industrial propriety, even if it made a lousy fill-up on page three.

The bad feeling – her oppressive sense of 'feyness' – had never left her, and she wanted to find grounds to dismiss it; to laugh at herself for . . . well, for succumbing to her own mental sensationalism. It had become intensely desirable to Fran that she leave Vaila reassured; with copy sympathetic to the gentle demonstration perhaps, but proclaiming that, for the majority of Vaila's inhabitants the Rora complex did indeed appear to have provided the economic miracle which had been so desperately needed.

By a quarter to one in the morning she had come to accept that such convenient assurance wasn't possible. The more doggedly she'd persisted in her line of questioning, armed not only with the contents of that fateful letter but also with the allegations made by District Councillor Mrs McLeish, the more discomfited Duggan had become. And the more concern for Vaila's future safety she herself had begun to feel.

181

Oh, she accepted that some accusations of negligence on the part of Panoco management were unjustified. The delayed certification of the offshore jetty escape rafts had proved an example; more advanced designs had been ordered some months before with delivery promised from week to week.

'A screw-up at the manufacturer's end. Hell, Fran, maybe we should've chased them, but you could hardly expect Charlie to have authorized the cost of having modules already scheduled for scrap re-certificated. We've been expecting their replacements to arrive at the gates every goddam day.'

Fair enough, perhaps, but it still meant that the men working out there now in the loch could only turn to out-moded escape facilities should an emergency occur. She hadn't pressed the point. There were other more wide-ranging concerns to explore.

'What about the terminal fire-fighting systems, Duggan? *Are* they being maintained in accordance with your original commitment to the Planning Committee?'

He'd hesitated, then growled, 'Of course.'

'Sure?'

He looked down at the tape recorder. 'Look, can't you switch that bloody thing off?'

She did. Then said quietly, 'Are you really sure, Duggan? Perhaps you could describe the system for me?'

'Only if you can spare the rest of tonight. Plus most of tomorrow.'

'Broadly. The general concept.'

Duggan shrugged. 'Okay. Then basically it's a ring main able to deliver water at a pressure of two-fifty pounds per square inch to any part of the tank farm or the offshore facility. Three one-thousand GPM pumps – one gasolene, two electrically-driven – draw from the loch itself into a twelve-inch manifold leading to roughly the centre of the tankage area. That manifold then spurs off into eight- and six-inch branches servicing hydrants throughout the complex as well as through sub-sea lines to the foam monitors mounted on the jetty out there.'

182

'How do you direct the supply to any particular location where a fire has started?'

'We don't need to. Each spur from the main manifold connects through a block valve; those valves are left permanently open. The emergency teams only need to crack the hydrant nearest the seat of the blaze and they get water.'

He stopped and eyed her challengingly, regaining confidence. 'You want more detail to fascinate your readers, Mrs Herschell? Like the gripping technical lowdown on the six-point pump-in manifolds located offshore to enable the fire-fighting tugs to back-charge the main? Or maybe an absorbing piece of reportage on how we've welded a twenty-four-inch continuous dam to the pontoon decks of each crude tank floating roof to conserve the foam effect? Or how about some edge-of-the-seat drama on the fusible link drop-weight system we've incorporated into the carbon diox . . .'

'What about the jockey pump in the main circuit, Duggan?' she interrupted coldly.

He broke off abruptly. '*What* about it?'

'Why does it exist?'

Duggan said, 'Christ, Fran: how bloody trivial do you want me to get?'

Her cheeks flushed angry pink. She'd tried to stay professionally detached, but it seemed he wouldn't let her. 'A lot less bloody trivial than your adolescent jibes suggest. I believe this is a deadly serious matter. I believe my questions concern the safety of a lot of people. You have the right to refuse to comment – but don't screw me around, Duggan. Just don't try it!'

'Well now, yet I'd kind of understood from the hints you dropped,' he retaliated impetuously, 'that that's exactly what I *was* expected to do tonight.'

She gazed at him for a very long moment. 'Not after that remark,' she said levelly, making sure he wouldn't read the hurt in her eyes. 'Not any more, Duggan.'

He rose, suddenly embarrassed, from his chair and came towards her. 'I'm sorry, Fran. I really didn't mean it the way it sounded.'

'Why was it considered necessary seven years ago, at the

time of the terminal's commissioning, to incorporate a low delivery capacity jockey pump in the main fire-fighting circuit?' she insisted, careless now of his feelings. 'Wasn't it because the original intention was to keep the entire system continuously charged at hose pressure? That the jockey pump is there in order to maintain such pressure so that in the event of a blaze – particularly in highly-inflammable locations where seconds of reaction time are vital for containment – your emergency teams really do only have to open the nearest hydrant to get water?'

Duggan looked uncertain for a moment, she didn't know whether because of her rejection or the question. Then he walked over to the window and stood staring out at the ship on the offshore jetty.

'Okay,' he said eventually. 'We don't keep that system permanently charged any longer. But pressure can still be initiated instantly – quicker than it takes for the firemen to connect foam branches to the local hydrants anyway.'

'But nevertheless you concede that five months ago Panoco knowingly approved a down-grading of the fire-fighting capability at the Rora terminal?'

'It was a local decision taken within Charlie's terms of reference. Dallas weren't consulted for approval.' He swung round to face her. 'Apart from which, I don't concede it *was* a down-grading for practical purposes. Do you have any idea of the maintenance problems we were facing before we discontinued twenty-four-hour priming through that jockey pump? We had five miles of goddam gland packing springing leaks; we had problems with grit working under two-hundred-plus hydrant valve seats; the bloody secondary pump couldn't cope with the seesawing drops in pressure and began breaking down, which meant the main diesel pumps automatically cut in as back-up. Until *they* were spending too much time under load . . .'

'You could have flushed the system through regularly. You could have reground the valve seatings; replaced faulty glands. In short, prudent local management could have reduced the load on the jockey pump to acceptable proportions. Why didn't you?'

184

He didn't reply.

'Cost!' Fran answered for him, finding it hard to keep the bitterness from her tone. 'Cost, and the loud clicking of top executive umbrellas over in Dallas. Panoco Head Office couldn't risk approving a down-grading of the Rora emergency facilities, so they put financial pressure on you local managers and left you with no alternative. Five months ago the States cut your plant maintenance budget so savagely Charlie had no option but to shut the pressurized system down. Since then you've both been compromising all along the line to keep some sort of fire cover going, but no doubt Dallas would rather not know about that.'

Duggan flared up. 'Christ, Fran: we *are* a commercial organization. The US Board has a responsibility to our international shareholders.'

'And an infinitely greater responsibility to the Scottish people sleeping so trustingly out there in Vaila. And to the worried fishermen at your own gates who *aren't* resting tonight because they sense Panoco isn't the benevolent giant your PR men would have them believe. They're frustrated by the seeming omnipotence of oil; secretly they're frightened.'

She took a grip on her passion; that sense of unease was back in the pit of her stomach. 'You claimed the water pressure throughout the system could still be initiated instantly in an emergency, Duggan. How?'

He looked unhappy, but still tried bravely to reassure her. 'By the Duty Expediter in the Control Room. He has a remote control button right in front of him on the console. He only needs to trigger it to start the main pumps running and charge the fire main. Those big fire pumps can also be activated under local control; either by the pumpman or a duty PPO from within the pumphouse itself.'

'What about a fire starting on the offshore jetty? Can they charge their own system by remote control from there without waiting for some shore-based Expediter to respond?'

He shook his head. 'No. But bear in mind we check that the VLCCs have their own first-aid capability at readiness before any cargo operations are permitted to begin; while our guys – the Pilots, the PCO, the jetty Foreman – they

185

only need to call the Expediter on VHF Ninety and they got water straight into the foam monitors and the spray curtain. There's a responsible man on watch at that console twenty-four hours a day, remember. He's also trained to implement the major emergency procedures: shut down the cargo transfer valves, alert the shorebased emergency services, call in the fire-fighting tugs . . .'

She looked up quickly. 'I was going to raise that point. About your stand-by safety vessels in heavy weather.'

'Ohhhhh, shit!' Duggan muttered, but this time with a wry, almost a resigned look. She liked him a lot better for it. She still frowned, though.

'What's wrong now?' he prompted tentatively.

'It seems your Duty Expediter forms the crux of every single operation within the terminal. He's the key to implementing any system; alerting all back-up facilities. Suppose an occasion arises when the Expediter *doesn't* respond to an emergency, Duggan. What happens in that case?'

'He will. They're carefully selected, usually ex-military. Totally reliable operatives.'

'Say he *can't*, then. Say he's incapacitated for some reason. A heart attack maybe – or a stroke.'

Duggan stared at the great ship seen through the rain-dashed windows for a long time.

'Then, Mrs Herschell,' he said grimly, and without any attempt to evade the question, 'there could be fifty-odd guys out there facing desperate trouble for a start!'

The youth, McLean, cut the perimeter wire and broke into the Rora terminal compound just before quarter to one. Shona Simpson followed him through the gap without hesitation, but it took a few moments of hoarse beckoning before Janey Menzies could be persuaded to wriggle with some difficulty to join them.

'I'm all wet,' she shrilled. 'The grass is soaking.'

'Keep your voice *down*, stupid,' Shona hissed.

'No' half as wet as Cairdy'll be, out in yon wee orange box he calls a boat,' John sniggered.

The three knelt for a minute, listening and gazing round.

186

The terminal appeared deserted. There wasn't a sign of movement anywhere between the glistening silver storage tanks towering above what must have been miles of piping and acres of wet-dappled concrete across which flurries of rain drifted in twinkling scatters. In that brief moment even John McLean's fettered imagination engendered visions of derring-do and devil-may-care achievement in the true Caird tradition.

'I'm getting cold,' Janey sniffled petulantly. But she had no imagination at all. John saw Shona open her mouth to make some acid retort and whispered hurriedly, 'Got your spray cans? Okay, let's go.'

They scuttled, crouching low, until they gained the shadow cast by a low brick pier carrying a block of giant valves. From there they could see right down to the water and the floodlit personnel jetty. The launch used for taking crews out to the offshore platform lay alongside, tossing fitfully and apparently unattended. A long low building ran off to the right, masking direct sight of the supertanker lying in the loch. There were lights on in the building.

McLean felt the blustering press of the wind against his face in that exposed location and was dearly glad it was Caird and Specky Bell who'd been foolhardy enough to go out in the boat tonight. He even felt a slight twinge of anxiety for them. The loch seas had increased considerably in the half-hour since he'd last viewed it from the old salmon fishers' bothie.

Shona didn't show signs of concern though. The girl seemed to be in her element; uncaring of the fact that her long blonde hair was plastered across her cheek by the wind. 'What about starting here?' she said.

'Are you sure we ought to?' Janey asked querulously.

'Ah'm sure we shouldn't,' John grinned, hard-man style. 'It's as good a reason as any to do it.'

'An' it'll show you a thing or two about me, you supercilious bastard,' he reflected as an afterthought. Though he wasn't quite sure whether he had his father or smart-ass Caird in mind when he did.

Abruptly Shona stood on tiptoe and sprayed the spidery

187

black letters as high across the brickwork as she could reach.

PETER CAIRD RULES OKAY!

'Christ!' McLean muttered, shocked. 'We're supposed to be writing "Oil Vandals go Home" or "Spill your filth somewhere else" or somethin'.'

'They'll *know* it was Peter now,' Janey blurted out. 'You'll get him into awfy trouble, Shona.'

'Aye, I will, won't I,' Shona Simpson giggled. She turned flashing eyes on the uncertain McLean. 'Well,' she challenged him provocatively. 'Are you coming, or do I have tae do it all myself then?'

Slowly he began to grin. It was expected of him, being the nonchalant hero, and besides, the damage was done now, no way could they remove Shona's damning condemnation of Cairdy without the right cleaning stuff. Besides, it wasn't he himself who'd so vindictively betrayed the doctor's boy, though it suited his book fine, too.

He shrugged, 'Och, in for a penny . . .'

But she'd already gone, impetuous as always; bending low and heading towards the front of the building showing lights. McLean and Janey – who was tight-lipped with protest by then but too scared to be left alone – caught up with her just as she beckoned urgently.

'There's a man in there. See? Through the big window.'

There was too. All on his own. Sitting in front of a range of instruments and writing something in a book. When he'd finished he sat back and opened what looked like a packet of sandwiches. He began to eat but not, it seemed, with great relish.

'Come *on*!' McLean muttered uneasily, scared the man might see them. But Shona didn't move.

'No, I want to watch for a wee while,' she said with a hint of devilment in her that made her two companions more than a little apprehensive. 'Maybe we can have some real fun now. Even more than Peter had in mind.'

The point Fran Herschell had barely touched upon with Duggan, but fully intended to return to, was that of the lack of seaward safety cover on vessels such as *Calauria* during Quarsdale's winter gales.

It wasn't so much the reason for the duty tug's leaving station she was concerned with – certainly few readers of the *Northern Citizen* would have expressed particular interest in the petty triumph of an unknown wee hard man called Wullie Gibb – as the fact that, following the *William Wallace*'s withdrawal, no fire-fighting vessel would be on call within two miles of the gargantuan tankship lying to the offshore jetty for the rest of that night. Under the press of heavy weather, and allowing time to manoeuvre from her sheltered berth again – it would be, say, some fifteen to twenty minutes steaming time away.

In some respects the *Wallace* might well have kept right on sailing a hundred miles over the horizon from *Calauria*. Within minutes of her abandoning station her crew wouldn't even be able to keep a visual watch on their charge until the weather eased again; the wild geography of Quarsdale was such that a rising granite spit called the Deil's Haund masked the man-made island tanker berth from the view of anyone unless they actually climbed to the top of the Neackie Harbour wall itself.

In addition, that same rocky protuberance also interfered with direct VHF communication between the low-powered portable handsets carried by the Pilots and PCOs aboard the VLCCs and the sheltering safety tugs. Very High Frequency transmits within a somewhat fickle wave band, efficient for line-of-sight operation only; you can speak clearly to the near side of the moon on VHF yet you cannot converse with a station thirty miles distant and below the dip of the earth's curvature. On occasions you may not even be able to contact a person hidden by some structure or by rising ground only a few hundred yards away.

Imagine christening an inanimate lump of rock *The Deil's Haund* – the Hand of the Devil? Or, when first the ancient Highlandmen were stirred to endow that great submarine crag off Neackie with an appropriate legend, could they have had some strange perception of the part it would play in future events?

Whether there had been or not, its existence meant that for the rest of that Sunday night not only was Expediter Blair the one man on duty who could activate the pressurized fire-fighting lines to the offshore jetty, but he was also the only man in a position to alert McFadyen's *Wallace* in a sudden emergency.

Still, as Duggan had properly claimed, Royal Navy-trained Blair *was* a most dependable operator. Dependable and utterly conscientious. Reg Blair wouldn't dream of allowing himself to nod off like, say, Ollie the Pumpman, just because a VLCC happened to be ballasting from sea and things were quiet in the terminal. That was why Panoco had selected him for a post carrying such grave responsibility in the first place.

Then you had to consider the statistical improbability of events turning sour at precisely the time when cover was scaled down. The chance of some serious emergency arising during the comparatively short periods when safety vessels were forced from station had to be so low as to be discounted. Everybody who worked the monster oil ships in Quarsdale accepted *that*.

At least, everybody accepted it other than Engineer Tam Burns, obsessed as he was with morbid predictions of the havoc which could be wreaked from 'wan wee spark'.

Well, Tam Burns – and most of the Pilots, to be truthful – men such as Archie McDonald who lived aboard and mothered the monster ships. They'd expressed anxiety regularly to management about the gaps in safety cover; but then, weren't they *paid* to be a professionally over-cautious lot?

Though mind you – some of the Pollution Control Officers weren't too happy with the system either, when you really came to think about it . . .

Reg Blair in Panoco Control logged the *Wallace*'s departure from safety station as being timed at 0044 hrs, then eased back into his chair and massaged his stomach. Christ, he felt lousy!

Briefly he toyed with the idea of phoning Duggan at his digs; telling him he needed to sign off sick and ask him to call one of the other Expediters to relieve him for the rest of the night. He was aware that it was the proper course of action to take – a man needed to be a hundred per cent attentive to handle Control efficiently.

But then he remembered Bill Thomson telling him Duggan was dining at the Meall Ness tonight – last night – and decided against disturbing whatever was going on at that late hour. He'd need all the tolerance he could muster from management when the news of the letter leaked out.

He unwrapped Ella's standard-issue lettuce and tomato sandwiches and began to chew without enthusiasm. He'd go through and make a cup of tea in a minute, it would help to pass the time. Reg dearly hoped McDonald's VLCC would soon complete ballasting and begin discharge of the Light Crude; some action on the transfer console was what he needed in order to take his mind off the rumbling discomfort of his bowels.

If ex-Chief Gunnery Instructor and usually conscientious key man Blair had allowed himself to dwell for one moment on just how crucial his role in any emergency might prove that night; if he'd truly considered the consequences, which Fran Herschell now foresaw so clearly, of his being indisposed to react to a first urgent appeal for help over that steadily whispering VHF radio before him . . .

Expediter Blair should have taken the first steps to sign himself off-duty there and then. But he didn't.

While within the Very Large Crude Carrier *Calauria* the thundering had already begun.

The Ship

———◆———

Just before one o'clock in the morning Pollution Control Officer Trelawney, accompanied by Second Officer De Mita, was walking *Calauria*'s deck on his routine safety check; shining his safety torch into the caverns below to enable him to make a visual assessment of *Calauria*'s ballasting progress. Hydrocarbon vapours were venting fast from each of those spaces examined, implying that sea water was still displacing the air within.

The PCO wasn't happy about the ullage ports being left open as they were, with lids simply resting on their clamps. Ideally all explosive gases should have been emitted through vapour lines travelling from deck level up through risers on the foremast and king post, thence into the open air some fifty feet above the ship. He accepted it as a necessary practice though; in all too many VLCCs the risers were inadequate for their task. This meant that an explosive-rich mixture could accumulate under light air conditions when wind speeds dropped below a velocity of some five metres per second. Fortunately tonight, with the gale whipping across *Calauria*'s exposed decks, there was no likelihood of such a potentially lethal build-up.

At that time Trelawney estimated that the tanks were topped to some eighty-five per cent of their capacity.

At four minutes to one he heard a further dull rumble of thunder which seemed to continue for several seconds. This time he also imagined he felt a slight vibration passing through the deck. The thunder didn't surprise him, Archie McDonald had already gone to some lengths about the inadequacy of meteorological forecasts; but that odd tremor . . .

Frowning, PCO Trelawney walked quickly to the starboard – seaward – side of the ship and flashed his torch to cover the heaving water some considerable distance below. He could detect nothing amiss. He did catch sight of the white stern and masthead lights of McFadyen's retiring duty tug, maybe half a mile distant now and heading back to Neackie. He didn't like that either, not as a safety officer, but the policy of continuing tankship operations even though afloat fire-fighting cover had been withdrawn was a top level Dallas decision. You didn't argue with Dallas. Christ, you couldn't even get to speak to Dallas!

It took him a further three minutes to cover the one hundred and twenty-seven feet required to reach the port side; stepping carefully through the maze of piping and under the ship's central fire main until he was gazing across at the jetty itself. He didn't need his torch to satisfy himself that all appeared normal over there; the white glare from the floodlamps beat like a frozen sun across the rainswept and deserted concrete. All the jetty watch would be huddled in the personnel canteen below the fire tower. There would be nothing for them to do until the discharge of *Calauria*'s Light Crude parcel commenced.

Trelawney couldn't really observe the condition of the water thrashing sullenly between jetty and ship; the contrast between direct light and black shadow was too intense. He did notice that the jetty slop tank – a fifteen-cubic-metre container situated below the lower platform and used to drain the still connected Chiksan arms once transfer operations were finally completed – showed obvious signs of external corrosion, and made a mental note to draw it to Duggan's attention on Monday morning. Not that anything would be done im-

194

mediately; a lot of Rora's plant was beginning to look faintly seedy since the maintenance budget had been reduced last year.

Dismissing the tremor through the deck as a figment of his imagination, he turned from the rail to see the dutiful Second Officer De Mita shivering miserably beside him. That made Trelawney himself conscious of the biting whip of the wind coming straight from the Atlantic. He conceded that they both deserved a respite and headed gratefully aft for the warm pumproom where Chief Officer Spedini watched over the gauges.

He hadn't detected the heaving black mulch between ship and jetty which marked the seeping of the first few tons of crude oil from *Calauria*'s hull, already spreading shorewards; creeping downwind around the piles of the offshore jetty. PCO Trelawney's nose had long become jaded by a lifelong bouquet of petroleum cargoes; the instant dispersion of these particular vapours by the rising gale would have prevented him from singling out its peculiar sick-sweet odour from all the other oil tanker smells anyway.

But it *was* a sort of cloying, 'garagey' smell. Precisely as the increasingly anxious Alec Bell had described it only a short time previously to Peter Caird.

Certainly Bell, geographically speaking, was in an excellent position to evaluate that direful substance in the wind. The slick – which had, of course, accounted for the waves seeming paradoxically less violent as they voyaged further from the shore – had nearly reached the youths' scrap of a boat by then.

By three minutes past one in the morning.

The Very Large Crude Carrier *Calauria* had finally begun to haemorrhage. She would die very quickly from that moment on.

195

CHAPTER TEN

Disaster Sunday: Phase Two

At about the time Shona Simpson was displaying an excessive interest in the doings of the unwitting Expediter Blair, and while careless adventurer Caird was on the verge of discovering for himself that the seemingly more benign waters of Quarsdale actually justified Specky's irrational concern, and during the period in which PCO Trelawney and Second Officer De Mita were savouring the welcome warmth of *Calauria*'s vast accommodation, young Police Constable Lawson, having completed the first step towards maintaining Law and Order by washing his Panda vehicle, was driving slowly along Reform Street, conscientiously scrutinizing the premises he passed, particularly those of shops now closed for the Sabbath, for any indications of forced entry.

Most law-abiding residents – which meant roughly ninety-nine per cent of Vaila's population, to career-conscious Lawson's constant chagrin – had completed whatever social visitings they'd embarked upon during the previous evening, so few cars travelled the roads by then, while the town's grey pavements had long since been deserted in favour either of warm beds or the closing minutes of the late film showing on BBC TV. Since Hamish had left the station he'd only overtaken one local stalwart in bonnet, anorak and rubber boots, striding out vigorously while trying to give the impression of thoroughly enjoying the slash of freezing rain across his face in the wee small hours of a winter's morning rather than submitting, as Hamish suspected was more likely, to being taken for a walk by a tongue-lolling, weather-contemptuous German shepherd.

When Hamish finally came upon the reported scene of

Thomas the cat's ill-judged merger with the near-side front wheel of Annie Clunie's motor, he discovered that the alleged corpse had mysteriously disappeared. After climbing from the Panda and walking up and down the flooded gutter just to make sure, he decided to take no further official action; the Case of the Disappearing Cat gave rise not so much to suspicions of feline necrophilia as to the assumption that some local householder had heaved the late unlamented Thomas into the nearest dustbin.

He returned to the car and decided to continue down to the Panoco terminal gates to confirm whether Auntie Jesse's demonstration had been rained off for the night. He sort of hoped the fisher lads *had* decided to give up; he felt sorry for them and sympathetic, for he himself had experienced the boredom of spending hour after hour hanging around that cruelly exposed place. He didn't want to watch their stubborn discomfort prolonged in what he personally considered a futile gesture.

The oil ships would keep coming to Quarsdale. Unless something disastrous occurred, of course. But that was hardly likely, no matter what Aunt Jesse claimed.

Police Constable Lawson checked his watch against the patrol car clock before he drove off. It was then one-thirteen in the morning.

While Hamish closed the file on Thomas, Fran Herschell was closing her interview with Duggan in an oddly strained and troubled mood.

'So despite Panoco's commitment made at the time of the planning negotiations seven years ago, to station one fire tug permanently by the offshore jetty, supported by a further two continuously-manned vessels on call in Neackie Harbour itself,' she summarized coldly, 'the reality is that safety cover has been gradually reduced so that now you provide one tug only to cope with a sudden emergency. Even worse – on occasions such as tonight there won't be ANY available for instant response.'

'Pretty infrequent occasions,' Duggan said defensively, much more reasonable now. 'And we've upgraded the delivery capabilities, remember. The new ships in particular, the *Wallace* and *The Bruce*, mount a cannon-throw of seventy metres. They can smother any section of a hot VLCC with five thousand gallons of foam per minute, Fran.'

'Not if they're over two miles away when the fire starts,' she countered. 'Not even within twenty minutes of the outbreak, should your Expediter also happen to suffer a heart attack while under pressure. Then, theoretically at least, the first your rescue crews would know of an accident at Rora is when they read about it in the newspapers the next day.'

'Now you're being silly.'

'Sarcastic, maybe; silly – no. I wish to God for Vaila's sake that I was.'

He got up and walked to the window again. The rain gusted against the glass, fretting the light from the middle of the loch into a thousand jigsawed patterns. He'd seen it all before, many times, but never with the same eye. Now it almost looked as though the ship itself had exploded. 'It's twenty past one,' he said. 'I don't suppose you'd consider going to bed with me now?'

She didn't answer. When he turned she was staring into the red-grey embers of the fire. 'I'm frightened, Duggan,' she whispered. 'I don't know why. I just am.'

'Of me?'

'No . . . of something within myself, I think.'

'You feel all right, don't you?'

Suddenly he was concerned for her, even though he knew she was duty-bound to do him harm. And Panoco. But as far as the company was concerned, press indignation would last only as long as the newspaper readers paid to support it. In a few weeks Panoco's public relations machine would have appeased the media; the Board would express grave concern; shrug the adverse publicity from broad international shoulders, spend a few hundred thousand dollars and restore the Rora safety balance while blaming local management inefficiency as the culprit. Charlie and himself would represent the sacrificial offerings to a by then already bored British public. Ultimately Dallas would compensate their corporate investors by implementing economies elsewhere, probably in some part of Panoco's Third World operation less vulnerable to external criticism. He still had a responsibility, though, to minimize the present threat.

'Is it the terminal?' Duggan asked. 'Because if it is, then you're over-reacting. That complex isn't a bomb down there, you know, whatever the antis claim. It's easy to criticize, to use emotive terms when referring to refineries and transit ports like Rora, but there has to be a limit to the precautions we take, or moving the world's energy becomes both economically and, for that matter, practically impossible.'

'It's more than that,' Fran said. 'It concerns that particular ship, *Calauria*. There's something . . . Do you believe in clairvoyancy, Duggan?'

'Second sight? Frankly, no.'

'Neither did I,' she muttered, and it seemed to Duggan that she shivered then, 'before I came to Vaila.'

Captain Bisaglia was turning restlessly in his sleep by twenty past one on Sunday morning. There was no apparent reason for such disturbance; it was quiet up there, six decks high in the sleeping quarters of the master's suite on the starboard side of the Captain's bridge deck. No crew member would dare to walk outside; for years no one had occupied the traditional owner's suite situated between Bisaglia's day-room and the equally palatial residence of Chief Engineer Borga.

It could have been a consequence of the ravages of lunch, of course. Tommaso Bisaglia normally being a man of frugal intake, it wasn't entirely outwith the bounds of possibility that Mrs McAllister's whisky-braised venison followed by a cheering immoderation of Drambuie, could have yielded a legacy of mild digestive shock. Also, his once wounded leg had troubled him slightly since the ship's arrival in Quarsdale; perhaps that had manifested itself as a result of the long-forgotten Scottish accents which caused images of drowning men and exploding shells to gurgle and scream afresh through his subconscious.

Or could it simply have been that the Captain felt his ship wasn't right? That a lifetime of sailor-sense was still at work

199

within his ageing brain; protesting through thickening layers of atrophy, and screaming, pleading with him to feel the pain within *Calauria*'s tormented hull as she relentlessly began to bleed to death below him.

But if it had been a last attempt on the part of the ship to commune with her master, Bisaglia did not understand it. And anyway, even had he done so, alerted himself and re-assumed the responsibility he had so unwisely renounced in favour of Chief Officer Spedini, then by that time in the morning it would have proved far too late.

At one twenty-four a.m. the steel plates forming the deserted and windswept deck just forward of *Calauria*'s manifold began to buckle ever so slightly.

At one twenty-five Expediter Blair couldn't stand the nerve pains in his stomach any longer. He picked up the phone and dialled Duggan's number, intending to ask for a relief, but Duggan's landlady, the Widow Doig, was away over to Fort William for the weekend to visit her sick sister so there was no reply.

Reg assumed Duggan must still be at the Meall Ness and reached for the phone again. Then the cramps hit him and he thought, 'Christ, this is ridiculous: get a grip of yourself, Blair!' but suddenly he felt he had to get to the heads – the bloody toilet! – and lurched from his console chair towards the passageway at the back of the Control Room.

For the first time ever he forgot to turn the volume of the VHF speaker to full.

From twenty feet away Shona Simpson watched Blair's less than dignified departure through the big windows. She began to snigger; the man looked so funny, unaware he was being observed from without. 'Where's he gone, d'you think?' she asked McLean.

The big lad grinned in the darkness. 'The toilet's my guess. Seems like yon sandwiches acted better than a dose of gunpowder, eh?'

Shona stood up with the wind clawing at her hair. 'Come *on* then. While we've got the chance,' she urged.

'Home?' Janey Menzies prompted hopefully.

'You go home if you want,' the blonde snapped impatiently. 'Me and John are going in there.'

'In where?' McLean frowned, conscious of a new surge of apprehension because he already guessed where she meant.

'Get her *back*, John!' Janey squealed, staring in horror after the already disappearing figure. 'She'll get us a' caught. She's daft as a brush, that one.'

'Ohhhhh, *shit*!' McLean snarled, hating all women, and took off anxiously in Shona's wake, but she'd slipped through the door and into the Control Room itself before he caught up. She turned as he entered, holding a finger to full mischievous lips.

'He's away down there,' she whispered, pointing along the corridor. 'I think he *is* in the toilet.'

McLean's eyes strayed nervously over the big grey-metallic console before the window. There were dials and switches everywhere: two red buttons marked *Commission Fire Main* and *Jetty Transfer Valve Shut-off* stood clear in the centre of the panel; there was a red telephone tabbed *Priority – Emergencies Only!*; a copper make-and-break switch behind a glass door in the wall bore the legend *Incident Siren*; to the left of the console sat two big radio sets with speakers emitting a gentle splutter of static. It was obvious to McLean that this was the nerve centre of the terminal; it was more than obvious they shouldn't bluidy well be in it.

'Let's get out of he . . .'

He ceased whispering abruptly – Shona had gone again.

Tiptoeing hurriedly to the corridor he found her once more. This time she was struggling with a heavy wooden batten leaning against some painter's trestles at the far end. A small kitchenette ran off to the right; to the left a closed door indicated, presumably, the toilet. The girl was attempting to drag the batten towards it without making a noise.

'The door opens out the way,' she panted. 'Gie's a hand to jam it with this.'

McLean shook his head violently. Shona fixed him with a contemptuous eye. 'Well, I must say I thought you had at least as much guts as Peter,' she hissed.

Maybe it was her tone – the cunning way she used the

201

challenging 'Peter' – that did it; maybe it was remembering the contempt in his father's criticism over tea-time. He managed a sickly leer of careless bravado, then took the batten from her and quietly wedged it with one end under the door handle and the other leading into the kitchen, supported against the base of the stove.

They were outside the Control Room again – McLean giggling and breathless with excitement just as much as his virago conspirator – before they heard the toilet flush.

When, as a final gesture of defiance, Shona sprayed the big observation window with the word *Cairdy was here!* the glass was so wet that even the oil-based paint floated down in great black runnels. It looked very like the mascara under Janey Menzies' eyes, for Janey had had enough of their doing stupid things and was tearful by then for fear of the consequences.

Of course, the big window could have been crying too. After all, it did gaze out over the loch.

Abruptly the dinghy stopped tossing altogether. Now it slid over hummocks of darkness, with a gentle undulating motion reminiscent of a pleasant summer day's cruise. Only the still surprisingly ebullient wind seemed at odds with the eerie quietude. That, and a stench now so overpowering that it bit acrid at the back of Peter's throat. Crude oil vapour, of course; but far more pungent than he'd previously imagined.

'See?' he said, gratefully resting a moment on the oars. 'We're well in the lee of the tanker now.'

'Ah thought a lee meant bein' *out* of the wind,' Specky Bell nit-picked uncertainly. 'It's near enough blowing a gale still, far as I c'n feel.'

Caird frowned. It did indeed seem illogical – that while there were no luminous whitecaps to be seen in their vicinity, the westerly still appeared to be gusting as strongly as ever. He pulled a few more experimental strokes. Even the feel of the oars seemed different: their blades plopping beneath the remarkably passive surface without registering that slight feather of foam you'd normally expect on entry.

Time to concentrate on practical matters. He swivelled on

202

the thwart to gaze ahead with narrowed eyes, needing to orientate himself for the final pull to the target's stern. His original intention had been to spray triumphant anti-pollution graffiti along both sides of *Calauria*'s hull, but the weather over the past hour had persuaded even Caird to compromise. Now he proposed to stick to the more sheltered landward side of the supership; there was ample visual clearance below the platform of the jetty. The whole population of Vaila would be able to read his contempt for Government-sanctioned vandalism from first light in the morning.

The Liberian dominated their seaward view now. Not more than two hundred yards ahead the mammoth black tanker towered from an equally black sea, oddly reluctant, it seemed, to reflect the sprawling incandescence flooding a deck line stretching such an awesome way on either side of them. From here it was necessary to turn their faces through considerably more than a right angle to encompass the mass between bow and stern. It was undeniable that the VLCC presented a majesty, and an immensity and – rather more intimidatingly – a sinister aspect previously unimagined by either youth, only previously accustomed as they were to watching Quarsdale's gargantuan callers from a greater distance. Now they had to crane their necks, force their heads back and bury them into the soft wetness of their lifejacket collars, simply to observe the rim of *Calauria*'s funnel which appeared – or so it seemed when viewed from flotsam level – to pierce a threat-heavy cloud base as sombre as the alien tankship itself.

'Let's go home, Peter. Please.'

Alec was gazing at him in bespectacled appeal from the stern, his face a pale shiny blob mirroring the light, magnified eyes wide and perturbed like some creature trapped in the headlamp glare from a car. For one fleeting second even Caird hesitated; this close he was just as overawed as Bell by the immensity of their undertaking; but Peter Caird thought again of Hornblower, a model of the sternest stuff, and dismissed any flutters of trepidation within.

'No – damned if we're going back just when we're good as there,' he hissed. 'An' take your lifejacket off.'

He knew it was silly, his whispering like that, but the general atmosphere seemed one of deathly quiet. Weird really. As if a sound-proofed baffle had been drawn across the previously voluble sea.

'Not bluidy likely,' Specky retorted, still spirited when it came to self-preservation. Then curiosity got the better of nervousness. 'Onyway – why?'

'Because you'll have to reach up to do the spraying and you're about as agile as a penguin wearin' a strait jacket in that thing,' Caird explained caustically. 'I'll need to keep at the oars to hold us alongside the hull.'

'Well, ah'm still no' taking mah jacket off. And ah'll tell you something else, Cairdy – there's something wrong out here. Sailor or no', I c'n sense it's not natural, an' I say we get the hell out of it. Now!'

'Okay.' Peter stopped rowing. Actually he was glad to for a moment, he wasn't proving as fit as he'd imagined. The oars had been getting heavier and heavier, like trying to scull through treacle. 'Anyway, I don't stay in the town now. At least I'll not get it cast up every time I see him in the next ten years.'

'See who? Get what cast up?'

'John McLean, of course. Och, but will he no' have the perfect excuse to take it out on you for giving in at the last minute, eh.'

There was a half-minute's delay while the short-term unattractive was weighed against the long-term unthinkable; then the boat rocked in the darkness as Bell struggled from his padded jacket. 'Hurry up then,' the crew muttered. 'Let's get it over with.'

'No, maybe you're right at that. Maybe we shou . . .'

'Oh, just get ON wi' it, Cairdy. F'r *Christ's* sake!'

Peter Caird's unworthy victory was to rebound on him. After a few more minutes the oil-heavy pungency seemed literally to envelop them until even breathing became difficult, particularly for the oarsman's straining lungs. He was beginning to regret not having aborted the operation when he'd had the chance of laying the whole blame on Bell, but he didn't dare let on now of course, not after provoking

204

Specky into continuing the mission. He'd never imagined the smell of oil could be so vile; he couldn't understand how the factory inspectorate or whatever would sanction men's employment in such an obviously debilitating atmosphere.

The ship loomed like some great sea cliff now, her after accommodation a dazzling city suspended high above them in the sky. It was even becoming possible to distinguish the lighter concrete-clad platform supports from the featureless density of *Calauria*'s hull. Caird rowed a bit longer in the oppressive silence until fatigue caused him to pull awkwardly on his starboard oar. The blade made a funny *glubbing* sound as it skidded flat across the surface.

Specky complained childishly, 'Watch it! You splashed me then.'

A moment later, puzzled, 'Here . . . wait a minute, Cairdy!'

Caird drew breath to make some acid retort but, panting with exertion as he was, the stench of crude speared to the back of his throat and he began to cough instead. A wave of alarm overtook him; suddenly he felt he was suffocating.

Alec Bell meanwhile was leaning out over the gunwhale and tentatively poking his hand down towards the water. Almost immediately he shrieked 'Ohhhh JESUS!' and drew his arm away as though he'd touched a red-hot coal.

'*What?*' Peter choked, the shock of Specky's reaction causing him to freeze briefly through terror of the unknown. But Alec wasn't stunned into inaction – he was rising unnerved from his seat in the boat while peering at his hand in the light from the ship. Cairdy could make it out too, by then. It looked exactly as if Alec Bell was wearing a thick glove.

'Oh, Jesus!' Specky began to sob. 'Ohhhhh Jesus, but you've got us floating in pure OIL, man!'

The dinghy began to rock with the sudden transfer of weight. 'Sit DOWN!' Peter shouted, suddenly galvanized by a very real fear of capsize. Then he did precisely the wrong thing – in his haste to confirm Bell's hysterical claim he dragged one oar inboard and fumbled desperately along the length of it. Immediately his fingers encountered a treacle slime smothering the smooth round of the loom which, in turn, transferred itself to his own palm. The ash-wood shaft, already yacht-varnished to a velvet smoothness, began to slide irresistibly through his lubricated grip.

'Help me!' he entreated. 'I'm goin' to lose the OAR!'

Alec Bell, by then panic-stricken, came blundering aft with his glasses smeared and awry and his paste-white features a bobbing moon against the darkness. The boat began to rock even more violently. 'Watch yourself,' Peter screamed, suddenly aware. 'There's oil everywhere: the bottom boards'll be like an *ice* rink!'

His warning was uttered far too late. For a hideously long moment Specky tottered, arms flailing wildly as rubber-shod feet skidded unavailingly for traction, then with only the slightest animal whimper of protest the ungainly youth over-balanced backwards to tumble clean over the side in company with the oar.

There wasn't even a splash, just that nightmarish *glubbing* of welcome, rather like the sound the mishandled stroke had made earlier, only sounding revolting now through awareness of its cause. Caird swivelled on the thwart to gape after his fellow conspirator, just in time to see Bell resurface.

But Peter didn't recognize the regurgitated apparition as Specky Bell any longer, for the Pitch Thing which now emerged alongside presented a chilling, shapeless aspect of elephantine horror; smothered by what appeared to be a perpetually shifting cowl of black-emulsifying globules sliding and oozing downwards to invade a red-mouthing hole still gurgling from somewhere in the middle.

'Oh, dear *God*!' Peter retched uncontrollably, flesh creeping at the monstrous fate which was engulfing Alec. 'Oh dear God HELP US SOMEBODEEEEEEEE . . .!'

The Elephant Creature uttered a sad little liquid grunt, then tendered a thick-dripping trunk which was really an arm held skywards in pathetic supplication. Caird was sobbing unrestrainedly by then, trying to stay on the thwart for the terror of what might happen to him too if he moved, and struggling to extend his last slip-slidey oar to meet the imploring claw that represented Specky Bell's hand.

Just for one exquisite moment the oil-glove grasped, and held. But then the SECOND oar slid through Peter's frantic grip, as the dinghy drifted to leeward under a press of vagrant wind.

The last glimpse anyone had of any part of poor Alec Bell was that of an arm rearing vertically from a carpet of glistening mulch, still clutching the black-gleaming Excalibur of ash now pointing directly towards the sky. And then the arm, followed by Excalibur, withdrew slowly below the surface, until there was nothing other than the moan of the wind and the gleeful chuckle of bilge water in the bottom of the tiny boat; and the harrowed sobs of a youth now finding himself adrift on an inflammable sea without means of propulsion. And distressed beyond any heroic measure.

It had just turned half-past one when Alec Bell became the first victim of the night. It was also the moment in which the thunder began again. Only it wouldn't be mistaken for thunder by any man aboard the ship this time. Not real thunder. A sort of thunderous overture heralding his own coming extinction possibly; hull plates grinding and tearing; the remorselessly escalating crescendo as thousands of tons of steel become overstressed to the point of destruction. Indeed, a tankerman's *Gotterdammerung*.

According to the town's Presbyterian church clock less than a quarter of a mile away it was precisely twenty-seven minutes to two – on what had otherwise promised to be a routinely dull Sunday morning for Vaila – when the long-predestined cataclysm finally overwhelmed Tommaso Bisaglia's so-weary supership.

The Ship

The formula for disaster – that amalgamation of chemistry and physics, human fallibility and pure chance which was to bring about *Calauria*'s destruction, had been years in the making. It would require only minutes now to achieve its end.

The second phase was nearing a close. Suffering an unequal distribution of ballast, the ship had already – long before Pilot McDonald raised any question of thunder with Expediter Blair – sagged past the point of no return. From the moment when the first severely corroded longitudinal had failed within her Port Permanent Ballast Tank the process of her dying assumed a rapid and ever-escalating momentum. The first Light Crude had already escaped through subtly fissured shell plating below her waterline to claim poor Alec Bell. As each subsequent plate or stiffener fractured so there became fewer to maintain the rigidity of the whole, and so those remaining critical parts tore or twisted or simply parted from their welds even more quickly.

The end came once compressive stress finally overcame all dwindling resistance in *Calauria*'s deck. The sequence of disintegration immediately converted to a thundering chain reaction. Her deck bulged and then buckled, deformed inwards on itself and thus fashioning a rude hinge. Still buoyed fore and aft by empty space, the excess weight amidships then exerted a downward force through that crude fulcrum which, in turn, inflicted an opposing and quite intolerable tensile strain on the keel section directly below. Instantly that giant member – the VLCC's spine, the most vital part of her skeleton – also ruptured in sympathy, ripped apart like rotten string and caused a cavernous split to drive upwards, shearing through both sides of her hull, cracking her clear from turn of bilge to main deck.

Within sixty seconds the second stage of catastrophe was complete. By the time the Vaila church clock hands jerked to one thirty-four in the morning, *Calauria*'s back was broken.

The next phase was to be the most awseome of all. Like subsea crags spewed forth by underwater cataclysm, *Calauria*'s streaming bow and stern began to soar skyward as her near-severed midparts lost flotation and sank, still screeling and roaring and tearing, into a gouting boil of foam. She could not settle far, only some four fathoms of water had cushioned her loaded draft from the rocky bed of Quarsdale. Very soon after there followed a muffled submarine *BOOOooooom* as the sundered faces of her partition – each drowning cross-girth equating in area to half a modest football pitch – brought up on the bottom of the sea loch. That sonorous death knell caused sleeping birds to rise from trees two miles away and startled deer to poise, alert for flight, on the snow-flecked slopes of the surrounding mountains.

The broken ship hesitated awhile then, making little immediate movement; an elongated 'vee' resting on the loch bed, bows and stern appealing forlornly towards the scudding night like the outstretched arms of some crucified giant. By then her midparts lay awash within a seething vortex, through which fingers of black-bubbling mulch already rose and sifted and weaved.

But awful as the supership's agony appeared, it was only then that the most dangerous prospect for any tankerman – a threat far more chilling than simple structural failure no matter how colossal – began to emerge.

210

Calauria's spine had snapped in way of her Permanent Ballast Tanks – her PBTs, topped by that stage to ninety per cent with salt water and producing no gas at all. But immediately forward of those inert spaces were located Numbers Three Wing cargo tanks – and they were still filled with Crude brought all the way from Mina al-Ahmadi in the Persian Gulf, a considerable part of her second Arabian Light parcel still awaiting discharge.

The line of hull failure zigzagged to crack and severely weaken the retaining after bulkheads of both cargo tanks. Denied of support they, too, breached under their own weight, instantly vomiting the contents of both cathedral spaces into the sea.

Within moments of her disembowelling some twelve thousand metric tonnes of potentially flammable crude were added to the loch waters creaming hysterically around her wound. They began to produce petro-chemical gas. As soon as that initially over-rich miasma mixed with the brisk night airs of Quarsdale it began to dilute. The more diluted it became, the closer it came to entering the explosive range of hydrocarbon vapour.

Suddenly there was a great deal of oil giving off vapour in the vicinity of *Calauria* and the Rora offshore jetty. All it would require now to trigger a holocaust was one incendiary micro-speck – 'Wan wee spark,' as Engineer Burns had always proclaimed. 'That's a' it wid need.'

Well, if you can conjure an image of two foundered sections of a Very Large Crude Carrier butting against each other, with ragged steel plates constantly moving and rubbing and screeling under the press of a gale . . .

Then, simultaneously, you've envisaged one of the largest lighter-and-flint arrangements ever resulting from the miscalculations of Technological Man.

CHAPTER ELEVEN

Disaster Sunday:
Phase Three

Guardia Marina Bisaglia felt *Fiume*'s director tower lean further and further while the warship reeled under the on-slaught of Cunningham's guns. There echoed a distant thundering as the cruiser's forward bulkheads collapsed and unsecured objects began to roll and tumble seawards; steel and men were screaming; fear-sweat stung his tightly closed eyes; his shrapnel-lacerated thigh burned as if acid were injected into each and every vein . . .

. . . seventy-two-year-old Master Mariner Bisaglia sur-faced through the sick-bitter smoke of Matapan and lay for a moment, blinking uncomprehendingly towards the deck-head. It seemed different this time – waking from the night-mare. Normally, during harbour working *Calauria*'s fore and mainmast lamps shining through the uncurtained forward windows of his sleeping cabin cast harsh but comfortingly predictable patterns – geometrically-etched light contrasting with intense shadow dappling the darkened room. On this occasion the patterns appeared unfamiliar and the level of illumination oddly reduced, ridiculously implying that their source – the masts themselves – had altered their positions relative to the berth in which he lay.

And then Bisaglia realized he could still hear the steady rumble of British guns. Only he knew without doubt that he was awake now, and that more than four decades of dream-plagued sleep separated him from the actuality of that terror-filled Mediterranean night. Yet nevertheless there *was* a great rumbling still carrying from without. And this . . . this massive ship of his present *was* falling forward; WAS going down by the head!

The tray carrying the jug of orange juice and glass, which Steward Gioia always left ready for him last thing at night, began to move, slid ever so slowly forward until it clattered impatiently against the low dressing table fiddle – then mounted that polished wood restrainer too and crashed to the deck.

Half-swinging, half-falling from his berth the Captain lurched towards the window cut high in the forr'ad face of the accommodation – only to halt abruptly, shocked beyond measure, staring with utter disbelief over the madman's vision rearing before him – for no longer did the rudely awakened Tommaso Bisaglia find himself looking ahead, out along one seventh of a mile of rusted steel plate and catwalk and piping and thence down towards *Calauria*'s bows. Now he gazed UP at the fo'c'sle head as it reared, impossibly elevated it seemed *above* the level of his uncomprehending eyes, with the wide expanse of tank deck viewed almost in plan rather than from the previously obtuse angle so familiar to him.

The harrowed Bisaglia stumbled desperately through his shadowed day room with its leather upholstered chairs and deep-piled if somewhat worn carpeting. As he passed the small refrigerator secured against the mahogany-panelled after bulkhead its door opened under an invisible hand – for Very Large Crude Carriers are not expected to pitch to the extent that retaining clips are required on athwartship-mounted refrigerator doors. The interior light shafted the gloom as a twinkle of ice cubes in company with the Captain's frugal stock of chilled wines and mineral water spewed forth unheeded.

He almost collided with Borga as he burst from his cabin. *Calauria*'s Chief Engineer was wearing one flip-flop and the jacket of his best uniform. Nothing else. His white paunch swelled ridiculously below the line of the reefer. Bisaglia was far too stunned to feel any embarrassment for him.

The Chief was dazed as well. 'She's broken her back on us, Tommaso,' he said incredulously. 'The bitch has broken her bloody BACK!'

'Go to your engine room,' the Captain entreated. 'We

213

must have light. Keep the generators running. And for God's sake maintain pressure to the foam monitors.'

'Chances are the intakes have hoisted clear of the water already,' Borga snarled, fighting for reality in a world gone berserk. 'My gennies will seize in minutes without coolant. Abandon, *Capitano*: give the word now!'

'Please, Chief,' Bisaglia heard himself beseeching. 'We must try . . .'

The Chief was getting a grip on himself now. Good, reliable, ever-practical Borga. 'And anyway,' the Engineer growled brutally, 'if she burns we'll need more than a spit of foam: we'll need a fucking miracle!'

The alleyway was sloping a crazy twenty degrees downwards. The open after door to the Captain's deck hung forlornly on its hinges, and through it Bisaglia could see *Calauria*'s dim-lit counter etched impossibly against black sky. He didn't think they would be able to launch the outboard lifeboats even now, their davits wouldn't cope with such violent inclination. High as they were above the loch surface there was no indication that one third of a mile of concrete jetty must still lie far below them.

He repeated urgently, 'Try for power. And hose pressure. If you fail, then get everyone from your department on to the jetty somehow, Moreno. Don't wait for my order. Forgive me for being abrupt, but I must go to the bridge.'

It was an old-fashioned, rather quaint apology from a man who suspected he was going to die very soon. But then, Captain Tommaso Bisaglia always had been a rather quaint, old-fashioned gentleman.

Men were bawling to each other from the inclining after decks now; there was naked fear in the voices. In that moment Bisaglia realized that he could never save his command, and that tragedy and panic were about to stalk arm in arm through whatever time was left to them.

Uncharacteristically the Chief grasped his hand before *Calauria*'s two elderly senior officers finally parted. 'Goodbye, old friend,' Moreno Borga said in a gruff but steady tone.

And the Captain understood with sad poignancy that

Borga also accepted that his own life was drawing to a violent close. They had both served in petro-chemical ships too long to cherish any false illusions about what would happen next.

He never did get the opportunity to reply though.

For it was at that moment that someone from below screamed above the thunder: '*Fiiiiire!* Mother of our Blessed Saviour – we have FIRE on the sea!'

While waiting for the interim ballasting phase to complete, Pilot McDonald had been chatting – or trying to make conversation despite considerable language difficulty – to Chief Officer Spedini, who was keeping watch in the cargo control room.

Actually Archie McDonald never liked lingering within that sterile fully-automated compartment aboard any VLCC. Vital nerve centres they might be, but to McDonald they presented a most unseamanlike environment for those obliged to man them in harbour. A seaman became blind once he entered these standard air-conditioned high-tech prisons, invariably lit only by the unremitting glare of arti-ficial light.

To Archie, never more content than when casting a fly across the exposed lochs or conning his cumbersome charges seaward through the wide wild Heads of Quarsdale, such functional spaces seemed remote from the real world of a mariner. He was accustomed to the snatch of the elements and an endless panorama of horizon. But because, during heavy weather passages, the seas broke over a deep-loaded supership – indeed frequently submerged that lowest weather deck to thunder aft and build against the structure with monstrous force – only ranks of calibrated glass *Teledip* gauges monitoring the various tank ullages occupied the forr'ad face of *Calauria*'s cargo room at main deck level, where windows might otherwise have been.

Chief Officer Spedini gave the impression that he fitted though, as he lounged easily in the watchkeeper's chair; a thoroughly modern maritime technocrat driving a remote control console, more space than sea-orientated, with its

215

array of meters and switches and valves and temperature displays.

Mike Trelawney entered in company with a chilled Second Officer De Mita. De Mita reached for the Rough Deck Log to enter his tour of inspection while the Duty PCO rubbed horny hands with relish, sniffed approvingly at the precisely-balanced warmth, and dripped all over the plastic deck.

'God help sailors on a night like this,' the ex-Captain growled cheerfully. 'How goes the ballasting, Chief Officer? I reckoned your tanks were ullaging to the order of eighty-five per cent a few minutes ago.'

Spedini looked confused. ''Ow goes what, *signore*? And to where, please?'

'Ah!' Trelawney coughed, slightly at a loss. Concealing a grin McDonald interposed, somewhat unnecessarily: 'Still raining topside, Mike?'

'Cats and seadogs! And thundering, to top it all.'

It came again then – the thunder. As if to underline Trelawney's comment. It was even louder than before, clearly heard within the virtually sealed compartment. The Pilot looked disgusted. 'Bloody forecasters!'

Both Panoco men eyed the twenty-four-hour clock on the bulkhead simultaneously. It indicated the time was approaching 01.33.

'Roughly half an hour to complete ballasting,' Archie speculated. 'What d'you think, Mike?'

A perceptible tremor ran through the ship. Chief Officer Spedini frowned to himself and leaned forward, scanning the gauges. The PCO hesitated, listening, then said flatly, 'I reckon we've got an electrical storm brewing. We should recommend delaying transfer of the second parcel – at least till you've checked again on the forecast.'

Behind them De Mita finished logging his deck round and laid his pencil on the desk secured to the after bulkhead. It rolled off. He picked it up and replaced it on the desk. It rolled off again.

Everyone turned to stare at it. Ever so slowly the pencil began to roll forward of its own volition, across the compo-surfaced deck towards Chief Officer Spedini's chair.

216

Pilot McDonald opened his mouth, swallowed uncertainly; thought a moment longer, then started to mutter, 'Mike . . .'

The whole compartment canted forward as a stentorian roar burst upon them. Spedini's chair overbalanced sideways against the console with a crash. Second Officer De Mita tottered downhill, grunting with fright, to collide with his senior shipmate while McDonald and the PCO clung ashen-faced to the desk for support.

To Archie it seemed the bedlam outwith their toppling steel-walled confinement would continue for ever. A claustrophobic fear of being incarcerated within this awful instrumented tomb suddenly seized him and he heard himself pleading, 'No, No, NO! Not trapped in HERE f'r *Christ's* SAAAAAKE!'

PCO Trelawney, dazed as he was, recognized instantly that the ultimate horror had occurred: the Liberian had broken her back. Hypnotically he watched as the ullage levels in the *Teledip* sight glasses bobbed and curtsied dementedly, dancing frantic attendance on the massive tidal waves caused by thousands of tons of liquid displacing abruptly within *Calauria*'s compartmented belly.

The deck itself continued its ponderous rise beneath them, compelled by some leviathan force acting upon the breaking VLCC's keel. De Mita began to sob quietly, black hair still plastered wet across his brow by the earlier Quarsdale rain. Spedini clung leech-like to the console and stared fixedly ahead . . . or down . . . or bloody SOMEWHERE in that sickeningly disoriented moment.

There came a final thunderclap of tearing steel, followed by a horrendous jolt which reverberated throughout the accommodation as *Calauria*'s severed mid parts struck bottom. The lights in the cargo control room died and then flickered back on.

Even then nobody moved for a few fearful seconds though Trelawney, white-faced, called gruffly to the sobbing De Mita: 'Belay that, laddie – she's stopped. F'r the moment.'

The Second Mate-child didn't understand the language, but read the look in the older man's eye and shut up.

Meanwhile McDonald took a deep breath and tried to think what to do next. Get out, that was the first priority! Get out into the clear night air of Quarsdale before they were faced with whatever threat would follow. Jesus! McFadyen's duty tug had withdrawn from station an hour ago! So he'd have to radio for help . . . the VLCC's generators were still running by some miracle, so her deck and accommodation lights would still be glaringly evident from Rora – even if those ashore hadn't heard the thunder they would surely have observed the emergency. A man could hardly fail to notice if a whole village of lights less than a quarter of a mile from him suddenly lifted into the air. Panoco Control; one of the patrolling PPOs; even old Phimister the Gateman . . . *someone* in the terminal must have recognized disaster. Reg Blair would already have alerted the emergency services and – most urgently of all – called on the *Wallace* to evacuate the ship and jetty crews.

Because an instant response from McFadyen's tug offered the only way by which they might survive. Even as he joined the scramble to escape from the cargo control room Pilot McDonald bleakly estimated that, including himself and Trelawney, there were nearly fifty men at risk aboard the Liberian. There would be a further five Panoco shift personnel just as dangerously marooned on the offshore jetty alongside – probably a long drop BELOW them now, f'r pity's sake! He had no faith in the inflatable escape rafts, certificated or not; an unmanageable rubber boat adrift on a sea of crude offered little promise of salvation if ignition did occur.

McDonald was thinking with chilling clarity. Already he'd dismissed any hope that something might be done to save *Calauria* herself – Christ, on a tinderbox pinnacle protruding through a cloud of increasingly volatile gas, and with the only practical means of rescue twenty minutes steaming time distant, it would need a very special miracle to preserve even human salvage from this night. And Archie wasn't a great believer in miracles; neither when they applied to trout taking a carelessly tied fly nor to breaking supertankers. Within moments of disaster occurring, the Liberian's Pilot – like her Captain and Chief Engineer Borga – anticipated

218

Death's bony claw would take him by the hand at any moment, along with his half-hundred-plus companions.

It was kinder perhaps that Archie McDonald, right from the start, did cherish so few illusions regarding his prospect for survival.

The first explosion within the ruptured Permanent Ballast Tanks occurred even before he'd reached *Calauria*'s deck.

Expediter Blair flushed the toilet and finished buckling his belt, then slipped the Timex watch Ella had given him last Christmas from his wrist before rinsing his hands in a none too clean basin. He noted anxiously that it was after half-past one and getting undiplomatically late for disturbing bosses. He'd have to phone Duggan as soon as he got back to the Control Room or dismiss any intention of requesting a relief during this shift.

The WC cistern was still noisily replenishing itself when he heard the first rumbling from outside. He thought, 'Bloody Met! That's *got* to be thunder,' and wryly reflected that he owed Archie McDonald an apology for being so brusque earlier.

The peals of atmospheric energy seemed to last a long time before they faded; then, just as the cistern quietened, they came again. Louder now but definitely thunder, and from the west; obviously approaching from the direction of the Heads to sweep down the reach of Quarsdale. Judging by their volume a lot of static must already be building in the air above the offshore jetty. He guessed either McDonald or the Duty PCO would be calling any minute to advise they'd decided to delay the final transfer operation until aft . . . .

Reg Blair growled 'Ohhhh, *bugger!*' out loud; he forgotten to turn the VHF speakers to full volume when he was caught short and had to fly along here. Hurriedly he slipped the Timex back over his wrist, then reached for the door handle. It turned freely enough, but nothing else happened; the door still didn't open.

Anxiously Blair checked the bolt though he remembered he hadn't had time to lock it earlier. It was free. He turned

219

the bloody handle and pushed again, but still the door was jammed.

He bellowed 'JESUS CHRIST!' and kicked the door in angry frustration – Sod's Law of the Sea: if anything can go wrong, it bloody will. And invariably all at the same time!

He tried putting his shoulder to it, but that only hurt him. It was a strong door, and jammed tight: didn't even give so much as the thickness of a coat o' paint. If Reg had been able to lay his hands on an axe he'd have used it with savage pleasure by then, an' screw Duggan, Panoco and the wholly bloody ill-maintained shooting match.

Expediter Blair thumped down on the toilet seat and glared morosely around the tiny compartment. There wasn't even a window; just an extractor fan which used to be activated by the light switch before it had expired two months previously. He was well and truly trapped until Downie or someone else came along and released him; Reginald bloody Blair – the proverbial old lady locked in a lavatory! He made his anxiety all the more exquisite by straining to detect any chatter from the VHF in the Control Room.

The next peal of thunder from the direction of the loch seemed to shake the whole building. It certainly shook Reg. By God but it was close; to his ears as an ex-gunnery instructor it had sounded more like an uncontained explosion than an electrical storm.

Alarmed now, he tried shouting for Downie and kicked the unyielding door a few more times for the masochistic satisfaction of it. Then he returned to squat uneasily, nervously, on the WC seat. There wasn't much more he could do.

Bloody Met experts . . . Bloody reporters . . . Bloody job insecurity . . .

Basically: bloody *Ella*!

Four fishermen-protesters were still hanging around the Panoco gates when PC Lawson drew his Panda alongside and wound the window down. McLean, owner of the lobster boat *The Vian*, was there, glowering resentment in his usual black-browed way at old gateman Phimister snug before a

TV set in the security hut. Lawson didn't like McLean senior; a man with an affinity for whisky and argument. He didn't go all that much on his son either, come to that. Hamish remembered Big John too well from school where he'd always shown a predilection towards bullying and over-conceit.

Jamie Kennerty was there too, with a couple of resigned and very wet supporters whom Lawson recognized only as hands from the boats. Kennerty was one of the fish porters and a nice wee man if a bit thick. Auntie Jesse always scolded him with a tolerance not usually granted to others should he dare betray more enthusiasm for supporting the public bar of the Stag than her political stratagems.

McLean bent to look in the Panda window and challenged Hamish curtly, 'No doubt you're here to be telling us to move along then, laddie?'

Hamish shrugged. 'Suit yourself, Mister McLean. There's no law against standing in the street.'

'More the pity,' Jamie Kennerty commented from the back. 'If there wis, it would gie us all a fine excuse tae go home, eh?'

He beamed amiably all round as though he'd made a great joke. 'You should be standing out here in the rain wi' us,' McLean grunted. 'Doing your duty like the auld polis did before they gie'd them these fancy motor cars.'

'We're soft now, Mr McLean. All us young ones,' Hamish said mildly. He didn't bother pointing out that, until tonight, he'd got just as wet as anybody through defending Vaila's interests.

A rumble of distant thunder came from the direction of the loch and McLean straightened to glance over the Panda's roof, out to where the beacon's flash on Roinn Tain was almost lost behind the rain-haloed glare from the big tanker at the jetty. The way the car was pointing, Constable Lawson had to crane awkwardly in his driving seat to follow the fisherman's gaze.

'We're getting a'thing tonight,' McLean commented sourly. 'Nae mention of thunder on the inshore forecast, yet we're still about to catch some.'

221

'It's the Lord's way of scolding us for picketing on the Sabbath,' one of the fisher hands intoned sonorously, and Hamish wasn't quite sure whether he was serious or joking. You never could be, in towns like Vaila.

Another peal of thunder rolled towards them as wee Kennerty sniggered, 'Ah'd rather hae the Lord displeased wi' me than Cooncillor Mrs McLeish.'

'What time is it, onyway?' the other hand asked, pulling his collar further up.

Hamish glanced at the clock on the dash. 'Just after one-thirty. Ah, twenty-seven minutes to two.'

'If ye want tae know the time, ask a pleecemannnn,' Kennerty hummed, good humour undampened by the appalling weather.

'Well, *I'm* bluidy brassed off,' the younger lad muttered plaintively. 'Ah think we should pack it in till the morn.'

'See,' McLean looked down on Lawson triumphantly as the thunder came again, even louder this time. 'Now *he* wants to go home. You're all soft, a' you young generation. You'll ken my son, John? Now, he's an example – soft, and as bone bluidy idle a . . .'

The owner of *The Vian* stopped speaking abruptly, staring intently at something out in the loch. Hamish frowned. Rude or no, it seemed a curious way to end a conversation.

Then wee Jamie Kennerty said, for no apparent reason, 'Christ! Och dear Jesus *Christ!*'

They were gazing fixedly above the roof of the patrol car and out towards Quarsdale now, all four of them. Blankly Hamish swivelled in the Panda's seat to follow their eyes – and immediately became transfixed himself.

. . . because the huge tanker out at the jetty was ever so slowly, ever so deliberately *rising* into the air . . . actually lifting from the sea loch itself.

Police Constable Lawson swallowed, trying desperately to understand. All lighting seemed to have been extinguished along the giant ship's forepart, yet aft the tiered brilliance of her accommodation – now high as a mountain, it appeared to the gaping onlookers – still blazed as if nothing extraordinary was taking place out there on Quarsdale.

But then, as their eyes adjusted to the subtle gradings of black shadow and marginally lighter night sky, they could detect a boil of monstrously disturbed water roughly midway between the extremities of the levitating Goliath; and see that the floodlit funnel was canting forward as well as soaring ever higher above the line of the jetty lights while – near enough a five-minute sprint from the stern of her – the silhouette of the supership's bows, with the grossly protruding chin of her forefoot pressure bulge already clear of the water, was angling just as surely backwards.

She wasn't lifting bodily at all. She was sagging into a long, spreadeagled 'vee' with its lower midpoint already submerged below Quarsdale's wind-frantic surface, while all the time the thundering rolled spectrally across the loch towards them.

'She's broken her back,' McLean whispered eventually, still staring hypnotized beside the police car. 'Och, man – she's broken her back!'

Constable Lawson never even thought to use the radio fitted in the Panda. Illogically he found himself fumbling for his pocketphone without taking his eyes off the unbelievable event unfolding a quarter of a mile away.

'Delta One to Romeo Tango. Romeo Tango . . . Delta ONE!'

'Keep the heid, laddie,' he thought, panicking a bit as the leather-cased personal radio hissed and dithered quietly in his hand without doing very much else. 'The Sergeant's at the station, sanity's at the station – an' guidance. They'll answer soon.'

The tenor of the thunder rose to a *boooom* which echoed and danced back from the eerie, snow-bleak slopes of the surrounding mountains.

'Och Jeeze but . . . can ah no' see *fire* doon there, amidships?' wee Kennerty exclaimed in awe.

'Romeo *Tango* – This is Delta ONE! *Do* you read?'

'She's on fire a'richt. Goad!'

'They'll hae to take them off! Where's McFadyen's *Wallace*, d'ye see her out there onywhere?'

Lawson's personal radio splurged. Night Sergeant Robertson's voice. Unhurried. Matter of fact. 'Aye, Lawson? Pass your message.'

'The tanker's breaking up, Sarge,' the young Constable called breathlessly. 'Out at the Panoco platform. Assistance required.'

He remembered to say, 'Over,' then there was a brief silence while the thunder subsided to a steady grumble again.

Until: 'Repeat your message, Delta One.'

Christ, there *were* flames out there all right – growing out of the sunken middle of the crucified black hull. Only a small glow, but spreading already; creeping like a pulsing red worm towards cocked bow and elevated stern. A monster worm . . . a monster *glow* worm. Demanding even more effort to credit than those scientist-devouring jokes on last night's telly!

'Yon big tanker lying in the loch. She's broken in half and she's burning, Sarn't. I . . . We'll need assistance across the board. Over.'

Sergeant Robertson's voice registered uneasy humour. Like it would questioning a lunatic. 'You havin' me on, Lawson?'

'No, Sergeant. Christ, no!'

Hamish released the pressel switch, then remembered procedure and triggered it again. '. . . over.'

There was a sudden explosion from the loch and the flames immediately spread wider along the dying ship's hull. They could see black smoke now, blacker than the blackest shadow, blacker than the clouds, beginning to billow in a rolling column torn by the wind. They must have heard that at the police station for Robertson's tone came back tight – and reassuring.

'The Inspector's away over to Lecky but ah'm instituting a major incident alert. Do what you can to keep the terminal access road clear for the emergency services, laddie; police assistance is on its way. Message timed at zero one three five. Confirm receipt, son. Over.'

'Message received. Delta One, out.'

Constable Lawson activated the Panda's blue flashing light, then hurled himself from the car and ran through the pouring

224

rain towards the locked gates. That bit closer to the terminal you couldn't actually see the loch for the bulk of the great silver storage tanks.

Old Gateman Phimister came wheezing out of his glass-fronted buckie and stared suspiciously through the wire at Hamish. 'Did ah hear a bang then?'

'Christ, you've got a disaster out there, man. Get these gates open.'

Phimister looked singularly unimpressed. But Constable Lawson didn't believe what was happening himself yet, and he'd bloody *seen* it.

'I'll need tae get Mr Duggan's authority to do that.'

McLean came running behind the young policeman and the Gateman said positively, 'Ah'm no' letting *him* in, for a start. He's a demonstrator.'

McLean shouted, 'We're away tae get *The Vian* startit in the harbour. They lads out there'll need a' the help they can . . . Yon big bastard could blow ony minute!'

Phimister looked grim. 'Who's he callin' a bastard?' the old man demanded.

The thunder rumbled frighteningly again from Quarsdale. Even above the Rora tank tops the rest of them could see the smoke rising. It was reflecting a flickering red now, from its rolling undersides. Auld Phimister didn't even glance round.

'If you don't open these bloody gates,' Constable Lawson snarled in frustration, 'I'll charge you with delayin' the Police in the execution of their Duty.'

'And if ah do,' the old Gateman retorted with an inflexible adherence to propriety, 'then *you'll* be held responsible tae Panoco Terminals PLC of America.'

There were lights coming on around the Cross and all down the length of Reform Street. The previously quiet borough of Vaila was beginning its rude awakening.

Well – apart from Thomas the Disappeared Cat, anyway. And Mister Leachan, who'd not long ago died of boiled eggs up on Craigie Drive.

. . . and Gateman Phimister, of course.

*

225

Wullie Gibb was frying bacon in the *Wallace*'s galley when the first thundering echoed from the loch. It had been a subtle diplomatic ploy really, offering tae make up a bacon sannie for the Skipper – but f'r the Skipper only, mind. None o' they ither unappreciative gannets – once his culinary skills could be extended to the full on a stable platform berthed comfortably by now in the lee of Neackie breakwater.

Wullie's uncharacteristic generosity had fine reasoning behind it; it was calculated to strike a balance somewhere between a compromise on principle and a job preservation exercise. Eck Dawson had implied motives somewhat less charitable when he'd stepped in to shelter briefly from the rain.

'Bluidy creeper!' the Mate had jeered, once Wullie had told him to go screw himself because there wis nae way he wis gettin' naethin' efter callin' Wullie an insec' an' near stranglin' him. 'You're jist a bootlicking wee toady when the chips is down, Wullie Gibb, so ye are.'

Wullie poked the smoking, already inedibly desiccated leather scraps critically with his finger; decided anither few minutes fryin' would see them cooked jist right, then buttered two slabs of bread big as elephant's paws.

He ignored his Chief Officer with lofty disdain. They'd soon enough find oot which one was the bootlicker.

The thunder came again. Dawson moved to the galley coaming and looked out, but there wasn't anything to see but a few dispirited harbour lights and the wet stone wall of the breakwater shielding them from the loch.

'Must be a warm front movin' in frae the Atlantic,' he diagnosed knowingly. 'Och, go on, gie's a bacon sannie, Wullie.'

Three minutes after *Calauria*'s cargo actually began to burn, normality still reigned aboard the only rescue vessel available in Quarsdale, other than a wee spit of an open personnel launch.

Councillor Mrs McLeish had worked in the study of her big house over on Fariskay until well after one o'clock before she finally completed her notes for the coming Vaila Council meeting, and decided to go to bed.

Mister McLeish – who had little interest in the affairs of the community but showed a remarkable tolerance for his wife's devotion to the good of others – had fallen asleep in front of a blank television screen. Constable Lawson's aunt eventually had to waken him. 'Cocoa or Ovaltine, Frank?'

'Cocoa, Jesse lass. I'll away and slip into my pyjamas while you're looking after me.'

She'd looked at the kitchen clock before she placed two mugs of milk in the microwave; the hands were just passing one-thirty. She knew it took precisely three and a quarter minutes to bring the milk to near-boiling point. While she was waiting Jesse McLeish sat gazing out of the kitchen window and down across the loch as she always did, with mixed feelings of pride and anger. The big foreign tanker lay ablaze with light; paling the streetlamps of Vaila to insignificance, blinding the eyes to every natural beauty. A monster of commerce making itself seem even more despicable by its very arrogance.

When she'd finished stirring the drinks she placed them on a tray, put the kitchen light out, glanced once more towards the ship now clearly framed in the dark window . . . and after a moment of terrible appraisal, went immediately to telephone the police station.

By the time Uncle Frank came down in his pyjamas and dressing gown to ask if anything was wrong, Jesse was sitting very quietly, still in the dark, at the kitchen table. When he lifted her chin gently and looked in her usually so determined eyes he saw – for the first time in the forty years he'd known her – that she was crying.

Young Ken Blair had still been reading a football book in his bedroom when he first heard the thunder. Secretly, even though he suspected the shift created a source of friction between his parents, he rather liked Dad's spells as night Expediter down at the terminal; if his father hadn't been working tonight, the ex-Chief G.I.'s son wouldn't have dared leave his room light on so late. Dad was a great stickler for the Navy ways. Lights out an' stuff. *When I was in the Navy, lad* . . .

The thunder kept on, rumbling and growling with an eerie insistence, until eventually the seventeen year old couldn't ignore it any longer. He slipped out of bed to gaze curiously towards the offshore jetty seen clearly above the roofs of company bungalows further down the hill. He noticed Captain Trelawney's house lights flick on across the road as he did so. In fact, quite a few lights seemed to be sparking to inquisitive life throughout the town.

He heard himself screaming 'MUUUUUUUM!' like some seven, never mind seven*teen* year old, waking from a nightmare. Except that he was quite clearly awake, and what Ken Blair had found himself faced by out there in the loch wasn't in any way a child's hallucination.

She came running into the bedroom looking pretty in a blue nightdress; took one glance at the monstrous happening through the window; whispered, 'Oh, God . . . Oh my GOD!' in a voice he'd never heard before, then rushed to the telephone.

The line to the police station was engaged. She hesitated, frightened to try the Panoco Control number, then dialled it anyway. It seemed to ring and ring for an eternity, but Reg didn't reply. No one answered, which was hardly credible and certainly alarming.

She composed herself with an effort, then ran back upstairs to Ken's bedroom where her son asked doubtfully, 'D'you think Dad's all right?' He didn't take his eyes off the great shadow of the tortured VLCC, though. He couldn't bring himself to at that moment – not when he thought he'd just detected the first glimmer of fire amidships.

Ella snapped with dangerous calm, 'Of course he is.'

She turned away from the awful thing Ken was watching with youthful fascination. 'I must get dressed, then go over to Mrs Trelawney. Ken. You listen by the phone and let me know the minute you hear from Dad.'

'Why?' the boy asked absently. 'Why Mrs Trelawney's?'

She didn't think he would understand. Perhaps she herself

was only just beginning to. To comprehend how Reg really felt over having left the Navy, and to appreciate what he meant by his insistence that they couldn't simply dismiss a way of life as though it had never happened.

Calauria's dying, even despite her fears for her own husband, was already demonstrating to Ella Blair that she, too, retained a sense of duty just as strong as Reg did. Miners' wives, fishermen's wives, Service wives: they all inherit the same sad community conscience born of disaster involving their men.

'Captain Trelawney's the Duty Pollution Control Officer out on that tanker, Ken,' she said simply. 'Madge will need somebody to wait with her through the night. For the news to arrive.'

Reporter Herschell was also deliberating the less happy aspects of conscience, and at much the same time as Ella Blair.

It was ironic, really, that despite Fran's continuously growing apprehension over that weekend, she wasn't actually thinking of the threat itself in the moment when it first assumed substance.

Certainly she'd been gazing through the big bay Meall Ness windows at the raindrop-diffused supership – but she had been reflecting more on the media monster she was constrained to unleash on Duggan and the guilt she suspected she would feel as a result. Then she saw the Liberian's foredeck lights suddenly extinguish.

Mrs McAllister's fire was dead by then, just grey wood ash and a few dulled embers left. Standing before it Duggan tried again, warily. 'Fran. Couldn't we maybe . . .'

The lights spaced along the third of a mile span of the jetty still registered a ruler-straight line across the dark surface, yet didn't something appear to be changing? Affecting the previously familiar lie of ship to berth? The still bright concentration of light around the after castle of the VLCC itself – was *that* it? Subtly altering its position relative to the level of the jetty as if . . . well, almost as if the stern of the tanker was – rising?

'Duggan?' Her voice was uncertain, strained. 'Duggan, please come over here.'

The after glare of *Calauria* flickered, went out, flooded back on again . . . then began to ascend, but this time with a ponderous and unmistakable certainty. As if in sympathy the bulk of the blacked-out foredeck also began to lift; buoyant, it seemed, like the bows of some joyously surfacing super-submarine, until it hung at a cocky, lunatic slant; actually reflecting a wash of light from below its streaming forefoot.

While, tenuously linking the two angled and otherwise apparently separate structures – bridging the empty cradle of a 'vee' where only a moment before had been ship – the prettily twinkling floodlamps spaced along the Rora offshore platform still insisted all was normal on Quarsdale.

'DUGGAAAAN!'

He took one instantly comprehending glance, blurted a curiously enigmatic, 'It's happened. Oh Jesus but it's *happened*!' then whirled for the door and began to run.

Sometimes Fran used to wonder how professionally detached she might remain if, instead of simply recording, she became an actual participant in crisis. Again like Ella Blair, she was to discover something more of herself in those first traumatic moments of disaster. Shocked as she was, it would be very much the Press Reporter Herschell, camera and tape recorder in hand, who finally caught up with Duggan in the Meall Ness car park, trying frantically to radio an apparently unobtainable Expediter Blair, to assess the situation at the offshore jetty, and to start the Range Rover all at the same time.

Even the first tongues of flame suddenly licking below the oil smoke already dominating Quarsdale stimulated journalistic description, in tandem with Fran Herschell's fear for the three score men presumably marooned out there.

Yet still Panoco Control either would not, or could not, respond to Duggan's radioed appeal. Even though the precious seconds of first-aid reaction time, conceded as being so critical even by the Official Duggan, were inexorably wasting away.

*

230

It is claimed that there is an overload of horror, a charitable circuit breaker, a point where the brain's ability to comprehend dreadful things trips out and enjoys a kind of merciful anaesthesia.

Certainly Peter Caird felt little pain in the brief period between Specky Bell's death and his own. Really it was more the simple mechanics of the process which struck him as being unnecessarily frightful – numbly he'd accepted from the moment of *Calauria*'s first Titanic convulsion that he *would* follow Alec. You can't expect a tiny dinghy to survive the sort of tidal wave that even a part of a submerging VLCC creates. Simple physics; not St Andrews University stuff at all. Archimedes' principle – jolly clever chap, Archimedes. Discovered the use of the lever, invented the Archimedean screw, *and* came up with a catechism about displacing liquids with masses, chanted by first-year school kids ever since.

By the time the maelstrom did expand to overtake Cairdy's little boat it consisted rather more of Mina al-Ahmadi Crude than Loch Quarsdale. It swamped the dinghy, but still didn't kill Peter. That was where his petulance over the mechanics of dying came in – the buoyancy bags wouldn't allow the craft to sink, so he was simply left sitting on the thwart, submerged to chest level in foetid sludge.

And then, when the first dull explosion midships was instantly followed by fire, and the fire reached, ever so slowly at first, towards him, he thought he would at least have a choice between cremation or suffocation. He was very brave to work that out, actually – probably quite as gallant in the face of certain death as Hornblower or most characters, even in novels, might have been – and would certainly have impressed Shona Simpson and infuriated John McLean by such sang-froid. Only it turned out that he didn't – have a choice, that was.

Because, back in two hundred and whatever BC, old Archimedes hadn't allowed for the principles embodied in the design of yachtsmen's lifejackets when it came to displacing liquid by lowering masses into it. So when the radiated heat achieved a level where Peter could actually see the oil-fouled skin on the backs of his hands bubbling and beginning to peel in thin, pink-revealing layers, and so *did* opt to drown himself in preference to being burned alive, he found he couldn't.

His life preserver wouldn't allow him to sink any further, nowhere near enough to force his nose and mouth below the morass. It did precisely what the man in the chandlers claimed it was intended to do – preserve life.

Unfortunately, in Peter's case, it was too efficient. It preserved his life for rather too long.

Until it burst into flames as well . . . but by then Peter Caird had ceased to plan ahead for reasons other than drowning.

The Hulk

Calauria was no longer a ship, though for a few further minutes she would continue to function as one in many respects. Her crew were still aboard; her harbour alternators were still running, as were her vittling cold stores and the short-wave radio tuned to night music from Rome in Bosun Egidi's deserted cabin, her air conditioning and internal telephone circuits, most of the heating coils within her after cargo spaces . . . and the single red light above her bridge still warning the world, somewhat unnecessarily by then: *I am taking in, or discharging, or carrying dangerous goods.*

Admittedly her Loadicator – her on-board stress computer up in Chief Officer Spedini's office – *wasn't* working. But that was another story.

The first explosion had occurred within the Port Ballast Tank at one thirty-six a.m. – three minutes after overt structural failure of Tommaso Bisaglia's unhappy command began.

That three minutes of grace provided ample time for twenty thousand tons of steel grinding against another twenty thousand tons of steel to generate considerably more than just the 'wan wee spark' essential for ignition. By then a volatile mix of hydrocarbon vapours and bracing Scottish night air had also accumulated just below deck level within the still cavernous envelopes of *Calauria*'s amputated Permanent Ballast Tanks.

Detonation occurred during the millisecond in which spark conjoined with contaminated atmosphere. Because both PBTs *were* already split wide open, the energy from the first eruption expended itself largely outwards into free space – that un-confined explosion which ex-Gunnery Instructor Blair had first identified as such, then quickly dismissed as being a bloody ridiculous thought.

Nevertheless it projected a rolling ball of flame upwards and outwards. The cloud of burning gas expanded across the twelve thousand tonnes of crude already vomited from Three Wings into Loch Quarsdale, licking them with thousand degree centigrade fingers, causing the surface of the sea to boil instantly, the oil to give off even more vapour which, in *its* turn, flashed across a wider span and eventually ignited the crude itself.

Three and a half minutes into the disaster and the submerged midships section of *Calauria* already presented the spectacle of a holocaust from which a dense column of jet black smoke rose into the frantic sky. From this gigantic central brazier, fire continued to reach hungrily fore and aft along the line of the hull.

And, urged by the westerly wind from the Heads, began to crawl in its white hot excitement below the offshore jetty itself.

There was an efficient and still surprisingly well maintained fire-fighting system aboard *Calauria*. There were seven platform-mounted foam monitors and twenty-six hydrant positions on her main deck alone. The sea-water supply to those was provided through a fire main running the full length of the deck, pressurized by three separate pumps in her engine room; all in good order thanks to the efforts of Chief Borga and his overworked gang.

The machinery space itself incorporated a foam-smothering system dispensed through forty-six diffusers. There were twelve more located in her pump room. She could provide steam-smothering facilities to her fuel and gas oil tanks, her store rooms, her paint and lamp lockers and her forepeak. She carried half a hundred portable fire extinguishers, three firemen's suits, twelve sets of self-contained breathing apparatus.

They were all to prove useless. In a cataclysm of such proportions it had become immediately apparent, not only to Pilot McDonald but to the majority of her complement, that the ship herself was lost; only retarding the spread of fire and thus delaying the prospect of explosion offered them a chance of survival.

Some attempt to take it – to blanket the midships failure point with foam while, simultaneously, creating a cooling water curtain between the seat of fire and after accommodation – might just have been made with a well-trained crew; but *Calauria*'s complement was not. They were inadequately led, and acted without cohesion.

And anyway that fire main running the vast length of the VLCC's main deck had snapped instantly on her initial breaking. Even had Second Engineer Visentini, her watchkeeping technical officer, engaged any one of the three fire pumps – which he didn't, because he abandoned the engine room immediately the disaster commenced – any hose pressure in the breached main would only have dissipated futilely into the loch.

Apart from which, even if the fire-fighting system *had* still retained its integrity, and her crew proved superlatively professional in its operation, they still wouldn't have been able to do a bloody thing to save themselves.

Because the whole stern, incorporating the vast engine space of *Calauria*, had lifted clear of the water within thirty seconds. From that calamitous moment her sea-pump intakes would only have sucked air.

Mixed with a lethal *soupçon* of pure hydrocarbon gas, of course.

235

It was at about that time – at around twenty to two according to the Vaila steeple clock which was now beginning to reflect an uneasy red gleam from the loch – that Chief Officer Spedini's earlier planning assumed an even grimmer significance.

As it spread aft along *Calauria*'s angled waterline, the burning crude eventually overtook the point where the supership's hull reared from the water. There the twin lava-like flows of flame conjoined, and continued their sternward passage.

The great steel structure crazily suspended above began to cook; a monstrous barbecueing cadaver.

Half the cargo spaces in that part of her would present little immediate threat even then. Five Centre was ballasted with harmless salt water. Number Five Wings still contained over sixteen thousand tonnes of undischarged Light Crude between them, but virtually no ullage space in which gasses could form to threaten explosion.

But Number *Six* cargo tanks across, situated immediately before the bridge, had been purposely left empty by Spedini in order to facilitate repairs to Chief Engineer Borga's precious sluice valves once they sailed.

Those mighty spaces contained no reassuringly inert ballast, merely the dregs of cargo unloaded on the previous day.

. . . and twenty thousand cubic metres of potentially volatile gas. But confined, this time. Just like the filling of any high explosive bomb.

CHAPTER TWELVE

Disaster Sunday:
Final Phase

Duggan had been justified in protesting to Reporter Herschell that the Rora fire-fighting systems were still good. They were. Particularly out on the offshore jetty where the greatest threat could be anticipated.

Forget all the extinguishers and back-charging points and hydrants and branches. Ignore, even, the thirteen lifebuoys and the two admittedly suspect escape rafts. There were two Pyrene Superjet monitors mounted on the Chiksan operating towers and thus seventeen metres above average deck level. Each of those could deliver finished foam at a rate of some five thousand gallons per minute into the seat of any fire aboard ship. Plus two type-MFG20s adding another three or four thousand GPM to the effort, enough in themselves to retard, if not smother outright, the spread of any burning fuel until the duty fire tug could come alongside and add its massive capability.

Then there was the water wall. The whole of the central part of the offshore jetty could be heat-shielded by a vertical curtain of high pressure water behind which any number of men could await rescue – even though the casualty itself had become untenable, abandoned, and with its crew retired to the rock-piled safety of the platform.

So of course Duggan had been right. Hundreds of thousands of dollars really *had* been invested in safety and personnel protection at the Rora terminal.

But as Fran Herschell had also argued, following broadly the philosophy of Duty Expediter Blair – Sod's Law of the Sea – if anything can conceivably go wrong it eventually will. And invariably at the same bloody time as everything else.

237

All that sophisticated kit out on the jetty still required a supply of water under pressure before it could perform its crisis-tailored function. For ease of maintenance that supply would only be available to the platform fire-fighters once a switch a quarter of a mile away had been activated. Six minutes after cataclysm the man who should have pressed the vital button – or, for that matter, implemented a host of other major incident measures – didn't even know a disaster had occurred.

Reg was still sitting on the toilet.

Shona Simpson reached the perimeter fence first, flushed with the euphoria of getting her own back on Caird. Any recriminations would affect him far more than the others; and Shona didn't care that much, anyway, about inviting her own parents' displeasure. Each family row made it that much easier to break from Vaila when the opportunity offered.

They'd become aware of the thunder while hurrying to make their escape. It was only the last knell, louder, more concussive than the rest, that caused McLean and Janey Menzies to halt in flight and look back.

Shona heard the other girl scream, and whirled round. 'Stop that, you stupid wee bitch!'

John McLean whispered sickly, 'She's on fire! Och Christ but she's burning all *ower*!'

They could see individual flames clearly despite the rain; burnishing the underside of the tanker's obscenely projected hull a flickering orange, with black rolling smoke already a thousand foot marker above.

'Peter!' Janey Menzies shrieked. 'He's out there!'

Nobody thought of Alec Bell. Not right away. But nobody ever had put Alec first, not at school, not later. Specky Bell had never claimed recognition against the clever ones like Caird, or the dominant ones like McLean.

The terminal itself remained eerily silent. You would have expected sirens; men running; some urgent response to crisis. But nothing was happening at all; not even now, maybe five or six minutes after the thunder had begun. Just a blue

238

flashing police light way up at the gate, and the great burning ship out in the loch.

Big John McLean recalled the room he and Shona had ventured into, and that man they'd locked in the toilet. And all those dials and switches – and emergency legends. And suddenly he realized they had done a terrible thing to-night.

Shona said calmly, unnervingly: 'The other two will be dead. Just go home now. Both of you. We don't know anything about it.'

Just like that. Cold. Emotionless. Terrifying.

Janey Menzies began to scream hysterically at the look in Shona Simpson's eyes. Screaming on and on into the night, a continual high-pitched lament, because after all their child-hood together she'd never understood until then that Shona was a very disturbed girl indeed – perhaps even a little bit mad.

John didn't see a group of men running down by the lovers' path at the side of the wire, he simply panicked. Scrambling desperately through the gap he collided with his own father, hastening by then with the others down the short cut to the fish harbour and *The Vian*.

McLean senior took one dreadful all-embracing look at his son and the screaming girl and the uncannily serene girl, and the hole in the fence and the holocaust on Quarsdale, and roared, 'My God, laddie, whit hae ye *done*?'

But then his rage and his contempt for the uselessness he had spawned took white heat and, before the others could stop him, he struck young McLean full on the side of the head. It was a savage blow, fracturing the lad's already shock-slack jaw and knocking him sobbing to the ground.

Police Constable Lawson would charge McLean senior later with causing grievous bodily harm, albeit to his own flesh and blood, just as others in higher authority were also to charge the same youth McLean and the girls Shona Simpson and Janey Menzies for their night's stupidity. The Law would eventually find no deliberate intent on their part to delay the process of saving life, in fact little serious offence in what, after all, had begun as an immature prank.

But that sad futility was all for the future.

Right then the flames were spreading unopposed around the Very Large Crude Carrier *Calauria*.

From two and a half miles away it was hardly possible to distinguish the ship at the offshore jetty through the banks of rain misting across Quarsdale. Not that Wullie Gibb was all that interested. He'd really only climbed to the top of the harbour wall as a welcome diversion from the rancid heat of the *Wallace*'s galley. Needless to say he'd delivered the Skipper's bacon sannie first, with carefully studied indifference to the covetous stares from Eck Dawson and the rest o' they gannets.

He turned to look down at the *Wallace*. He had to admit she looked fine all the same, especially snug alongside on a night like this. White topsides flawless through the darkness and the black hull almost as smart as she'd come from the builders six months before. Just lying there waiting patiently with her stubby, powerful lines and the high wheelhouse reflecting its warm, red night lighting. Like a fox's eyes, Wullie imagined them to be; with the two highest superjet monitors cocked either side of the flying bridge like alert ears.

Wullie wondered idly what his dad would've thought about her, old drowned Chippie Gibb with his sardine tin sou'wester and his bag o' carpenter's tools that had been around the world three score times and then some. Probably he wouldn't even have considered the *Wallace* as being a ship, no more than his laddie as being a proper sailor – slabbing bacon sannies an' frying sausisgis less than a spit fae shore, and aye arguin' wi' the Chief Officer.

Dad wisnae dressed so daft, though. Thon sou'wester may look odd on the photie, but it would have been braw gear for Quarsdale weather.

Wullie glanced casually towards the lock again as he turned for the stone steps leading down to the waterborne plant jetty. Above the jagged rock silhouette of the Deil's Haund it seemed an unusual glow had developed in the sky. Reddish, like the cosy gleam from the wheelhouse.

Quite bonny in fact. Like wan o' they Mediterranean sunsets he'd observed down in Torremolinos on holidays. Only this wis getting on for a quarter to two on a winter's morning. In bluidy *Scotland*.

Then the curtain of rain drifted clear of the offshore jetty, and Gibby could see plainly that the whole midships section of the Liberian VLCC was enveloped in flame.

The clatter of boots on the steel deck caused Eck Dawson to stick his head through the saloon door when Wullie leapt precariously across the narrow gap between ship and quay. 'Go away,' he said. 'There's nae room aboard here for insects.'

'She's afire!' Gibb shouted. 'Burning all ower. The big tanker on the jetty.'

'Oh, aye?' the Mate retorted. 'I may be soft, but ah'm no' egg-shaped, so jus' bugger off, Deckhand Gibb.'

'Please, Eck,' Wullie appealed through drained lips. 'She's on *fire*, man. We've got a major disaster oot there!'

Engineer Burns materialized at the engine room fiddley looking black-oiled disenchanted. 'Stop yon row! Dae you lads no' ken ah've got a heart condition?'

'Awwwww, look at the fucking *sky*!' Gibby screamed.

Mate Dawson did, then blurted a disbelieving, 'Jeeeeesus!'

Tam Burns took one glance and said, surprisingly calmly for a man with a serious heart condition, 'Call the Skipper. Ah'll away and start the engine.'

But then, Engineer Burns had known it would happen onc day. Hadn't he always claimed that? Insisted that all it needed wis just the wan wee spark?'

Skipper McFadyen noted in the *William Wallace*'s Log that they cleared Neackie Harbour entrance en route to the casualty at 0146 GMT – thirteen full minutes after *Calauria* actually broke her back. The Skipper's hand shook as he did so.

Had he resisted Wullie Gibb's mixture of blandishment and blackmail a little more resolutely; had he remained on station just three quarters of an hour longer; then he could surely have helped contain the spread of the fire with the *Wallace*'s foam smothering capability – even more vitally, he would have evacuated all personnel from both VLCC and jetty and thus ensured their survival.

McFadyen, having been a tanker man himself, knew *Calauria* was lost from the moment he first saw her. And the jetty too. The fire had instantly grown to massive proportions following a detonation amidships; through binoculars he could observe flame already reaching for Numbers Six across. He also knew from earlier VHF chat between Panoco Control and the Pilot that those tanks were empty and not yet gas-freed. If they went up now he grimly anticipated that the *Wallace* would save very few crewmen indeed. If they exploded in approximately ten to fifteen minutes: while the *Wallace* was close alongside . . .

Beside the Skipper in the corkscrewing wheelhouse, Dawson was trying urgently to raise a still inexplicably silent Reg Blair: 'Control, Control, Panoco CONTROL, this is Watchdog – do you read? Control, Cont . . .'

The Mate threw the handset down and shouted, 'The BASTARD! Where is the useless wee man? Christ, but does he no' ken they're *dyin'* ower there?'

'Easy, Eck. Easy, lad. Away down and take charge o' the lads, eh.'

McFadyen at the wheel added nothing about Reg Blair, for there was little he could bring himself to say. He was sick-aware that, had the usually reliable Expediter alerted them in the instant when the emergency first became evident from the Control building, then his *Wallace* would have been at least thirteen minutes closer to plucking fifty, sixty men from the holocaust now reflecting from the disturbed sea pounding their bows. He further suspected that no attempt had been made even to contain the outbreak from either the jetty or aboard the tanker itself. Was that the consequence of panic? Or had Blair, for whatever unimaginable reason, also denied *them* the necessary water supply from Control?

Wullie Gibb and the other two deckies, Stuart and McDade, were readying the monitors and preparing the recovery gear in virtual silence. Every so often each of them would lift his head and gaze with awe towards the broken tanker, now less than half a mile ahead. There seemed to be fire under the jetty; fire on the sea, racing to encircle the giant hull as it reared ever more self-destructive in death, constantly fuelling its own pyre beneath a flickering column of smoke linking loch and sky.

Where in pity's name *was* yon Blair man? Why hadn't he called them even now?

Reg was *still* barricaded in the bloody toilet.

Every so often rage had overwhelmed him and he'd flung himself uncaringly at the solidly barricaded door. Still it mocked him, scarred but impenetrable, leaving the Expediter sick and miserable and ever more agitated.

The fright hit him an almost physical blow the moment he heard Downie's voice yelling for him from the Control Room. He knew immediately that something terrible had happened. Downie was normally an unflappable man. The Downie out there must have been under a dreadful strain. Reg found himself bellowing for help from the edge of hysteria.

Downie flung the door open and stood, a light of panic in his eyes, looking like death.

'She's burning, Reg. Jesus Christ, man, d'ye not know she's burning all OVER?'

Blair hurled himself past the shocked PPO and tumbled into the Control Room – then halted aghast. Disbelieving. The whole window revealed a hellish panorama of flame and smoke with the ends of a great red ship extended crazily from the infero.

There was a voice calling desperately over the VHF. Archie McDonald's voice. 'Help us! Send help IMMEDIATELY!'

'Ohhhhhh dear God!' Expediter Blair sobbed, paralysed by the ultimate nightmare. 'Ohhhhhh dear merciful GOD!'

'Mayday, Mayday, MAYDAY! All stations, this is Liberian Tanker *Calauria* – send help immediately . . .'

'React, Reg! You're NAVY, Reg! Discipline! Self Control! DO YOUR DUTY, REG.'

'They can't get the personnel launch started. *Do* somethin',' Downie was pleading in mounting horror. 'DO something, Blair!'

Ex-Chief Gunnery Instructor Blair hit the jetty fire main

243

commissioning button, then shut down the emergency block valves in the cargo transfer lines from the jetty. He activated the foam flooding system protecting the foreshore of the Rora terminal and brutally switched Channel Ninety out of circuit, cutting McDonald's appeal off the air.

'Watchdog – Panoco Control. Emergency!'

McFadyen's voice came back instantly. 'Watchdog. We're a'ready on our way, Control. ETA at the casualty; aboot nine minutes. Over.'

No recriminations – they would come later. Just professional now. Pertinent.

'Affirmative, Jimmie. Give priority to getting them off if you can. Out.'

Blair called the emergency Telecom operator on the red phone and requested her to advise all essential services, then swung to make the terminal siren switch on the wall. Immediately the sadness of it began to wail across the night hush over Vaila.

He felt dead inside, and knew everything he had done had been far too late.

Finally he performed his most difficult duty of all. He re-called Pilot McDonald so very far from aid out there on the blazing *Calauria*.

Archie's voice sounded calm. Not really hurt or angry, or even resentful of Reg who had let him and all the others down so terribly.

'Nine minutes yet,' Blair said. 'I'm sorry, Archie.'

'We'll have to go over the side before then,' McDonald replied after a long moment. 'I'm up in the wheelhouse. We've got it sealed off but the windows are beginning to explode with the heat.'

Blair closed his eyes tightly for a minute. He heard Downie draw a shocked breath behind him. 'Can't you make it to the jetty?' Reg asked with enormous care. 'The water wall should be operating now.'

'The jetty's on fire. Everything's on fire out here . . .'

Expediter Blair heard bells clanging in the distance. The first fire tenders were arriving at the gate. Their task would be largely prophylactic: fight the blazing oil as it drove ashore

244

under the westerly wind, prevent the holocaust spreading through Rora itself, possibly even to the town.

They wouldn't be able to help Archie, though. Or those half hundred other men trapped out there with him. They had needed a rescue ship, and a better system, and the few so-incredibly precious minutes which Reg had failed to give them.

'I'm sorry, Archie,' Blair said again, staring sightlessly through the rain-spattered window at the great doomed ship in the loch. 'Christ but I'm sorry!'

At 0151 GMT – eighteen minutes after the first indications of disaster – *Calauria*'s Number Six tanks across finally exploded, sending a monstrous pressure wave approaching furnace heat clear across Loch Quarsdale.

Duty Expediter Blair knew Archie was dead then, and Mike Trelawney and that Captain . . . Bisagleri, was it? And all the others.

Even before the plate-glass window of Panoco Control blasted inwards to bury him and PPO Downie under a storm of lacerating splinters.

Post-Disaster

District Councillor Mrs McLeish was wrong in one important detail, just as the worst of Fran Herschell's fears were proved groundless. There was little loss of life caused by *Calauria*'s leviathan dismemberment among those who actually lived by the shores of Quarsdale.

Though there might well have been had *Calauria* caught fire under different loading conditions; with less inert ballast and even more hydrocarbon gas within her hull for instance, in which case she would indeed have carried the blast-destructive potential of a small nuclear weapon.

But because major tanker disasters do occur with distressing frequency – something in the order of fourteen times every year – then by definition something appalling *will* happen to a giant Crude Carrier loaded in that critical manner, and possibly quite soon, perhaps tomorrow, perhaps next time in a much more densely populated area. And when it does, it won't necessarily take place because some V or ULCC actually breaks apart at her berth – though unhappily that isn't an unheard of circumstance – but merely as a result of somebody doing something quite ordinary, only doing it in the wrong place and at the wrong time; dropping a metal object like a spanner, crushing a grain of sand under a shoe. Even the static generated by a nylon shirt could trigger a holocaust. Wan wee spark. That's all it needs. Not a complicated recipe for cataclysm.

Anyway, Reg Blair failed to recover from his injuries and so he was never able to answer the question of why he didn't try to evade the blast which he must surely have known was coming. PPO Downie had managed to. Travelling from the offshore jetty, the pressure wave from the detonation had taken a moment longer to impact against that massive plate-glass window. Downie had found enough time to take partial cover below the level of Reg's console and thus escape the more dreadful aspects of what those imploding shards did to Expediter Blair. So why didn't Reg?

Police Constable Lawson, who had to take note of many unpleasant details during the post-disaster period, often wondered about that. It even occurred to Hamish occasionally that . . . well – that maybe Mr Blair hadn't even *tried* to take cover.

But twenty-year-old Constable Lawson was inclined towards grim reflection during the traumatic hours which followed. He performed many hours of extra duty at the temporary mortuary the police established in the Presbyterian church hall – the very same venue where Peter Caird and Specky Bell had attended a disco on that previous Friday night.

An elderly and totally deaf crofter called Meally Doug died asleep in bed in his wee cottage at the back of Fariskay when *Calauria*'s anchor, weighing all of fifteen tons, travelled a mile through the air like a glowing meteor before joining him. There were a number of residents of Vaila itself, including Reg's own son Ken, who also suffered unpleasant injuries as their windows blew in on them, but nothing half so grievous as those of Expediter Blair.

The church clock stopped at the instant of the final explosion – nine minutes to two on that Sunday morning – and was never restarted again at the suggestion of the Reverend Johnson, the gesture being intended as a form of timeless memorial for the fifty-odd Italian seamen and Panoco employees who died in the disaster. Mind you, some claimed uncharitably that it was a crafty move for the Meenister to make. It meant that from then on every day in Vaila remained, according to his steeple timepiece, the Sabbath Day.

Even Thomas the cat wasn't allowed to rest in feline peace. The dustbin within which he'd been so rudely interred was blown across Reform Street. But this was only a temporary hiccup in the funeral process. Thomas still finished up in the back of the Council refuse lorry a few hours later.

The duty tug *William Wallace* was too late on the scene, fortunately for her. It wasn't the fault of her crew that she was still a full half-mile away when *Calauria*'s Numbers Six across exploded, and it did mean that Engineer Burns was her only casualty – he got blown fifteen feet all the way from the fiddley back down into his roaring engine room by the blast.

When Wullie Gibb picked him up and asked if he wis a'right, Tam shrugged him off in outraged fury. "*Course* ah'm a'richt. Christ man, ah'm no' bothered about a wee bump on the heid – ah'm no' a bluidy hypnochondriac!'

The *Wallace*, in company with *Robert The Bruce*, *The Vian* and the other boats of the Vaila inshore fishing fleet, recovered one deflated liferaft and thirty-nine bodies following dawn light on that Sunday. In subsequent weeks Quarsdale was to give up a further seven. Most of them were fully clothed and wore lifejackets, which suggested that they would have had ample time to abandon had there been any safe place to go. Some of them had died from asphyxia due to drowning in crude oil, the majority from body tissue destruction as a result of explosive force and fire.

It was a very long Sunday for the men aboard the sad little ships. Wullie Gibb didn't cook a meal at sea for the first time in months. Nobody wanted one, not even Eck Dawson.

The salvors did find four unidentified corpses –
one of which may have been PCO Trelawney's –
huddled below the jetty fire control tower. Also,
twelve days later and after everything had cooled,
what were believed to be the remains of Captain
Tommaso Bisaglia in company with Pilot McDonald
and Second Officer De Mita in the burned-out shell
of *Calauria*'s bridge deck. A week later divers recovered the unmarked body of her Chief Officer
from the flooded cargo control room. It seemed that
Mario Spedini, rather like Expediter Blair oddly
enough, had never attempted to save himself when
the end came.

No one would ever learn what had happened
to Chief Engineer Borga, nor to Bosun Egidi, nor
elderly and faithful Steward Gioia; certainly not to
Peter Caird or to quiet Alec Bell. Loch Quarsdale
had existed in one form or another for two million
years; it would demand more than a microscopic
thundering during one night of one brief century
fo make it surrender those secrets it intended to
keep.

When in May 1970 the Norwegian *Polycommander*,
a tanker of a mere fifty thousand tons, grounded
and caught fire on Muxieirio Point near the Spanish
port of Vigo, the thermal flux from the blazing
wreck became so intense that it created a firestorm
– hurricane winds which sucked fine particles of oil
into the high atmosphere where they condensed,
formed clouds and, within a few days, returned to
the coastal farmlands around the villages of Bayona
and Panjón.

On the Tuesday following the Rora disaster the
same legacy of black rain began to fall on Quarsdale.
It turned the snow to hideous pitch on the great
mountains flanking the loch, and polluted the crys-
tal waters of the many wee lochans once fished by
Archie McDonald with such pleasure. It destroyed

the early crops just planted, it poisoned sheep and cattle and deer grazing on the tainted grass for twenty miles around. It fouled the forests. It caused traffic accidents on skidpan roads and killed small birds and insects and furry creatures alike with horrible efficiency. For many weeks it made the gentle town of Vaila a noxious place in which to live.

Six thousand tonnes of unburned Arabian Crude emulsified and sank to the bottom of Quarsdale to pollute the mussel beds and shellfish grounds and destroy the families of fish, and thus to cripple for a generation the livelihoods of those very men who had protested vainly against just such a possibility. Either that, or the black tide which had been brought all the way from Mina al-Ahmadi in the Persian Gulf, drifted sullenly ashore to coat Scots granite coves with a gelatinous, corrosive mulch as deep as a man's knees, and to melt the yellow webbed feet of, or otherwise smother or mutilate, four thousand once beautiful seabirds.

Three months later District Councillor Mrs Mc-Leish suddenly passed away. Dr Caird said her death was caused by a massive coronary thrombosis, but there were many on Quarsdale who claimed that what happened on that awful morning had killed her too, that Jesse simply died of a broken heart.

So it may have been that   when the Very Large Crude Carrier *Calauria* first materialized through the wreathing gossamer strands of that bleak winter's sea mist, and thus came both to destroy and to be destroyed – for Vaila, and for those who lived by it, the Thundering had only just begun.

Author's Note

At 00.31 hrs on the morning of Monday 8 January, 1979, the French supertanker *Betelgeuse*, while discharging some one hundred and fifteen thousand metric tonnes of Arabian Crude, broke her back at the offshore jetty of the Whiddy Island oil terminal situated in Bantry Bay, County Cork, Ireland.

As a tragic consequence of the fire and explosions which followed, fifty persons lost their lives. There were no survivors from either ship or jetty. An Order appointing a Tribunal of Inquiry was later made by the Irish Minster for Tourism and Transport. The Tribunal sat for a total of seventy-two days throughout the year 1979; heard the evidence of one hundred and eighty-four witnesses; and finally published one of the most exhaustive and searching reports ever produced on the circumstances leading to a maritime disaster.

Certain delays in implementing rescue procedures were considered, particularly arising from the alleged absence from the Control Room of the dispatcher when the disaster began, the position of the duty tug at that critical time, the absence of suitable escape craft, and the alterations which had been effected in the fire-fighting systems on the jetty.

The Report on the Whiddy Island Disaster is a matter of public record, and it would be disingenuous of me to claim ignorance of its contents. I would stress, however, that the characters and events described in this novel are quite fictitious, that no intention exists to draw parallels with any persons living or dead, or with commercial organizations or places, or with any particular ship.

Only to entertain. And, perhaps, to help promote a greater awareness of the price paid for, and the risks inherent in, energy transport operations.

BRIAN CALLISON
Dundee, Scotland
1986

Fontana Paperbacks: Fiction

Fontana is a leading paperback publisher of both non-fiction, popular and academic, and fiction. Below are some recent fiction titles.

- ☐ GLITTER BABY Susan Elizabeth Phillips £2.95
- ☐ EMERALD DECISION Craig Thomas £3.50
- ☐ THE GOLDEN CUP Belva Plain £3.50
- ☐ A THUNDER OF CRUDE Brian Callison £2.95
- ☐ DESERT QUEEN Julia Fitzgerald £3.50
- ☐ THE GREEN FLASH Winston Graham £3.50
- ☐ UNDER CONTRACT Liza Cody £2.95
- ☐ THE LATCHKEY KID Helen Forrester £2.95
- ☐ IN HARM'S WAY Geoffrey Jenkins £2.95
- ☐ THE DOOR TO DECEMBER Leigh Nichols £3.50
- ☐ THE MIRROR OF HER DREAMS Stephen Donaldson £3.95
- ☐ A SONG IN THE MORNING Gerald Seymour £2.95

You can buy Fontana paperbacks at your local bookshop or newsagent. Or you can order them from Fontana Paperbacks, Cash Sales Department, Box 29, Douglas, Isle of Man. Please send a cheque, postal or money order (not currency) worth the purchase price plus 22p per book for postage (maximum postage required is £3.00 for orders within the UK).

NAME (Block letters) _____

ADDRESS _____

_____

_____